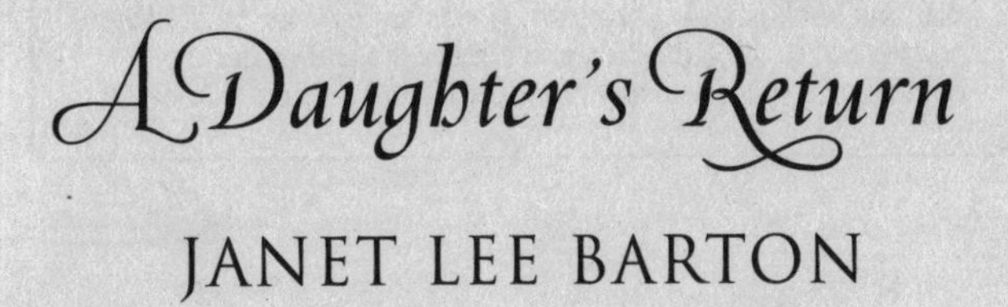

JANET LEE BARTON

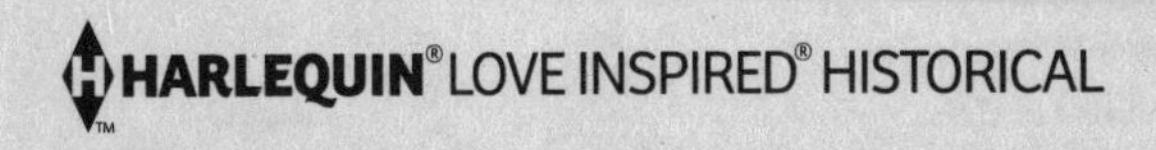

Recycling programs for this product may not exist in your area.

ISBN-13: 978-0-373-28301-9

A Daughter's Return

This edition published by arrangement with Love Inspired Books.

www.Harlequin.com

Printed in U.S.A.

If we confess our sins, he is faithful
and just to forgive us *our* sins,
and to cleanse us from all unrighteousness.
—*1 John* 1:9

To my readers who love this series as much as I do,
To my family who always encourages me to keep writing,
And always,
To my Lord and Savior for showing me the way.

Chapter One

Heaton House, New York City,
January 1897

After helping her mother take down the last of the Christmas decorations, Rebecca hurried upstairs to check on her napping daughter. It was the Monday after New Year's, and she still found it hard to believe she and Jenny were finally moved into her mother's boardinghouse.

The past few months had sped by—reuniting with her family, staying with her brother, Michael, and his wife Violet, to help out with her sweet nephew, who had been born two weeks before Christmas, and the weddings of several of her mother's boarders.

Here it was, 1897 already—a new year and a whole new life for her and Jenny. What would the Lord have in store for them this year?

Rebecca entered the suite her mother had given them and still couldn't believe the space they each had. Compared to the tiny apartment in the tenements she'd left only a few months ago, the suite seemed huge and sumptuous. Her room was done in the blues and yellows she loved and the colors in Jenny's were her favorites—pink and lavender. After living in the colorless tenements, she loved having color around them once again. The two rooms were connected by a bathroom they shared—a real luxury after having to share a bathroom with everyone on one floor of the building they'd lived in.

"What do you think, Jenny? Are you going to like living here at Granma's?" she'd asked that very morning. Rebecca had smiled, realizing she'd begun to say granma like Jenny did—without the d.

"Oh yes, Mama." Jenny's eyes had sparkled. "I love being with Granma every day and I like all the others here, too," Jenny had said. "And you won't be so sad anymore. We're going to have good days now, aren't we, Mama?"

Rebecca's breath had caught and her heart twisted in her chest at Jenny's words. Suddenly, she'd realized her child's daily moods in the past had been a reflection of her own. *O Lord, please forgive me. Again.*

Determination had risen up strong and swift and Rebecca had bent down, gathered her young daughter in her arms and hugged her tight. "Yes, Jenny. We are going to have much better days from now on."

If she had a bad day, she'd make sure she didn't drag her daughter down with her. "I love you so much!"

"I love you, too, Mama." Jenny's small hands patted her on the back.

Rebecca was always amazed at how comforting her daughter's hugs and pats could be.

Now, she crossed her room and went through the bathroom to sit on the side of Jenny's bed. She gave her a gentle shake and kissed her forehead. "Wake up, sleepyhead. We need to wash up and go see what Gretchen and Maida are cooking for dinner. Something smells really yummy downstairs."

Jenny stretched, smiled and opened her eyes. "I hope she's making chocolate cake!"

"Oh, I'm sure Gretchen will make something you'll like." Dessert was a real treat for Jenny. Living in the tenements, Rebecca could rarely afford any kind of indulgence for them. She'd done well most days to provide the basic meal, which had been awfully skimpy at times. She still found it difficult to believe she didn't have to worry about where their next meal would come from. "Let's go wash your face and hands."

Once they'd both freshened up, Rebecca took her daughter's hand and left her room. What a wonderful feeling not to have to lock her door or worry about someone breaking in. She and Jenny swung hands and then the child giggled, let go of Rebecca and ran to the staircase.

"Jenny, not so fast!" Rebecca watched in horror as her daughter grasped the newel post and swung a leg over the side, leaving her in a kind of lopsided position as she started to slide. "Jenny! No!"

Jenny's descent built up speed while Rebecca ran down the stairs on legs that had suddenly gone weak, terrified she wouldn't reach her in time. The front door of Heaton House opened and Benjamin Roth, one of the boarders, walked in. Rebecca yelled, "Ben, catch her, please!"

She saw him glance up and run to the bottom of the staircase just as Jenny flew off the end and plopped into his arms. Her child's delighted giggle helped Rebecca breathe once more as she reached the foyer, took her child from him and hugged her close. She looked up at the man who'd kept her from getting hurt. "Oh, Ben, thank you!"

He let out a huge breath. "You're welcome. That was a bit frightening."

"I was terrified." Rebecca turned her daughter's face to hers. "Jennifer Dickerson! I told you not to ever slide down the banister. You nearly scared the life right out of me and Mr. Ben."

She set her daughter down and grasped her hand. "You deserve a paddling for disobeying me, Jenny!"

"What's all the commotion about?" her mother asked, hurrying down the hall from her study.

"Granma!" Jenny reached out to her grandmother, sounding as if she'd been saved from the sound spanking Rebecca knew she needed.

Rebecca relinquished her to her mother and let out a huge sigh before explaining. "Jenny decided to slide down the banister and Ben caught her right before she flew across the foyer, Mama."

She still trembled at the thought of what might have happened had Ben not arrived when he did.

"Oh, my sweet Jenny, we don't want you to get hurt. Granma has a rule in this house. Never, ever slide down the banister. You won't try it again, will you?"

Rebecca watched her blond-haired, blue-eyed child shake her head.

"You promise?"

Jenny hesitated only a moment before nodding.

"Now what do you need to say to your mama?"

"I'm sorry, Mama."

Rebecca felt torn between hugging her close again and punishing her for disobeying. "I forgive you. But you still deserve a spanking. You slide down again and you'll get one, you hear?"

Jenny's head bobbed up and down once more.

"You received a reprieve this time, sweetheart," Mrs. Heaton said, patting her granddaughter's back. "I'm not sure you will a second time. May I take her to the kitchen to check on dinner, dear?"

"I suppose, but no treats before dinner."

"Of course not." She turned and headed for the kitchen. "You heard your mama, Jenny. You have to wait until after dinner for dessert."

"I know, Granma."

Rebecca shook her head, let out a shaky breath and looked up at Ben. Her trembles had only now begun to subside. "Oh, Ben, I am so glad you came home when you did. My legs felt like water as I tried to hurry down the stairs and I was sure I wouldn't make it down in time."

"I wasn't too sure I'd be in time, either." He ran a hand through his blond hair, then chuckled and shook his head. "She thought it was great fun."

"And it is. I tried the same thing when I was around her age."

"Was anyone there to catch you?" His blue eyes twinkled as he waited for her answer.

"Thankfully my papa heard Mama yell, much the same as I just did, and he caught me."

"Then what happened?"

Rebecca chuckled. "The outcome was about the same as now. Mama came running down the stairs and Papa said almost the exact same things Mama told Jenny."

"Like mother, like daughter?" He grinned at her.

She thought for a moment and then sighed. "I'm afraid so. I pray she's not as rebellious as I was when she gets older."

"Well, it appears you turned out fine. I'm sure Jenny will, too."

"I pray so. I hope our move hasn't changed life at Heaton House too much for all of you."

Ben grinned. "You and Jenny have livened things up a lot around here. It's wonderful to see your mother so happy. So don't worry about changing life around here. We're all enjoying whatever changes you and Jenny have made."

"Thank you, Ben. Still, I probably should be making her take her meals in the kitchen, but Mama will have none of it."

"I'm glad! Jenny is not a problem, Rebecca. You've taught her good manners and she mostly listens to the conversations around her. Makes it feel more like we are part of a family. Having you both here made Christmas especially wonderful."

Ben's smile went a long way in convincing Rebecca that he meant what he said. Then he bent down, tipped Rebecca's chin up and looked her in the eyes. "Please…let yourself enjoy being with your family again. And don't for a minute worry about what the boarders think. We're all very happy to have you and Jenny here. You've been through a lot, trying to raise your daughter by yourself. Some women would have given up their children for—"

"Oh! I could never have given Jenny up. Having her is what gave me reason to keep going." She stopped herself from saying more.

How much did Ben know about her past? Her mother had told her that all most of them knew was that she'd been found after having been missing for over four years—except perhaps for Kathleen and Luke Patterson, who'd been responsible for finding her.

"It's your story to tell, Rebecca dear," her mother had said. "If you decide you need to, when and to whom is your choice. As for your brother and I, we're overjoyed to have you back in our lives."

The Lord had more than answered Rebecca's deepest prayers in sending Kathleen to her apartment as a liaison for the Ladies' Aid Society. Because of her, Rebecca had faced her past and been reunited with her loved ones—but she wasn't sure she'd ever share that past with anyone else.

The door opened and boarders Julia Olsen and Millicent Faircloud came in. They'd barely removed their outer wraps when Mathew Sterling, another of her mother's boarders, entered. Greeting each one,

Rebecca had no chance to say more to Ben alone. Everyone rushed upstairs or down to get ready for dinner, but as Ben turned to go down to the men's quarters, Rebecca reached out and touched his arm. "I…thank you again for catching Jenny."

"You're welcome. I doubt she'll be sliding downstairs anytime soon." Ben reached out and covered her hand with his.

Rebecca was a bit disturbed by the way her pulse raced with the touch of his hand on hers and she quickly slipped hers out from under his. "I'd better go find out if Jenny is getting in the way in the kitchen."

"And I need to go wash up. See you in a bit."

Rebecca nodded and smiled. She headed toward the dining room, trying to tell herself her racing pulse had nothing at all to do with Ben and everything to do with seeing her daughter sail down the banister. Still, her reaction to his touch unsettled her. She hadn't reacted quite like that in years and she was determined to tamp down the fluttery feeling inside. She would not—could not—let herself become attracted to another man. She'd been through enough heartbreak to last a lifetime and she wasn't going there again.

She hurried to the kitchen to give a huge hug to the only worthwhile thing to come out of her time of rebellion and reprimand her one more time about ever trying to slide down the banister again. Then she sent up a silent prayer of thankfulness that Ben had been there to catch her precious daughter.

When Ben entered the dining room a short while later, he was glad Rebecca and her mother seemed to have recovered from Jenny's near tragedy. Rebecca must have been terrified when Jenny began her slide down—he'd been quite alarmed himself in trying to get to her in time. The little girl was a bit quieter than normal, but she gave him a sweet smile as he held out a chair for Rebecca and then took his own seat across from her.

He smiled back. Jenny had her mother's beautiful blue eyes, but her hair was blonder with no red in it. Rebecca had just enough red in her hair to make him finally realize what strawberry blonde looked like. She was very pretty, petite and delicate to look at, but she was also a strong woman. She had to be, to have lived in the tenements and raised a child by herself.

He knew little about the circumstances that had taken Rebecca away from her family or kept them from finding her, but he admired her for the simple fact that she'd kept her child and tried to do the best she could by her. Jenny was a happy little girl and Ben was certain her mother deserved the credit for it.

His heart went out to women raising children alone. Always had. His own mother had abandoned him when he was a baby, dropped him off at an orphanage, leaving him to grow up wondering why she'd left him and what had been wrong with him to cause her to…desert him.

He was thankful for Mrs. Butler, the director of the orphanage, who'd taken him in and been there for him all those years. And he'd been blessed in having an anonymous benefactor who'd paid for his education. Because of the generosity afforded him, Ben had made a vow to help other orphans in whatever way he could. He visited the orphanage often and mentored the young people who were of an age to go out on their own. Still, the thought that his mother had deserted him—

Ben swallowed around the tightness in his throat and turned his attention back to his fellow boarders.

With Kathleen and Luke Patterson married and starting their life together a couple of blocks away, and Elizabeth and John Talbot doing the same thing several blocks in the opposite direction, the table seemed very empty. Two couples—four boarders—had moved out within a few months of each other. If not for Rebecca and Jenny moving into Heaton House, it would only be him and Matt, Millicent and Julia left as boarders.

The four of them had wondered what would happen next. Would Mrs. Heaton close her boardinghouse now that her daughter and granddaughter had moved in? Or would she take in more boarders? There was room for at least two more men downstairs and several more female boarders upstairs, if Mrs. Heaton utilized a room or two on the third floor. They might be a bit smaller on that floor, but still larger than many rooms to let in the city, and he had no doubt they'd be filled quickly if his landlady decided to rent them out.

He hoped she did. For some reason, the upcoming changes in boarders left him feeling odd, longing for something more and he wasn't even sure what that was.

Ben looked at Jenny, who was staring at him. He smiled and she grinned at him—right before she ducked her head, touching his heart. He looked up and found her mother's gaze on him. Something stirred inside as their eyes met.

"I've been thinking," Mrs. Heaton said from the head of the table. "Before I put in an advertisement for new boarders, I want to tell you all what I'd like to do and hear what you think about it."

"What is it, Mrs. Heaton?" Matt asked from the other end of the table.

"Well, even gaining Rebecca and Jenny, this place has begun to feel a little empty with our married couples moved out."

"That's for sure," Julia Olsen said. "I'm certainly glad Rebecca and Jenny moved in. We barely have enough to play a good game of charades as it is."

"I'm more than thrilled my girls are here," Mrs. Heaton said. "And I'd like us to have a full table again, but I want to do a little remodeling first. I'd like to change things up a bit on the third floor." She lowered her voice. "I want to give Gretchen and Maida a small sitting room between their rooms and then redo several more rooms for more possible boarders, making sure I keep at least two for emergency arrivals. It's going to be a bit of an inconvenience for a few weeks, but the work will be done while you're all out for the day and—"

"Mrs. Heaton, this is your home. Whatever you want to do is fine with me," Julia said. "If you need me to move into another room, I'll be glad to. I'm just happy to be here and glad there'll be more boarders coming in."

"So am I," Millicent said. "I'll be happy with anything you choose to do."

Everyone chimed in, telling her she had their support, including Ben. "Will you be changing the downstairs, as well?" he asked.

"Not right away. You men are fairly safe for the time being."

"I feared you might decide to close Heaton House to boarders now that—" Millicent clapped a hand over her mouth.

"Rebecca and Jenny are here?" Mrs. Heaton asked. "I did think about it, but I had good reasons for opening Heaton House and those reasons still remain and, in fact, are stronger in knowing my Rebecca could have used a place like this."

"Oh, I'm glad you've made that decision," Julia said.

So was Ben. The last thing he'd want would be for Heaton House to close. This was home to him and the others.

"I'm thinking of taking some business courses," Rebecca said. "Jenny and I love being here, and I want to help Mama out some, to give her more time to spend with her grandchildren," Rebecca said. "I'd like to be able to learn the skills I'll need to do that, and to make a decent living should I ever need to, without counting on my family to provide for us." She turned to Ben. "Mama says you teach business, Ben, but I'm not sure I want to go to school full-time and leave Jenny that long. When does the next session begin?"

"I do teach business classes. The new term at college is under way, but I also teach two nights a week at the YWCA. I mostly teach young women who are struggling to get out of the tenements and need to make a living. Some want to add to the family income, and others have to provide for their children."

"Two nights a week? That wouldn't be too bad. That way I wouldn't have to be away from Jenny too much while we're getting adjusted to the changes in our life."

"I think you'd be quite an asset to the class—and you'd be able to meet your goals, too. You'd only be gone a couple of hours this way."

"I'll be glad to get Jenny ready for bed while you take some classes, Rebecca," Mrs. Heaton said.

"Thank you, Mama. I know you will. When could I start, Ben?"

"Well, classes are under way at the Y, too, but I can get you caught up with the others pretty quickly, if you're willing to study here for a week or so. Then you'd be able to start as soon as you feel ready to," Ben offered.

"You would do that after working all day?" Rebecca sounded as if she couldn't believe his offer.

"Of course I would."

"I'd really appreciate it, Ben." Rebecca looked relieved. "I'd like to begin as soon as possible."

He smiled at her. "I've got some books you'll need downstairs. I'll get them after you put Jenny to bed and give you your first assignment. Let's meet in the small parlor."

Rebecca rewarded him with the biggest smile he'd ever seen from her. "Thank you."

"Yes, Ben. Thank you very much." Mrs. Heaton's look of gratitude would have warmed Ben's heart even if Rebecca hadn't looked so happy, but the expression in the young woman's eyes touched him to his core. And yet he was the one who should be grateful. They were giving him an opportunity to do what he felt called to do—help a young woman with no man to support her provide for herself and her child.

Rebecca was with her family again and she wouldn't have to worry about taking care of Jenny. But it was obvious she had an independent streak and wanted to be able to provide a good life for herself and her daughter, no matter what happened, which was understandable after struggling on her own for so long. And he wanted to do all he could to help her reach that goal.

Chapter Two

After the excitement of the afternoon, it only took a few minutes for Jenny to go to sleep. And, once asleep, her daughter usually didn't stir until Rebecca woke her the next morning. Even so, she was sure her mother would slip upstairs and check on Jenny in her absence.

She smiled as she freshened up before meeting Ben. Her mother seemed overjoyed to have them finally at Heaton House and Rebecca felt the same way. She wished she could make up for the lost years. But she couldn't, and she'd do her best to never put her family through the kind of pain they'd endured during those years thinking they might never find her.

She splashed water on eyes that suddenly filled with tears. Her family had forgiven her; even more important, the Lord had forgiven her. One day, she hoped and prayed she'd be able to forgive herself for what she'd put them through.

Rebecca dried her face and let out a deep breath. Until then she would go forward, thanking the Lord for seeing to it that she and her family were reunited and for all the blessings in her life.

She quickly neatened her hair, smoothing back an errant strand, then went to kiss Jenny's sweet brow before heading downstairs to the back parlor—excitement warring with nervousness. She reached her mother's study and peeked in.

Her mother glanced up from her desk and smiled. "Jenny asleep?"

"She is."

"I'll check on her in a bit."

"I know you will." Rebecca smiled at her mother and crossed the room to kiss her cheek. "I've caught you coming in to check on the two of us."

Her mother nodded. "I still can't believe you're both here. I love you, Becca."

"I love you, too, Mama. I'm sor—"

Her mother lifted her hand and sliced the air in a way that told Rebecca no more needed to be said. "Becca, the past is just that and we're going forward now, remember? I'm so glad you want to take business courses. I understand you want to know you can make your own way and if you ever feel you must, I want you to be able to find a position that will make doing so easier on you. And until then, I'll enjoy your help with Heaton House. I'm sure Ben is a great teacher. I've heard wonderful things about him."

"I'm relieved he's willing to help me until I can enroll for the next term. He's going out of his way to make this easier for me."

"As long as I've known Ben, he has always reached out to help anyone in need. He's a good man."

Rebecca nodded. Although she couldn't imagine putting her complete trust in another man ever again, she did realize there were a few good ones out there. "Guess I'd better go see if he's waiting for me. I don't want to take up any more of his time than I need to."

She hurried out the door and down to the back parlor, but Ben wasn't there yet. Rebecca let out an uneven breath, unsure of why she felt so jittery. She'd always done well at school and loved learning. She shouldn't be nervous about this.

She took a seat at the round table in the middle of the room and looked around. The parlor was decorated in blues and greens and Rebecca loved it. The colors always seemed to comfort her and she and Jenny had already spent a lot of time there. During the day, the boarders were at work and the small parlor wasn't used much at all. Her mother had set up an area to keep some of Jenny's toys where she could get to them and Jenny loved playing there.

It would take a while to get used to living in such a large home after their apartment in the tenements, and in the meantime this parlor would work wonderfully for the two of them, as Rebecca would be able to study while Jenny played.

"I'm sorry I'm late," Ben said from the doorway. "I had to do some hunting to find what I wanted to bring. I hope you haven't been waiting too long."

"No. Just a few minutes." She smiled at him.

Ben brought a stack of books and dropped them on the table before taking a seat adjacent to her. "I suppose we need to determine what classes you might be interested in."

"Anything that will let me take some of the work off my mother. Michael has been keeping the books for her, but now that he's starting his own family, Mama doesn't want to burden him with the day-to-day business."

"I understand," Ben said. "So, let's start with what you already know and are accomplished at. Did you take math in school?"

"Actually, I did very well in it. I graduated at the top of my class." For some reason, she didn't want Ben to think she'd never finished her schooling. At least she had managed to graduate. But with a child to raise alone, her degree hadn't helped much in finding the kind of work she needed.

"That's a plus. I suppose you might like a course in accounting?"

"That would be wonderful."

"What about typing? Do you want to—"

"Oh, yes! Mama said she wants to buy a typewriter like the one at the Ladies' Aide Society, to keep up with the times, and I'd love to learn to type."

Ben nodded. "I think you should. It's a great skill to acquire. Many large companies hire typing pools now and I believe the future for typists will only get brighter." He chuckled. "Maybe Mrs. Heaton would like to learn to type, too?"

Rebecca laughed. "She might, but I think mostly she wants me to learn."

"We'll make sure you do, then. I'll speak to her about typewriters. The new Underwood is a wonderful machine. So right now, we'll get you started on basic accounting—some of which you may be familiar with from high school, and then we'll move on to advanced accounting—more in keeping with running a boardinghouse or any business."

"That sounds wonderful."

"Once we get you a typewriter, I'll give you practice lessons you can do here." He handed her a small manual. "In the meantime, look this over. There are illustrations showing the keys on the keyboard so you can become familiar with them—they will be the same no matter what typewriter your mother buys."

"Thank you, Ben. I'm excited to get started."

"I can tell, and I'm glad you are. It's always easier to teach someone who wants to learn." He pulled out a book and tablet from his stack. "The first few chapters of this math book might be familiar to you. There are problems at the end of each chapter you can work and I'll check them tomorrow."

Rebecca flipped through the first few pages and nodded. "I should be able to manage, although it's been a while since I had to study."

Ben sat back in his chair and smiled. "You'll get caught up with the class in no time, I'm sure. And you'll be learning other things from your mother about how she runs Heaton House, too. That should definitely be counted as a business course, for it's directly connected to what you'll be doing here. Hands-on experience is the very best kind."

"Mama said she'll start me off with the meal planning and shopping, so I know what we should be spending and can tell if we've been charged too much. And I need to learn how to order enough food for everyone, but not be wasteful with it."

Ben chuckled. "She does do a wonderful job of keeping us from going hungry. Your mother is a very special woman and there isn't anyone here who would want to live in any other boardinghouse."

"She loves you all, you know." And she did. Her mother's boarders were some of the nicest people Rebecca had ever met and suddenly she realized how grateful she should be to each one of them. For, while her mother and brother had constantly searched for her, having these people in their lives must have made the wait a bit easier. Once more she fought back the guilt for what she'd put her loved ones through.

"We're thankful for her. And we're all very glad you and Jenny are here with her now."

The compassion in Ben's eyes made Rebecca wonder again how much he knew about what had happened. But she wasn't going to ask. She gathered the books Ben had given her. "I've taken up enough of your time this evening. I—thank you again, Ben. For this and especially for coming to Jenny's rescue today."

"I'm glad to do it, Rebecca. Anytime. I'll have a better lesson plan for you tomorrow evening."

"All right. I'd best go check in on Jenny. Good night, Ben."

"Good night, Rebecca."

Something in the way Ben looked at her made Rebecca a little breathless and sent her hurrying out of the room, down the hall and up the stairs before she could give any thought to why.

The next afternoon, Ben tidied up his desk after the last class and was on his way out when one of his students knocked on the door.

"Mr. Roth? Do you have a minute?" Josh Benson asked. He was one of the orphans Ben had helped get a scholarship and would be graduating with honors at the end of the spring term.

"I always have time for you, Josh. Come on in. What can I help you with?" He pulled a chair up to his desk and motioned to the young man to take a seat.

"Well, I have some news to tell you and I want your advice about it."

"Fill me in."

"I'm applying for a position teaching math at the new Morris High School opening this fall, and I'd surely like an endorsement from you."

"Are you sure this is what you want to do, Josh? Teaching isn't the best-paying job out there, at least at first."

"Yet, you do it. I've admired you for years, Mr. Roth. I want to follow in your footsteps and help others get ahead the way you do for so many."

Ben couldn't contain his smile. "Thank you, Josh. You will make an excellent teacher and I'll be more than happy to give you a solid recommendation. What does Annie think about all this?" Annie was Josh's fiancée and Ben hoped she loved Josh more than Mary Reynolds had cared for him. Ben had thought he and Mary would have a wonderful life together—until he'd proposed and Mary told him she couldn't live on the salary of a teacher, that there would never be enough money.

A grin split Josh's face. "She's behind me one hundred percent, sir. She knows we won't be making much, but she shares my dream of helping others."

"I'm glad to hear it. Annie is an admirable young woman. Don't let her get away."

"I won't."

"I've got an errand to run this afternoon, but stop by tomorrow and I'll have the recommendation ready for you."

Both men stood and shook hands. "Thank you, sir. I appreciate everything you've done to help me."

"You're welcome. I wish you all the best." Ben quickly locked up his room after Josh left, and headed down the stairs. He prayed things worked out well for Josh and Annie. They deserved a wonderful life together.

At the corner, Ben caught a trolley to pick up paper and extra ribbon for the typewriter he'd ordered for Mrs. Heaton at her request last night. He'd spoken with her after Rebecca went upstairs and they'd made arrangements for him to order her a brand-new Underwood. Ben eased the front door open and made sure no one was around before hurrying to Mrs. Heaton's study. The Underwood had been delivered and Mrs. Heaton clasped her hands together and watched as he unpacked the box.

"I'm glad Rebecca was out when the delivery boy came, so we can surprise her," Mrs. Heaton said. "I can't wait to show it to her."

"Neither can I." Ben set the gleaming typewriter on her desk. "Here it is. What do you think?"

"Oh, my, it is a beauty, isn't it?" Mrs. Heaton said.

"It's the newest model out. I realize it cost a bit, but it should last you for years to come."

"I'm sure it will. I want the best for Rebecca to use."

Ben set the typewriter up, installed the ribbon and put in a sheet of paper. "Want to try it?"

Mrs. Heaton grinned. "I suppose I should find out if it works before we surprise Rebecca with it, shouldn't I?"

She looked as excited as he hoped Rebecca would when she saw it. "Oh, I think so."

Mrs. Heaton sat down at her desk and began to peck at the keys. "Oh! These keys are much easier to press than the one I've tried at the Ladies' Aide Society! They sometimes stick."

Ben chuckled. "Probably needs some servicing."

"Most likely." Mrs. Heaton tapped a few more keys and then got up from her desk. "Maybe I'll learn how to do more than hunt and peck, too. Thank you for picking this up for me, Ben, and for getting me a good discount. We'd better get out of here before Rebecca finds out what we're up to. I need to check on dinner, anyway. We'll surprise her afterward."

They had barely made it out of the study before Ben heard Jenny's voice. "Hurry, Mama. I'm hungry!"

"I'm coming, but we can't eat until we're called to dinner, you know."

"Can't I go to the kitchen and find out what Gretchen is cooking? Do you think she'll give me a taste?"

"She might."

They reached the bottom of the stairs just as Ben and Mrs. Heaton did.

"Come with me, Jenny, and we'll see how dinner is coming along." Mrs. Heaton held out her hand.

"May I, Mama?" Jenny smiled up at her mother.

"You may. Aren't you going to say hello to Mr. Ben, first?"

Jenny waved to him, her smile a little shy. "Hello."

"Hello, Jenny. Have you had a nice day?" Ben asked.

She nodded. "And I didn't try to fly down the banister today."

"That's good. I'm sure your mama is happy about that."

The little girl giggled and nodded before turning to her grandmother. "Come on, Granma. Let's hurry things up."

"Let's go." Mrs. Heaton gave a little wave and they hurried off, leaving Ben and Rebecca in the foyer.

"Sounds as if you had a pretty good day since Jenny didn't try to repeat yesterday." Ben grinned at her.

"That child..." Rebecca smiled at him. "Yes, it's been a nice day. I worked on the assignments you gave me and I think I did all right."

"I'm sure you did. I'll check them over this evening, if that works for you?"

"Whenever is convenient for you is fine with me. You're helping me, remember?"

"I am. But I don't have a child to take into consideration. If you need to wait until you put her down for the night, I don't mind. It'll give us more time anyway. I will be going to the YWCA around seven-thirty to teach for about an hour or so."

"Oh, that will work out well for me, Ben. By the time you get back, Jenny should be asleep and I'll be able to concentrate a little better."

"Good. Where shall we meet?"

"I'll be in the small parlor."

She smiled and Ben's chest tightened. Something about Rebecca had him not only wanting to help her but to get to know her. He told himself it was because she was his landlady's daughter who'd had a hard time, and if he knew more about her, he'd know how to help her better.

Yes, he'd always had a soft spot for women who raised children by themselves—but he wasn't totally sure that was all there was to it. Those women didn't make him feel quite like this...he couldn't name it, didn't have any idea what to call it. He only knew he'd never felt quite this way before.

Mrs. Heaton appeared just then, with Jenny in tow, and announced dinner was ready. Other boarders hurried out of the big parlor or down the stairs to the dining room.

Ben held out both arms, thinking Mrs. Heaton would take one and Rebecca would take the other. His landlady did take an arm, but when Rebecca hesitated, Jenny rushed forward and placed her small hand inside the crook of his arm. She smiled up at him and in that moment Ben realized the little girl had claimed a very special place in his heart.

After putting Jenny to bed, Rebecca checked her hair, pinned up a few stray curls and then gathered her math book and started downstairs as the clock in the foyer chimed the half-hour.

She hurried down the hall and was surprised when both Ben and her mother came out of her study. "Rebecca! We've been waiting for you. Please come here for a moment before you and Ben get started on your lessons," her mother said.

"Of course. What's happened, Mama?"

"Well, we have a surprise for you."

"A surprise?" Rebecca looked from her mother to Ben and they both grinned at her. She followed them back inside, where her mother pointed at her desk. In the center of it sat a gleaming black typewriter.

"Mama! You bought one already?" The typewriter was beautiful, big and black with gold lettering proclaiming it an Underwood.

"I did. Ben recommended this brand and said he could get one at a discount for us. It was delivered this afternoon."

"That was very nice of you, Ben." Rebecca turned to him. His smile seemed to be contagious and she found herself grinning back at him.

"You're both very welcome. Now you can start those practice lessons."

"Speaking of lessons, I'll let the two of you get to them."

"Thank you, Mama." She hugged the mother, who kept showing her, in every way she could, how very happy she was to have her back in her life. "I'm going to learn quickly so we can put it to good use."

"I'm sure you will, dear." Her mother hugged her

back. “I’ll check on Jenny and send some tea in when I get back down.”

“I’ll probably need a cup,” Rebecca said as her mother left the room.

“Well, are you going to try it out?” Ben asked.

“I suppose I should.” Rebecca sat down at the desk. There was a fresh sheet of paper in the machine and she put her hands on the keys. They were laid out exactly as the picture showed in the manual Ben had given her the night before.

She looked ahead and began to hit the keys in the order of the alphabet as she tried to remember each one’s placement on the keyboard. Once she’d hit what she hoped were all the right keys, she glanced down.

“Oh, no! It appears I’m going to need a lot of practice.”

Ben came up behind her and began to chuckle as he examined the paper.

“I don’t think it’s very funny,” Rebecca said, but she couldn’t help but join in. She’d been wrong on each and every key.

“I have an idea what the problem is. You had your hands on the wrong keys to begin with.”

“What do you mean?”

“Here, let me show you. I’m going to place your hands in the right position.” He stood behind her and leaned over one shoulder.

Rebecca wondered if he heard her quick intake of breath at his nearness. She could smell his aftershave and feel the warmth in his hands as they took hold of hers.

"Keep your thumbs free and place your fingers on the four keys on either side of the *g* and the *h* keys."

"Like this?" Rebecca's voice sounded breathless to her own ears as she turned to him and found his face so close to hers she saw tiny flecks of gold in his blue eyes, giving them a blue-green tint. Her heart began to beat erratically and she quickly returned her attention to the keyboard.

"Exactly like that." Ben cleared his throat and backed away.

Rebecca could tell because some of the warmth that had been surrounding her suddenly disappeared.

"Now try again," Ben said. "But be sure to keep your fingers on those keys when you aren't using them."

Rebecca took a deep breath and began to tap out each letter as she had before, only a little slower than before. She smiled when she finished. This time, she'd only missed a few letters.

"Very good," Ben said. "You'll get better with practice. Did you bring your math with you?"

"I did. It's right here." She picked up the book and the notebook she'd done her problems in from the corner of the desk and handed them to him.

"I'll check them over while you practice and then we'll go over your problems together."

"All right." Rebecca was happy trying again. Learning to master this machine had quickly become a goal and she wouldn't settle until she had accomplished that.

She began again, trying to keep from looking over at Ben sitting in one of the chairs flanking the fireplace. It wasn't easy to do and her next set of letters showed she'd better get her mind off the man and on to concentrating on typing. This time she looked at the fire in the grate and not Ben. And she had only two mistakes.

She smiled and tried again. And again. After about three more tries she looked over to see if Ben was still going over her math, only to find him looking at her with a smile on his face. When she thought to smile back, she realized she already was.

"You must've done very well, you look quite pleased with yourself," Ben said as he got up and came over to inspect her typing.

Gretchen came in with a pot of tea for her and Ben and several cookies. "Your timing is great, Gretchen. Rebecca just finished her practice and I must say she deserves a treat. She's had a great practice run."

Gretchen chuckled. "That's good. Mrs. Heaton said you might be ready for some refreshment about now." She set the tray down, poured two cups, handed them out and made her exit.

Rebecca reached for a cookie, took her tea and went to sit in one of the chairs flanking the fireplace. Ben followed with a cookie and his cup and returned to the seat he'd vacated.

"You really did great. What did you do? Memorize the keys?"

"I worked at it today." Rebecca sipped her tea.

"Your memory must be excellent."

"What makes you think so?"

"You remembered your high school math quite

well, too. You're a very intelligent woman, Rebecca. You'll have no problems at all with your courses."

Rebecca flushed at his compliment. "Thank you. I always liked school—but I was impatient to graduate and be an adult."

"That's the way a lot of us were."

"Yes, and I thought I was ready for what the world held. I had a lot of lessons to learn." She caught her breath at her own words. What was she doing talking to him like this? She didn't share those kinds of thoughts with anyone.

"Some lessons are difficult for us."

She wanted to ask if he'd had to learn anything the hard way, but that would be much too nosy. She only nodded and changed the subject instead. "Do you have new assignments for me?"

"I do." He handed her a sheet of paper. "I'll check this tomorrow and see what progress you're making on your typing." He gave her a booklet. "Work on your letters tomorrow and then when you think you're ready, this will get you started on the first real typing lesson, sentences and all. I think you'll be ready to start your math classes at the Y next week."

"So soon?" Rebecca asked. "Oh, I'm not sure, I—"

"You'll do fine, I'm sure of it. You can keep doing your typing here. You'll get more practice in working from home. As for your math, maybe next term, you might consider taking a more advanced business accounting class at the Y."

"I—if you think I'll be ready."

"I do." Ben said.

They both seemed to finish their tea and cookies

at the same time. Ben stood and stretched. "I guess I'll look in and see what's going on in the front parlor. Are you coming in?"

She shook her head and placed their cups on the tray. "No. I'm going to take these to the kitchen and call it a day. Good night, Ben, and thank you for all your help."

"You're very welcome. Good night, Rebecca."

She put her lesson books under one arm and took the tray to the kitchen, where Gretchen was kneading dough for sweet rolls the next morning.

Rebecca went down the hall to the foyer. In the front parlor, Julia was playing the piano while the others sang along. Rebecca headed up the stairs. For a moment she thought of going back and joining them. The few times she had, she'd enjoyed singing with everyone.

But she was tired. Jenny had been active all day, talking of little else than how Ben had caught her from flying off the banister the day before. Rebecca had no doubt Benjamin Roth had become her daughter's hero in that instant.

Truth be told, he might have become Rebecca's, too—*if* she didn't know all too well how quickly a hero could turn into a villain. Sadness welled up inside. She prayed her daughter never had to learn that lesson.

Chapter Three

Over the next few days Rebecca's typing improved greatly and by the weekend her papers showed few mistakes but little speed.

"You will get faster, I promise," Ben said as they waited to be called to dinner on Friday. "That's what all the practice is about. You haven't been at it even a week yet. Give yourself a break. You're doing really well with your math assignments."

"Thank you. You're right. I suppose I am being impatient. I'm taking a break tonight. I promised Jenny I'd take her over to Michael and Violet's to see baby Marcus."

"That's a good idea. It will do you both good to get out. I'll be glad to escort you over and come and get you."

"Thank you. I'll accept your offer." She lowered her voice. "I'm not used to living under my mother's rules again, but I understand why she put them in place and I certainly can't go against them now I'm making my home here."

Mrs. Heaton had a hard-and-fast rule that young

women living at Heaton House did not go out and about alone after dark. They had to be in a group or one of the male boarders had to escort them. "I'm sure she appreciates your attitude."

"It's the least I can do. Besides, I wouldn't put Mama through that kind of worry again."

Ben wanted to ask more, to know what exactly she'd done that she felt so bad about. Oh, he knew she'd left home and never gone back until Kathleen and Luke had found her last year. And he'd worked with many young women living on their own. Their stories were sad, most regretted whatever they had done that had brought them to the place they were—having to learn a skill to provide for themselves and their child, or in the case of some, their children.

But they volunteered the information on their own, and Rebecca's past wasn't something he thought he should ask about no matter how badly he wanted to. It was none of his business and he didn't want to bring her more pain by having to dredge up what she'd been through. In the meantime, he sensed she needed a friend and he could be that for her. "What time do you want to leave?"

"Soon as we finish dinner. Violet said she wouldn't put little Marcus down until about eight-thirty, so we won't be there long. I hate for you to take us, come back, and then have to turn around and come get us, though. Why don't you stay and visit, too?"

"I will. I haven't visited with them in a while."

Mrs. Heaton called everyone to dinner and once they were all seated, she asked Ben to say the blessing.

As always, dinner was very good and tonight the conversation centered on the building Matt was working on. It was one of the tallest in the city and his tales of working his way into the sky kept the interest of everyone at the table.

"I can't imagine working up so high." Rebecca waved her hand toward the ceiling.

Millicent dipped her spoon into her soup. "Neither can I. I'd love to get photographs from up there, but I—" She broke off and shivered.

"I'd sure like to see the city from up high." Ben turned to Matt. "It must be some view."

"It's something, that's for sure." Matt nodded. "I think that's why I love working on these buildings. The view is breathtaking."

"If you don't fall off the scaffolding!" Millicent said.

"Believe me, I don't intend to."

The subject of heights and the danger of Matt's profession always seemed to be a sore spot between the two, and Ben often wondered if they had feelings for each other.

Once dinner was finished, Rebecca turned to Jenny. "Run up and wash your hands, so we can go visit Aunt Violet and Uncle Michael, and baby Marcus, of course. We need to get going."

"I'll hurry, Mama," Jenny said, slipping out of her chair and running out of the room.

Rebecca turned to her mother. "Ben has offered to escort us there and back, Mama."

"How nice of you, Ben," her mother said, giving him a smile before turning back to her daughter. "The outing will be good for you, dear. Cuddle baby Marcus for me."

"I will. I'd better go freshen up a bit myself. We'll be back down in a few minutes, Ben."

"I'll be here."

Once they left the room, Mrs. Heaton turned to Ben. "Thank you for offering to escort them, Ben. Rebecca has been on her own for a long time, having to do things by herself. But I do so appreciate her trying to live by the rules I've set for the other women at Heaton House."

"You're welcome. And I'm sure Rebecca wouldn't want to undermine your rules for the others."

"No. She wouldn't." Mrs. Heaton nodded. "I do hope she'll start joining you all on your outings and leave Jenny with me before too long. Rebecca needs to have a little fun in her life."

"I'm sure we'll be able to talk her into some outings, Mrs. Heaton. We'll do our best." He certainly would.

"Thank you, Ben. I think being around you all is exactly what my daughter needs right now."

She didn't elaborate and Ben didn't press.

"We're here!" Jenny bounded back into the dining room. "Are you ready, Mr. Ben?"

Ben jumped up and grinned at the child. "I am, Miss Jenny. But where's your mama? Isn't she going with us?"

Jenny giggled. "Of course she is, but she's not as fast as I am."

"She's right, I'm not." Rebecca said, entering the room. "I must be getting old."

"You're not old, Mama," Jenny said. "Even Granma isn't old yet."

Mrs. Heaton laughed. "Oh, Jenny, darling, you are so good for your grandma! Come give me a kiss before you go."

Jenny ran into her grandmother's arms as her mother smiled and watched. The love in her eyes for her child and her mother touched Ben's heart. Rebecca *was* happy to be with her family again. One could see it—feel it even.

Rebecca's smile lit her face and Ben hoped she'd be smiling more in the days to come. It wasn't that she frowned. And it wasn't that she appeared to be in a bad mood. There seemed to be something keeping her from enjoying being back with her family to its fullest—as if she were afraid her joy would be taken away from her. As if she didn't deserve it.

Ben related—somewhat. At least he knew what it was to deny himself something he feared wouldn't last. His own mother had cast him aside, and then the woman he'd hoped to make a life with had rejected him. How could he ever trust that *any* other woman he might fall in love with wouldn't do the same?

"Ben? Are you ready?" He seemed lost in thought when Rebecca spoke to him, but he quickly turned to her and smiled.

"I'm sorry. I must have been woolgathering. Let's go."

"Better grab your wraps. It's getting cold out," Mrs. Heaton said.

"We will, Mama," Rebecca said. She couldn't help

but smile as they went to the foyer to get their jackets. She supposed she'd be telling Jenny the same thing when Jenny was her age. Since she'd become a mother, Rebecca had appreciated her own more than ever. Now she welcomed the chance to show her how much.

She helped Jenny on with her new jacket, thankful she had one warm enough for the cooler weather. Not long after she'd been found, Michael and her mother had called her into her office and told her that her father had left a small inheritance to her for when she turned twenty-one. But she'd gone missing by then. Still, they'd invested the money, trusting she'd be found one day and they turned it over to her.

What they called small had seemed like a fortune to Rebecca, although she realized she'd need to handle her inheritance well and she was determined to make sure she saved for Jenny's future. However, it had enabled her to purchase new wardrobes and to buy Jenny the doll she'd wanted so long for Christmas with plenty left over in savings—even after letting Michael invest some of it. Rebecca felt truly blessed as Ben helped her on with her coat and they hurried out into the brisk evening air.

Lights were on in most of the homes surrounding Gramercy Park, helping to guide the way to the trolley stop. The leafless trees stood stark against the night sky, but Rebecca knew that in a few months they'd be budding out to give much needed shade.

Rebecca loved the small park and was glad she had access to it because of living at Heaton House. She could take Jenny outside to play anytime—without worrying about the filth in the street or in the hallway of the building they'd lived in. She was so very thankful they were out of those tenements.

Now she smiled as she watched Jenny hop, skip and jump to the trolley stop, but she never got too far ahead. Once they got on, she climbed up onto Rebecca's lap and looked out of the window. They'd walked most places when they lived in the tenements and getting to ride anywhere was quite a treat for them both.

The ride wasn't a long one, which was a good thing because Jenny was very excited about seeing her baby cousin. As they stepped off the trolley and walked the block to Michael's home, she ran ahead just far enough to ring the doorbell as Rebecca and Ben reached the steps. The door flung wide to let them in.

"Hello, Uncle Michael! Is baby Marcus still awake?"

Michael swept Jenny up into his arms and gave her a kiss on the cheek, while Rebecca and Ben came in and took off their coats. "Yes. He's been waiting for you. We've missed you, Jenny!"

"I've missed you, too, but I do love being at Granma's."

"We're glad you do, but our house sure has been quieter since you've been gone."

"Doesn't Marcus make any noise?"

"Well, yes, but he can't talk, you know." Michael set her down and helped her off with her coat before handing it to Rebecca. "He's in the parlor with Aunt Violet."

Jenny took off in a run and Rebecca followed her into the parlor to ooh and aah over the baby. He was adorable, with Michael's hair and Violet's eyes, and holding him made Rebecca wish life might be different and she'd have a loving husband and more children. But that wasn't in her future and she pushed the thought to the back of her mind.

Michael and Ben joined them and they began talking sports while Rebecca and Violet talked about the upcoming housewarmings they'd all been invited to. Kathleen and Luke's party was first up for the next weekend and then Elizabeth and John Talbot's would be a few weeks later.

"I can't wait to see their homes," Violet said.

"Neither can I. I'm sure Elizabeth's aunt is helping her, but I should find out if Kathleen needs any help," Rebecca said.

It seemed odd to Rebecca that although her mother owned Heaton House and her background wasn't very different from those living at the boardinghouse, Rebecca sometimes felt more at ease around Kathleen than anyone. Perhaps it was because she'd been the one to persuade her to come back to her family.

Kathleen had lived in the tenements, too, although they hadn't known each other then. Still, there seemed to be a kinship in having lived in similar places. There was no need to discuss the conditions there, for they were much the same for all of them. It was comforting to be around others who'd wondered if they would ever be able to get out.

They were all proof one *could*, and as Kathleen and her sister, Colleen, had been able to help others in those situations, now Rebecca found she wanted to lend a helping hand in a similar way. She just wasn't sure how.

"I imagine Kathleen would appreciate some help," Violet said. "I am so happy for them all, but things must be a lot quieter at Heaton House."

"Things aren't quite as lively as they used to be with everyone there. Mama plans to put an advertisement in the paper as soon as the remodeling she wants to do is finished."

"I'm glad you're there to help her with all that, sis. How's everything else going for you?" Michael asked. "Ben told me you're taking classes from him."

Rebecca nodded. "Everything is going well, and yes, I start classes this coming Tuesday. Ben has been helping me catch up with his students."

"She's excellent at math and she's going to do really well in the business classes," Ben said

"She's always been very smart," Michael said with a smile. "Thanks for helping her out, Ben."

"It's been my pleasure. I like helping people, just as everyone else at Heaton House does. Mrs. Heaton's good works are an inspiration to us all."

Rebecca had a feeling Ben had helped others long before he moved to Heaton House. He was that kind of person. "I am so proud of Mother and all of you for helping others in this city the way you have," Rebecca said. "I hope to find a way to help, too. But I'm not sure where to start."

"Being with mother and living at Heaton House, I'm sure you'll have many chances to do what you can," Michael said.

"I do hope so," Rebecca said.

"Oh, no doubt about it," Ben said. "The opportunity to help others will come your way."

* * *

They chatted for a while longer, until baby Marcus began to fuss, signaling it was time for company to leave. They put on their coats and Ben waited as Rebecca and Jenny gave kisses and hugs, and then the three of them hurried out into the brisk night air.

A sudden gust of wind made it even colder as they started toward the trolley, and Jenny surprised Ben by holding up her arms to him. "Will you carry me, Mr. Ben?"

"Jenny, I'll carry you," Rebecca said.

The child shook her head. "I want Mr. Ben to."

"I don't mind, Rebecca," Ben said, bending down to lift the child into his arms.

"But—"

"Hurry, Mr. Ben. Here comes the trolley and it's cold!" Jenny said. "Run, Mama!"

Rebecca had no choice but to keep pace with Ben as he rushed toward the trolley stop, trying to keep her child warm. They entered the streetcar and Rebecca quickly found a seat by the window and then held out her arms to Jenny. "Come on, sweetie. Mama will hold you now."

Again, Jenny shook her head before laying it on Ben's shoulder, turning his heart to mush as he slid into the seat by her mother. He looked down at Rebecca, who seemed taken aback by the fact that Jenny wanted him to hold her and unsure as to whether or not to pull her daughter out of his arms and into hers. "She's fine, Rebecca. I don't mind at all."

Rebecca sighed and nodded her head. "All right. This time."

He had a feeling she was as surprised as he'd been that Jenny wanted him to hold her. After only a few moments, one of the child's arms relaxed and dropped down from around his neck. He looked at Rebecca and whispered, "I think she's already asleep."

Rebecca leaned over to look at her daughter. "You're right. She is."

Lowering his voice so as not to waken the child, he broached the subject he'd wanted to bring up. "You know…you said you'd like to help others?"

"Yes, I would. I'm just not sure—"

"I have an opportunity for you."

"Oh?"

Ben nodded. "Remember, I mentioned how you'd be an asset to the classes I teach at the Y?"

"Yes. What are you thinking?"

Ben took a deep breath and looked her in the eyes. "Most of the women I teach have a really tough life and they could use a mentor—someone who's come through some hard times, too, who can listen to them, give them encouragement and advice. I think you would be the perfect person."

"Oh, Ben, I'm not sure. I—"

"You don't need to answer just now. Wait until after you meet them and get to know them and then make your decision. Please."

"I…all right. I'll meet them. I'm not sure I'm the right person for this, though."

"I'm certain you are, but the decision is yours. I won't push."

Rebecca nodded. "We'll see what happens."

"That's all I can ask." Jenny stirred in his arms and

flung an arm tighter around his neck. This child had wormed her way into his heart in the past few weeks and he had no idea what—if anything—to do about it.

There was no getting around the fact that he liked holding Jenny and sitting next to her mother. It felt... right. He glanced down at Rebecca. He'd enjoyed the evening a great deal. Maybe too much for his own good. Having a child steal his heart was one thing. Losing it to her mother was something entirely different. He couldn't let it happen.

By Tuesday evening, Rebecca was a bundle of nerves. Ben had assured her she would do fine and he'd help with any problems she might encounter. Still, leaving Jenny and meeting new people, some of whom Ben wanted her to mentor, had her wondering if she should have delayed taking classes for a few months.

But Jenny was excited about Granma putting her to bed—most probably because she hoped to get an extra snack—and Rebecca was sure her mother would be disappointed if she backed out.

So she did what was expected of her and was ready when Ben came up from downstairs. He helped her on with her wrap and she kissed Jenny. "You be a good girl for Granma, okay?"

"I will, Mama. I promise. Don't worry. We'll be fine."

"I know. Love you."

"Love you, too, Mama."

Rebecca turned so no one could see the sudden rush of tears to her eyes at her four-and-a-half-year-old daughter's reassurance. How did she know it was exactly what Rebecca needed?

She and Ben walked out into the cold night air and he took her arm as they headed toward the trolley stop. "That's some daughter you have."

Rebecca swallowed hard. "Yes, I know. I don't know what I'd do without her. Sometimes she's wise beyond her years."

"She will be fine, you know."

Ben's understanding that she had mixed emotions about leaving Jenny made her feel better.

Their trolley arrived and they hurried on. It felt warmer inside but not by a lot, and Rebecca was thankful for Ben's warm shoulder next to hers. It wasn't nearly long enough before they arrived at the stop a couple of blocks from the Y and they stepped out into the cold once more.

Ben took her arm and pulled her close as they hurried down the walk. He led her into the building and upstairs to the third floor and into his classroom. The room was nearly filled with women, some younger than Rebecca, most about her age and a few older. They chattered amongst themselves in small groups, but the moment Ben entered, they all quieted and hurried to their seats.

There was one seat in the second row and Ben motioned for her to take it. Then he turned to smile at everyone.

"Good evening, ladies. It's nippy out this evening, isn't it? Glad you all could make it. You might've noticed there's a new classmate with us tonight." He motioned to Rebecca. "This is Rebecca Dickerson and she's my landlady's daughter. I'd like you all to meet her, so if you stay over after class, I'll introduce you."

Then he opened his book and went to the chalkboard where the same math problems she'd worked on earlier in the day were written out on the board. Rebecca relaxed a bit when she realized she could work them all. Maybe starting class now would be easier than she'd thought.

She loved Ben's style of teaching. He made it fun and had them all laughing from time to time as they worked through the problems. She could tell his students all liked him…some probably more than a little. He lavished praise when one got a problem right and was encouraging when the answer was wrong.

Rebecca realized class was over only when Ben gave out the next assignments. The time had flown by. Evidently the others thought so, too, for no one seemed to be in a rush to leave, and she was pleased when a couple of them introduced themselves to her.

A young woman named Sarah came up first. She had blond hair and hazel eyes and a sweet smile. Molly introduced herself next. Her hair was brown, her eyes green and fairly sparkling with liveliness. She would probably be fun to be around. Rebecca had a feeling they wanted to know how well she and Ben knew each other, but they didn't have a chance to ask.

Ben came up right then and introduced some others to her, explaining that Rebecca had a young daughter and wanted to be able to make a good living to support herself and her child, like many others there.

A few appeared skeptical but still welcomed her to

the class. She wouldn't remember all of their names right away, but hopefully she'd put names to faces before long.

As they all said good-night and went their separate ways, Rebecca realized she looked forward to the next class. Ben erased the board and then they headed back outside. It had turned even colder and she was glad when Ben drew her arm through his and took the brunt of the cold breeze as they hurried toward the trolley stop.

He stopped abruptly at a small café near the stop and looked down at her. "Want to get some hot chocolate to warm us up for the ride home?"

Rebecca hesitated only a moment. There was no need to hurry. Jenny would be fast asleep by the time they got back anyway and she was really cold. "That sounds wonderful."

The small café felt cozy and warm—probably because it was nearly full of customers. But Ben seemed to know the proprietor and they were quickly shown to a table near the front window. Ben gave the order for two hot chocolates and smiled at her as the waiter hurried away. "At least it's warmer in here."

Rebecca shivered and chuckled. "It'd have to be. I hope this cold spell eases soon."

"So do I. But I'm not ready for it to get too warm. I'm looking forward to doing some ice-skating soon."

"Oh, that would be fun. Jenny's been asking to learn, but I haven't skated in a long while."

"I'll be glad to teach her."

"That's very nice of you, Ben."

The waiter brought their drinks, and Rebecca

wrapped her hands around the cup, warming them before she lifted it to her lips. She took a small sip and let the warm liquid thaw her insides. "Mmm, this is delicious. Thank you for thinking of this, Ben. I'm warmer already."

"You're welcome. I stop here often." He smiled and took a sip of his own hot chocolate. "How did you like class?"

"I enjoyed it. You really are a very good teacher, Ben. Those women hung on every word. I think there might be a few students who are a little sweet on you."

"Oh, no. I don't think so. They are quick learners, though. I'm pleased with their progress. Do you remember any of their names?"

"I seem to recall…Sarah. I think that's it? Blond hair."

"Yes, that would be Sarah Jarvis. She's one of the women I thought might benefit from getting to know you. She seems a little lost at times and I think she needs another woman to talk to."

"She seems a little shy. But very sweet."

Ben nodded. "Then, to her opposite, is Molly, who doesn't have a shy bone in her. She's very outspoken, but kind."

Rebecca nodded. "I remember her, too. How old are they?"

"Sarah is seventeen going on eighteen and Molly is almost nineteen."

"I thought they might be around those ages. And they are very nice. But, Ben, I'm still not sure I can help."

"Please don't say no until you get to know them and their situations better, Rebecca."

The plea in his eyes had her asking, "Why is helping these women so important to you, Ben?"

He took a sip of his chocolate and leaned back in his seat. "Over half of the women I teach are living in the tenements, raising children by themselves with no man around to help support them. As you saw, several young women in class are obviously expecting babies." Ben shrugged. "They aren't all married and I fear any of them might give their children away if things get too hard for them. I want to help them be able to find positions that will provide a living for them, so they won't do...what my own mother did. Drop those babies off at an orphanage."

Rebecca's heart seemed to shatter at his words. The very thought that Ben's mother had abandoned him made her want to weep. She blinked to hold back tears. "I'm so sorry, Ben. I didn't know."

"It's not something I talk about. But you wanted to know why I care so much and that's it. However, I am a man and their teacher, and I must be careful in how I help. I feel my job is to teach them the skills they must have to get a decent job."

He looked out the window for a moment before continuing. "But I believe they need to talk to a woman who has lived in similar conditions, who knows things can change for the better. They need someone to encourage them on a level I can't. That's why I asked you to help."

Rebecca couldn't resist—not after he'd opened up

to her. Besides, she wanted to help others and he'd just given her an opportunity to do so. "I'll do what I can."

"Thank you, Rebecca. That's all I ask."

Wanting to comfort him, Rebecca impulsively reached over and touched his hand. "Ben, for what it's worth, and speaking as a mother...I'm sure *your* mother must have thought she had no choice. And giving you up *had* to have been the most difficult thing she ever had to do."

Ben's fingers curled around hers and squeezed, sending a shot of electricity straight to her heart. "Thank you, Rebecca. Your thoughts are worth more than you realize."

The expression in his eyes warmed her as much as the hot chocolate she'd been sipping had and she quickly slipped her fingers away from his. "I guess we'd better be going."

"I suppose so." He looked out the window. "I think our trolley is coming now."

They took one more sip of their drinks before heading outside. Rebecca almost hated for the evening to end, but the sudden burst of cold air took her breath away and brought her to her senses. She couldn't start weaving sweet moments into impossible dreams—no matter how very much she longed to.

Chapter Four

The ride back to Heaton House was quiet. Ben seemed lost in his thoughts and Rebecca didn't know what to say. Her own thoughts were in turmoil, wondering how he must have felt all these years to know his mother gave him up, and trying to keep from thinking about how her heart had skittered at his touch.

She liked this man sitting next to her very much but she couldn't begin to care for him in any way except as a friend. There would only be heartache to follow if she did.

She was more like those women in his class than he knew. And even though he wanted to help them all, when it came to his heart, no man wanted to court a *used* woman and that was a fact she'd accepted long ago. She must take care not to let herself forget it now.

"Thank you again for agreeing to help, Rebecca," Ben said, breaking into her thoughts. "Please don't think I expect you to fix these women's lives. I know they are the only ones who can do that…and then only with God's help. I'd just like them to realize they can get through it all and make a good life for themselves. But I don't expect you to have to do any more than listen and encourage them, if they come to you. And if it becomes too much..."

The expression in his eyes was so earnest she had to reassure him. "I'll let you know."

Their trolley came to a stop and it was so cold out that Rebecca was relieved when he said, "Let's make a run for it!"

"Let's!" It was just what she wanted to do.

They took off laughing and she wondered if Ben felt as much like a child as she did. They reached Heaton House and hurried inside to the fireplace in the parlor.

"I'm so cold my teeth are chattering," Rebecca said, proving her point.

"Gretchen is making hot chocolate. That should warm you up," her mother said.

"We had some already and it didn't help for long." Ben shivered.

"It will this time," Mrs. Heaton said. "You aren't going back out into the cold tonight."

"How was Jenny, Mama? Did she give you any trouble?"

"None at all. I read her a story and listened to her prayers just a little while ago. I think she was asleep before I left the room."

"She usually is." Rebecca turned to warm her hands at the same time Ben did. Both of them were still shaking.

"She played charades with us before Mrs. Heaton put her to bed," Julia said. "She's very smart, Rebecca."

Rebecca turned back around with a smile. "Thank you. I think so, too."

"She takes after you," Ben whispered to her.

"Do you think so?" Rebecca felt heat rise in her face, but was it because she was standing at the fireplace or because of Ben's compliment?

"I do."

Maida, Gretchen's sister, came in with a loaded tray of steaming hot chocolate and they all took a cup. Rebecca sipped hers and let it slide down her throat. "Finally, I'm beginning to feel warm again."

Ben smiled at her over the brim of his cup. "Me, too."

"So how did your first class go, Rebecca?" Millicent asked.

"It went very well. Ben is a very good teacher. He managed to hold everyone's attention through math. And I think he has a few admirers in his class."

Ben shook his head. "No, I don't think so."

He seemed flushed and she wondered if she'd embarrassed him. She hoped not. But she was afraid to say more in case she made it worse.

"Well, I'm going to go check on Jenny. And I have homework to do, thanks to my teacher." She grinned at Ben before crossing the room to kiss her mother on the cheek. "Thank you for watching over my girl, Mama."

Her mother leaned close and whispered, "You know Ben has been added to her prayer list, don't you?"

Rebecca glanced over at the man and then back to her mother. "I do. He's kind of become her hero since he caught her that day."

"I figured as much. And that's good. Every girl needs one."

And every woman needed a hero, too. But Rebecca couldn't allow herself to start thinking of Ben that way. "I'm going up now."

"Good night, dear."

"Night, Mama." Rebecca turned back to the others in the room. "See you all tomorrow."

She left the room with a chorus of "Good night" behind her and headed up the stairs.

Rebecca quietly entered Jenny's room and looked down on her daughter. One arm was flung over her head, and her even breathing told Rebecca she was sleeping peacefully. She leaned down and planted a kiss on her forehead and almost wished Jenny would wake up so she could tell her she loved her. But Jenny slept on and Rebecca didn't disturb her dreams.

She tiptoed to the bathroom separating their rooms and pulled the door shut most of the way, but left it open enough to hear Jenny should she awake in the night. Not that she would, but Rebecca had shared a room with her for so long that she couldn't bring herself to shut the doors between them at night, except while she readied herself for bed.

Still a little chilled, she made quick work of it and opened the door once more. She went to her bedside and knelt to say her prayers, thanking the Lord for her daughter, for being reunited with her family and for forgiving her for bringing them pain.

And then she whispered, "Dear Lord, please comfort Ben tonight. I know it couldn't have been easy for him to open up to me and tell me about his mother. The memories must be terribly painful for him. Please give him peace. In Jesus' precious name, amen."

Rebecca slid beneath the covers and pulled them up high. Then she closed her eyes and listened…yes, in the quiet of the night she could hear Jenny's light breathing. She smiled and turned over. What would she do without her?

People around her in the tenements had urged Rebecca to give her up when she began showing—put her in an orphanage like Ben's mother had done. And she had given it some thought. But much as she knew she'd done wrong by trusting Jenny's father, she couldn't add to her sins by deserting her child.

She wondered what it had been like for Ben when he was Jenny's age…to know that he'd been left on the doorstep of an orphanage and that his own mother had deserted him. Her heart squeezed tight just thinking of it. Still, he'd grown up to be a wonderful man—but without the love of his mother. Suddenly, the tears Rebecca had fought when Ben told her about what his mother had done flooded her eyes and she buried her head in her pillow and wept for him.

Ben didn't tarry in the parlor long after Rebecca left. He went down to his room thinking back over her remark at the café about some of the women being sweet on him. The thought had him a bit unsettled. He sincerely hoped not. He tried to be very careful not to give the impression that he might be attracted to any of them, because he truly didn't return any interest like that. He wasn't there to find romance—he wanted to help those women better their lives. He cared about them to that extent only.

However...Rebecca was different. Something about her touched him in a way no one else ever had; otherwise, he'd never have been so open with her tonight. He couldn't put a name to what drew him to her, but the pull was strong and tonight he'd had to remind himself that he'd vowed never to fall in love again.

But the way Rebecca had reached out to him after he'd told her about his mother abandoning him, and her effort to comfort him with her assurance that his mother must have thought she had no choice had him on the verge of rethinking the vow he'd made.

Only for a moment, though, because Rebecca seemed to draw away and whatever dreams he'd thought to weave had disappeared before they ever formed. Which was probably for the best—he couldn't let himself begin to care too much for her.

Ben had a feeling Rebecca was as determined as he was not to trust her heart to another. Besides, she had Jenny to think of and that would most likely add to her resolve.

Still, he had enjoyed the evening in her company a great deal and he looked forward to class on Thursday, too. Surely they could be good friends. He didn't realize until tonight how much he needed to have someone *he* could confide in. Oh, the people at Heaton House were his friends. He even considered them his family, and he probably could have told any of them what he'd told Rebecca and they would have cared. But he'd never felt the need or desire to tell them.

If Rebecca hadn't asked such a straightforward question tonight, he probably never would have told her. But he was glad he had. Hard as it was to tell her he'd been dumped at the orphanage by his mother, Ben felt as if a load of baggage had been lifted from his shoulders. He didn't feel the need to tell others, but he also no longer felt the dread of telling anyone and seeing the pity in their eyes.

He'd never liked to think about it at all, and up until tonight, he'd always assumed his mother just didn't want him. Rebecca's insistence that his mother must have felt she had no other choice gave him something more to think about now. He wasn't sure he agreed with her, but he found he very much wanted to.

He was glad Rebecca had agreed to help some of the ladies in his class however she could, especially after tonight. If she could make him feel better, he was certain she'd be able to encourage those women.

All *he* had to do now was keep his attraction to her from growing. Ben had a feeling that was going to be much easier said than done.

The next morning, Ben came up from downstairs just as Rebecca and Jenny entered the foyer. Jenny's smile was contagious and he answered it with one of his own. "Good morning, Miss Jenny."

"Good morning, Mr. Ben," Jenny said. "How did Mama do in class last night?"

"She did very well."

"I knew she would. Granma and I prayed she would last night."

"I'm sure those prayers helped." Rebecca smiled down at her daughter as they entered the dining room. "Keep them up, okay?"

"I will, Mama."

"Good morning, everyone," Mrs. Heaton said from the end of the table.

"Morning, Granma!" Jenny held her plate while Rebecca filled it from the sideboard. Her grandmother helped Jenny get settled at the table while Rebecca filled her own plate.

Ben helped himself to sausage, eggs and the best biscuits around and took his seat at the table. "You two are up earlier than usual today. Do you have a big day planned?" he asked.

"We're going to drop Jenny off to help Aunt Violet with baby Marcus while Mama and I do the shopping this morning. And I might visit Kathleen later today to see if she needs any help getting ready for the housewarming this weekend," Rebecca said. "I'm going to telephone her after breakfast."

"That is coming up, isn't it? It will be good to get together with everyone again," Ben said.

"It certainly will," Mrs. Heaton said. "And next week the workers will be here to start remodeling the third floor. It shouldn't take too long to make the changes. Once it's finished, I'll put an advertisement in the paper. Or do you think I should just put a sign out?"

"I'd put the sign out. You're more likely to get people who know of or have heard of Heaton House that way and I think you'd have your new boarders in no time," Ben said.

"I think Ben's right, Mama," Rebecca added.

"I'll give it a try. If it doesn't work, I'll put an ad in the paper. I've always acquired new boarders quickly and I do hate to keep turning down people who see the ad after I've let the rooms.

Ben stood. "I'd better get going. You all have a nice day and I'll see you later."

"Bye, Mr. Ben," Jenny said. "See you later."

"I look forward to it, Jenny. You have fun with baby Marcus."

She nodded. "I will."

Ben's gaze met Rebecca's and her smile warmed him clear through to his heart. Funny how none of the other woman here had ever had that effect on him. He liked them all, but he'd never felt…quite the same way about them. He still didn't know why it'd been so easy to open up to Rebecca as he had the night before. But he wasn't sorry. He hoped one day she'd open up to him.

After dropping Jenny off at Michael and Violet's to play with baby Marcus, and having some hug-and-kisses time with him themselves, Rebecca and her mother were on their way to the grocer's. The day before, they'd taken stock of the kitchen pantry, made a menu for the rest of the week and then prepared a shopping list from the menu.

The grocer welcomed them in and her mother introduced them. "Mr. Hale, this is my daughter, Rebecca Dickerson. She'll be doing some of the shopping in the future and I'm going to show her how I go about it."

"I'm pleased to meet you, Mrs. Dickerson. There's no one better to teach a person about ordering for a boardinghouse than your mother. You'll learn a lot from her. I do hope we'll still be seeing you, too, Mrs. Heaton?"

"Of course you will. But I have two precious grandchildren to spend time with now and I won't mind giving up grocery-buying time to do that when I can."

"Ah, well, I can understand that. I've a couple grandchildren of my own I like to spend time with. It's too bad my wife passed away before they were born. She would have loved being a grandmother, just as you do."

The expression in Mr. Hale's eyes as he looked at her mother made Rebecca wonder if he might be a bit attracted to her. She could definitely see he had great respect for her mother and within a few minutes she knew why.

She was very precise in the amounts she ordered, she had no problem asking for the best price he could give her and she insisted on the freshest of everything she ordered, from vegetables to dairy products. She zipped around the store faster than Rebecca could keep up with her.

"Mama, slow down a bit. I'm trying to take notes, but you're going much too fast for me."

The proprietor chuckled. "She goes too fast for me sometimes, too, Mrs. Dickerson."

Her mother came to a sudden stop and turned

to them with a smile. "I'm sorry. I didn't realize I was being hard to keep up with. I'll try to go a little slower."

She did just that, which gave Rebecca a chance to make a list of things she needed to remember on the small note pad she'd brought with her.

When they had finished giving the grocer their order for staples—flour, sugar and the like, then fruits, mostly canned this time of year, and vegetables, some canned and some fresh—Rebecca was surprised that the end price wasn't higher.

The grocer promised to have everything delivered as soon as possible, and then it was on to the butcher's for the meat. The day was quite chilly, but nothing like it'd been the night before. The wind had died down and while the air was brisk, it didn't take one's breath away and they were able to converse along the way.

"Mama, I think Mr. Hale might be sweet on you."

Her mother looked at her and laughed. "Oh, Rebecca. No. I don't think so. He just likes my business."

"I don't think that's all he likes. I saw the way he looked at you. He is a widower. Perhaps he's in the market for a wife."

"Well, it certainly wouldn't be me. I enjoy watching my boarders' romances, but remarrying is not something I ever give a thought to for myself. Your papa was my first and only love, dear."

"I know. But that doesn't mean you couldn't fall in love again. You should give it some thought."

Her mother chuckled and shook her head. "I don't think so. I like my life just as it is and I have so much to be thankful for. I have my family reunited and two precious grandchildren, I have Heaton House and the boarders—my life is full and I don't have time for courting or romance. But you're still young, dear. I hope one day you'll start thinking of finding Jenny a papa."

That was not something Rebecca wanted to talk about at all, and she was relieved that they'd arrived at the butcher shop so she didn't have to comment. But she had a feeling her mother would be bringing the subject up at another time.

They entered the shop and Rebecca was introduced to Mr. Kelly. He was behind the meat counter and she wondered how he kept his white apron so pristine.

"Nice to meet the daughter of one of my best customers," Mr. Kelly said. "She is also one of my most demanding. Nothing but the best for her boarders, she always says."

Rebecca smiled, then stood back and made notes as her mother tried to get the very best deal she could on the meat she ordered to be delivered on different days that week.

"And you know I want the freshest you have on the day it gets to Heaton House." Her mother smiled at the butcher.

He smiled back with a twinkle in his eye. "I do know that, Mrs. Heaton. And I know that if I don't deliver what I promise, you'll be back in here with it, demanding your money back."

"You're certainly right about that, Mr. Kelly," her mother agreed.

"Your word of mouth has gotten me many a new

customer over the years, Mrs. Heaton. I'll not be disappointing you."

"Thank you. I think you are the best butcher in the neighborhood and you haven't let me down yet."

"Nor do I intend to. You ladies have a nice day."

"The same to you," Rebecca's mother said.

They walked out and Rebecca linked arms with her mother. "You certainly know how to do business with these people, Mama. I have much to learn."

"You'll do fine. You catch on quickly. Ben told me you'll be ready for advanced bookkeeping in no time at all."

"He did?"

"Yes, he did."

The fact that Ben truly did think she was intelligent made Rebecca feel she could learn whatever she needed to so that she could find a good position when the time was right. For right now, she was enjoying learning again and spending time with her mother. And she found herself looking forward to attending class at the Y the next evening.

"I've been wanting to ask you more about the class last night. Were the other women there nice?"

"They seem to be. I'll get to know them better over time, I'm sure. Ben seems to think I can be an encouragement to them—the fact that I lived in the tenements and all, but I'm not sure—"

"I agree with Ben. I believe you will be an asset to the class just as he suggested, dear. Many times people just need to realize there are others who've walked down a similar path, to give them hope and belief that they can get through their trials, too."

"I did tell him I'd do what I can to help."

"I'm so glad you did, Becca, dear."

Rebecca still wasn't certain she'd be able to help anyone, but she suddenly realized she wanted to very much. Without Kathleen's assistance, she'd never have been united with her family. She had to do what she could.

Chapter Five

Rebecca and her mother arrived back at Violet's to find that she had lunch waiting for them.

"Mama, Granma! Guess what? We're eating with Aunt Vi!"

"We are?" Rebecca loved seeing her daughter so excited and happy.

"Uh-huh. She said it was the least she could do with all the help I gave her with baby Marcus!"

"I telephoned Heaton House and told Gretchen not to expect you all home for lunch," Violet said. "I hope it's all right, Mother Heaton."

"Of course it is, dear," Rebecca's mother said. "That was very nice of you and it will be good to spend more time with you."

Hilda—Violet and Michael's housekeeper and Gretchen and Maida's younger sister—had made them creamed chicken with crusty rolls.

"This is wonderful, Hilda," said Mrs. Heaton when the young woman cleared their places and brought in warm gingerbread for dessert.

"Thank you, ma'am. I'm glad you like it. I used Gretchen's recipe." Hilda flashed a dimple when she smiled and headed toward the kitchen.

"We are so fortunate to have those sisters in our employment," Rebecca's mother said.

"Oh, I agree," Violet said. "I don't know what I'd do without her, especially now that we have Marcus. Michael gave her a raise and said she was worth every penny."

Rebecca's mother lowered her voice, "That's why I want to give Gretchen and Maida a sitting room of their own. They work long hours for me and it just doesn't seem right for them not to have any place to relax in their free time."

"I know they're going to love it, Mama."

"I'm so excited that work on it will be starting soon. They're sharing a room for now, thinking I just want to spruce up all the others, and they don't know what I'm doing for them."

"They'll be thrilled," Violet said. "All this remodeling, and Kathleen and Elizabeth moving into their own homes and decorating them is very exciting. I can't wait to see what they've done to their homes."

"I'm going over this afternoon to see if I can help Kathleen get ready for her party," Rebecca said. "I can't wait to see her."

"She and Luke stopped over to see how much Marcus had grown last night. They both seem very happy," Violet said. "I believe you ought to go into the matchmaking business, Mother Heaton," Violet added.

"I think she should, too," Rebecca said.

"What's matchmaking, Mama?" Jenny asked. "I'm not supposed to play with matches."

"No, you aren't. But matchmaking the way we're talking about is getting a man and a woman together so that they can fall in love and get married."

"Oh! That sounds like fun," Jenny said.

"Well, I haven't done anything except take in boarders so far and it has been fun watching them fall in love, Jenny. Sometimes it takes a while before they realize what's happening and it seems everyone else knows before they do. Only bad thing about it is I keep losing boarders and have to get new ones."

"Wonder what new boarders you'll have next? Maybe you can matchmake them," Jenny said.

Her grandmother chuckled. "Maybe. Or just let the Lord do the matchmaking. So far He's done a wonderful job of it. I just furnish the place for them to get to know each other and watch what happens."

"It is fun," Violet said. "Michael and I knew Luke and Kathleen were falling in love long before they did. And everyone knew that John and Elizabeth's sparring was in denial of the attraction they felt for each other."

"But they're all married now," Rebecca's mother said. "I have begun to wonder about Millicent and Mathew, but I'm not sure about them. He loves working on those tall buildings and she's afraid of heights."

"And of him getting hurt, I think," Rebecca said. "But there does seem to be something between them—although I haven't lived there long enough to know if it is attraction for one another or just that they are so opposite that makes the sparks fly."

"You know, I've never sensed that Ben and Julia were attracted to one another," Violet said.

Rebecca felt a funny little stab near her heart at the mention of Ben being attracted to Julia. Yet, she'd never seen anything to indicate he was, either.

"Nor have I sensed he was romantically attracted to Millicent," her mother responded.

"He's always been a good friend to us all. But if he ever wanted to court anyone at Heaton House, I never saw any evidence of it," Violet commented.

"No, neither have I," Rebecca's mother said.

That revelation left Rebecca feeling…relieved. And yet, he'd been through so much growing up in an orphanage, surely he must long to have someone to love…and especially to be loved by someone.

"I like Mr. Ben," Jenny piped up.

"We all like Mr. Ben, Jenny," Violet said. "Maybe one day he'll fall in love and there'll be another match made at Heaton House."

"Maybe…" Jenny looked at her mother. "Maybe you and Mr. Ben could make a match, Mama."

Rebecca felt the heat rush to her face. "Oh, I don't think so, Jenny. Mama isn't looking to fall in love with anyone. And besides, Mr. Ben is my teacher now, and…" She didn't know what to say next.

"But I sure like him, Mama."

"He is hard not to like, Rebecca," Violet teased with a smile and a gleam in her eye.

"Now, you all stop. Just because Heaton House is a bit empty at present doesn't mean you need to start pairing people up."

"At least not yet," her mother said. "I hope I don't

lose as many boarders at one time as I did this past year. I'm all for seeing people fall in love, but I do need to bring a few more renters in first. I think Julia may be seriously thinking of going out west before too long and, I really hope I have a full house by then."

"You really think she'll leave, Mama?" Rebecca asked.

"I do. Every time I get a letter from your aunt Pauline, describing Oklahoma to us, she seems to get more excited about it. But it will be hard to see her leave. She was one of my first boarders."

Rebecca could feel her sadness and realized it must be very hard for her mother to see her boarders go. She knew that they were like family to her and she was happy her mother had people to care for and who had loved her during the time they'd been apart. And once again, she hated that she'd put her mother through so much.

But she thanked the Lord for His forgiveness and that her mother had welcomed her home like the prodigal son's father had welcomed him. How blessed she was.

"Well, I hope there are going to be lots more matches made at Heaton House, Granma!" Jenny exclaimed, lightening the mood once more. By the time they finished lunch, they'd decided that Heaton House definitely needed new boarders—and as quickly as possible if there was going to be much matchmaking in the future.

Later that afternoon, Rebecca and Jenny caught a trolley to take them to Kathleen and Luke's home. It wasn't far from Heaton House, only in a different direction. The neighborhood was one of smaller homes than those surrounding Gramercy Park, but they were very well kept and Rebecca thought it a perfect area for the newlyweds.

Kathleen opened the door wide and enveloped them both in a hug. "It's so wonderful to see you two! Come in and I'll take your wraps, then I'll show you our home before we have a cup of tea."

Kathleen took Rebecca's jacket while she helped Jenny off with hers, and then hung them on a standing coatrack. Rebecca looked around at the foyer where a small table was set next to the staircase. It held a lamp and a dish for calling cards. She handed Jenny one of her cards that her mother had given her for Christmas to put in it.

On the right, the hallway opened up to the parlor, and behind the staircase a hall led down to what Rebecca presumed was the kitchen. "This is so nice, Kathleen."

"Thank you. We love it," Kathleen answered. "Come follow me. I'll show you the downstairs and then we'll go up."

The parlor was a nice size with windows on two sides, one a bay that looked out onto the street. The room was light and bright and done in burgundy and cream, and opened up into a nice-sized dining room, large enough to accommodate at least twelve guests.

"I love your table and sideboard, Kathleen. They're beautiful."

"We found them for sale in the paper and hurried over to see them before they were snapped up. We had to do a little refurbishing, but I think they turned out very nice."

"They're very pretty," Jenny added in her most grown-up voice.

"Thank you, Jenny," Kathleen answered, treating her like a lady.

The kitchen was nice and bright, and big enough to hold a breakfast table near a window looking out to their small backyard. "We have some of our meals in here because it's cozy, but we're so looking forward to having guests over so we can put our dining room to good use. It feels a little empty in there with just the two of us."

"Heaton House feels quite empty with you and Luke, and Elizabeth and John, all gone. Mama's going to put a sign out soon. Everyone is teasing her about having more of a matchmaking business than a boardinghouse one."

Kathleen chuckled as she put the kettle on. "That is certainly understandable. Plenty of matches have been made there. I'm very grateful for mine."

She led them up the back staircase to the second floor where there were two bedrooms and a smaller room, which they'd made into an office. Kathleen was allowed to work from home for the Ladies' Aid Society and Luke was a writer known for his dime novels, but with Kathleen and her family as inspiration, he'd written one on the living conditions in the tenements and how it was possible to get out of them and have a better life.

"Where is Luke, by the way?"

"He still works in here sometimes," Kathleen said

as she motioned to them to go back downstairs. Jenny hurried down and as she did, Kathleen whispered, "He says working in the same room with me is a bit distracting, so he rented a small office in Michael's building and has begun writing there. I must admit it makes the housekeeping easier, too, for I find him just as distracting as he does me." She smiled and her face flushed as they entered the kitchen.

Happy as she was that her best friend was so blissful, Rebecca couldn't help but feel a stab of regret for her past actions that she was certain would prevent her from ever having the kind of joy Kathleen was experiencing now.

But as Kathleen poured their tea and brought out some cookies for Jenny, she concentrated on her blessings—including being friends with this woman. Kathleen had become a true friend over the past several months and was the first person Rebecca told about how she ran away from her home in Virginia and came to live in New York City, and why she'd never gone back. She felt she could tell her anything.

"How are you doing? You've started classes at the Y, right?"

"I have. Ben is a very good teacher. He seems to come alive in that environment."

"Really? It's always been hard for me to picture him as a teacher. He's always seemed so mild mannered. Come to think of it, I don't really know all that much about Ben, but I always enjoyed his company along with the others. I suppose there is much more to him than I realized."

Very much more. But Rebecca couldn't share what

he'd confided to her. His being abandoned was his story to tell and not hers. "I suppose there's more to us all. You know all there is to tell about me, and you've shared things with me—"

"That not everyone knows. I'm glad to have you as one of my best friends, Rebecca."

"As I am you. Mine and Jenny's lives have been changed so much by you finding us and convincing me that my family loved me and—"

"Thank you, Mrs. Kathleen!" Jenny jumped up from her chair and hugged her.

"You're very welcome, Jenny." Kathleen hugged her back.

"Jenny loves her grandma, Uncle Michael, Aunt Violet and of course, baby Marcus. And she loves playing with your nephews at Colleen's, too."

"Uh-huh." Jenny nodded. "I love all the people at Heaton House and you and Mr. Luke, too."

"We love you, also, Jenny." Rebecca's and Kathleen's gazes met over the child's head. Sometimes it was too easy to forget how much young children were capable of comprehending. And just how much did Jenny understand? She was going to have to watch what she said in front of her daughter from now on.

Kathleen really hadn't needed her help in getting ready for the party, but Rebecca insisted on doing something, so they spent an hour polishing the silverware she and Luke had received as a wedding present. But that was all Kathleen would let them do.

Rebecca and Jenny hugged her goodbye and when they arrived back at Heaton House, Jenny opted for resting in her room while Rebecca did her typing exercises before dinner.

She headed down to the back parlor where she'd moved the typewriter so as not to bother her mother if she needed to work in her office. Jenny probably wouldn't sleep for long—if at all. She seemed to be growing out of her naps, but she loved her new room and liked playing with her dolls there.

Rebecca looked at the chime clock in the foyer. She had just about enough time to get a good practice in before the boarders started getting home. But first she went to the kitchen and found her mother having a cup of tea with Gretchen and Maida as she did many afternoons.

"Do you have enough left for me to have a cup? I'd like to take it to the parlor if you do."

"Of course," Maida said. "We always have the kettle on."

"You've had a busy day between shopping with me and visiting with Violet and Kathleen."

It had been a busy day, but Rebecca loved it. No longer were she and Jenny stuck in the tiny apartment in the tenements—they had family and friends and were free to visit them. She was busy with her lessons and learning how to shop. It had been a very long time since she'd felt as happy as she did right now.

"Where's that grandchild of mine?"

"She's resting…or playing in her room. I think all the clacking of the typewriter keys annoy her a bit."

Her mother chuckled. "Maybe I'll go up and see what she's up to while you practice."

"I'm sure she'd love your company, Mama."

Rebecca thanked Maida for her cup of tea and headed for the small parlor. She settled in front of the typewriter and enjoyed her tea, then set it aside and started on her practice lessons.

Ben would be giving her a real test that evening after dinner and she hoped to be able to beat her previous time with no mistakes. She checked the small clock she used to time herself, fastened her attention on her lesson and began typing as fast as she could read. Once she was finished, she glanced at the clock again. She was very close to beating her previous record but wasn't there yet, and she had several mistakes she circled.

Rebecca took a sip of now-lukewarm tea and began again. By the time she heard the front door open and the boarders coming in, she'd typed the same lesson four times, getting closer to beating herself each time. She was almost there. Maybe tonight she'd get it.

Ben put the next day's problems up on the blackboard, but his mind wasn't really on the task. He'd pushed thoughts of Rebecca from his mind all day. But now that his classes were over, she'd sneaked back in and he had no desire to push those reflections away.

When he'd seen her and Jenny first thing that morning, he'd realized how quickly he'd come to enjoy them being part of his day. Watching Jenny get used to living at Heaton House was heartwarming. Seeing her mother's reaction to her happiness had him wondering—again—what life had been like for them in the tenements and why they'd been living there in the first place. Perhaps one day she'd open up to him, but he had a feeling he'd have to earn her trust, be the kind of friend she needed, for that to ever happen.

He slipped on his jacket and headed out the door of his classroom, locking it behind him. Friendship like that took time to build, but it would be time well spent. Instead of taking the trolley to Heaton House, he hired a hack and had the driver take him the long way home through Central Park. He was happy to see skaters out on the ice in the lake. If there was no huge weather warm-up, perhaps he could convince Rebecca and some of the other boarders to go skating on Saturday. If so, he'd give Jenny her first lesson.

Heaton House was quiet when he arrived, except for the sound of typewriter keys coming from the back parlor. He hurried down the hall to peek inside. Rebecca was practicing, concentrating so hard she never heard his footsteps or saw him at the door.

He smiled and backed away. No sense disturbing her. It was near dinnertime and she'd be stopping soon. Besides, they'd be going over her work that evening anyway and he looked forward to spending some time with her.

Ben turned and took the stairs down to the ground floor to freshen up. He hoped Rebecca's shopping trip with her mother had gone well and wondered if she'd gone to visit Kathleen. He couldn't wait to find out what kind of day she'd had.

Rebecca glanced at the clock and jumped up. It was time to go check on Jenny and get ready for dinner. She neatened her work area and hurried upstairs to find her mother and daughter on their way down.

"Mama, Granma played dollies with me. We had such fun!" Jenny's eyes were shining and so were her mother's, for that matter. "She helped me get ready for dinner so I could come help Maida set the table."

"I hope that was all right, dear?" Rebecca's mother asked.

"Of course it is. I'll go freshen up and be right back down."

"No need to rush. Take your time."

Rebecca watched the two head off to the kitchen before going upstairs. She still felt a little strange not having Jenny along with her at all times. Should she feel guilty or rejoice that she knew Jenny was well taken care of and she could relax and enjoy some time to herself? She chose the latter and did as her mother suggested. She took her time getting ready for dinner.

She even changed into a different shirtwaist, one a little more appropriate for dinner than the one she'd worn shopping and over to tea with Kathleen. Then she repinned her hair and turned this way and that before a full-length mirror, suddenly realizing that she cared more about how she looked than she had in a long while.

Not that she didn't want to look neat and clean, but now she found she wanted to look pretty. Rebecca didn't want to think about why too deeply, so she turned on her heel and hurried out the door.

Going downstairs, she could hear the boarders had begun gathering in the parlor awaiting her mother's announcement that dinner was ready. Sometimes she wasn't sure if she should join them or not. Not that they hadn't made her feel welcome when she did, but she still didn't feel she quite belonged. She was a mother and had responsibilities they didn't. At least that's what she told herself.

Part of it was because they didn't know her past and that wasn't something she wanted to go into, although she felt that she wasn't being totally truthful with them. But...did they need to know every last detail about her life? She didn't know theirs.

Unsure what to do, Rebecca decided to check on Jenny. Maybe she'd join them tonight after she put her daughter to bed. Instead of going through the dining room to get to the kitchen, she turned down the hall to go in the back way and didn't see Ben as he came up from downstairs. She ran slapdab into his chest.

He reached out to steady her. "Whoa, there. Where are you going in such a hurry?"

They'd never stood quite this close, except when he'd handed Jenny to her that day she'd slid down the banister, and Rebecca felt a little breathless at his nearness. "I was...on my way to check on Jenny. I think she's in the kitchen."

"Did I knock the air out of you?" His hands still held her upper arms.

"No, I'm all right. I'm sorry I didn't see you. I was woolgathering, I guess."

She took a step back and he let go of her arms. "No need to be sorry. I'll let you go look for Jenny."

Before Rebecca made a move, her mother was announcing that dinner was ready.

Jenny came running down the hall. "I was just coming to tell you to come downstairs, Mama."

"And I was just coming to find you." She took

hold of Jenny's hand, but her daughter turned to Ben. "Hi, Mr. Ben."

He smiled down at her child and crooked his arm. "Hello, Jenny. Would you like an escort to dinner?"

Jenny nodded and slipped her small hand through his arm. His kindness to her daughter turned Rebecca's heart to mush.

Ben crooked his other arm and smiled down at Jenny. "I can escort your mama, too."

That same mushy heart gave a weak flutter as Rebecca put her hand through his arm. "Thank you, Ben."

They were the last ones at the table and Rebecca was relieved when no one seemed to notice as Ben seated Rebecca and then Jenny before taking his seat. She felt flustered and she wasn't sure why. The men at Heaton House had always escorted women to the table, or pulled chairs out for them—it was common courtesy, after all.

So why did she feel all fluttery on the inside?

Chapter Six

Once everyone found out Rebecca and Jenny had visited Kathleen, the conversation at dinner turned to the upcoming housewarming.

"What is her house like, Rebecca?" Julia took a serving of roast chicken from the platter being passed around.

"It's lovely, but I won't spoil her fun in describing it to you all. She's so excited about having everyone over."

"Are we supposed to give a gift for a housewarming?" Ben took a portion of creamed potatoes and passed the dish on. "I don't have the slightest idea what to get."

"Nor do I," Mathew said. "I'd be glad for any ideas you can give us."

"Why don't we all go together and buy something really nice for them?" Rebecca's mother suggested.

"That's a great idea, Mrs. Heaton," Millicent said. "But what should we get?"

"You know, she has a beautiful bay window that could use something...a plant or bowl maybe?" Rebecca asked. "She could put it in the window or set it the middle of her dining table."

"That's an excellent suggestion," her mother said. "What about a brass bowl large enough to hold a plant or pretty enough by itself?"

"Do you know where we'd find one?" Julia asked.

"I'm sure Macy's or Lord and Taylor will have something nice. Rebecca and I can go look tomorrow."

"May I go, too?" Jenny asked. "I love going to Macy's."

"Of course you may," Rebecca said. They'd rarely gone shopping for anything other than food when they lived in the tenements, but occasionally she'd managed to take Jenny to Macy's to look around.

"Let me know how much I need to put in," Ben said. "I'm relieved I don't have to go shopping for a gift. I had no idea what to begin looking for."

"We will. The cost shouldn't be too bad with all of us going in together."

Rebecca knew her mother could afford something herself, but she loved how she was trying to help the others with their gift giving.

"We'll do the same for Elizabeth and John's housewarming, too, if you'd like," her mother suggested.

"Yes, and we could choose it tomorrow, too," Rebecca added.

"Maybe we should get them the same thing?" Millicent asked. "That way, they'll know we love them all just the same."

"Good idea," Julia agreed.

"I'm glad we got that settled," Rebecca's mother

said. "We'll go shopping for two of the same item tomorrow, and make it clear that if they don't like the bowls, they can exchange them for anything else in the store."

With the subject of the housewarming party exhausted and dessert served, Ben took the opportunity to introduce a new topic. "I checked out Central Park today. Lot's of people were ice-skating. Want to try to go on Saturday?"

"That sounds fun," Mathew said. "What do you all think?"

"I think we should, if the weather lets us and the ice stays frozen firm," Millicent said.

Rebecca heard Jenny catch her breath and saw the hope in her eyes. "Oh, can we, Mama? Will you teach me how?"

There was no way she could refuse. "Well, I might be too rusty to teach you, but Mr. Ben has offered to, so yes, if the weather cooperates, we'll go."

"Oh, thank you, Mama and Mr. Ben."

"At the housewarming on Friday, we could ask the others if they'd like to join us," her mother suggested.

"Let's do." Julia smiled. "It'd be great if we all can make it. It's been a while since we've all gone on an outing together."

By the time dinner was over, everyone seemed quite excited about the upcoming weekend as they left the dining room.

Rebecca's mother offered to watch Jenny while she and Ben met in the small parlor so that she could take her first typing test.

"Thank you, Mama. Jenny is bound to be excited

about going skating for the first time and I'm sure it'll take a while for her to get sleepy. After the test I can get her ready for bed." She kissed both her mother and daughter on the cheek and turned to Ben. "Will now work for you, Ben?"

"Whenever you're ready is fine with me. I'll go get the test we use at school and be right up," Ben said.

"I'm not sure I'm prepared enough for this, but I'll be waiting in the parlor."

"You're going to do fine."

Ben headed downstairs while Rebecca continued on down the hall to the small parlor. She did feel nervous, although she'd practiced well. Maybe it was because Ben would be right there in the room with her, or that she didn't want to disappoint him or her mother.

She let out a big breath trying to let go of her anxieties. She'd do the best she could and if she didn't do well, she'd practice more. She wasn't going to quit. She was going to make sure she had the ability to take care of her and her daughter no matter what happened in her future.

Whatever she did, she'd do it to the best of her ability. She wanted to be treated with the same kind of esteem the merchants had shown her mother that morning. And...she wanted to feel respectable again.

Rebecca seemed lost in thought as Ben entered the room. "You ready?"

He must have startled her for she seemed to jerk out of her reverie and put a hand to her chest. "I'm sorry. I didn't mean to alarm you."

"I'm fine. I was just woolgathering. And I'm as ready as I'll ever be, I suppose." Rebecca took her seat in front of the typewriter.

Ben handed her a sheet of paper and pulled his watch out of his pocket. "Just type this as fast and accurately as you can. You tell me when you're ready and I'll start timing you soon as I say to begin."

Rebecca nodded and Ben watched as she rolled her neck and shoulders, then put her fingers in the correct position on the keyboard. As much practice as she'd been getting in, Ben didn't think she'd be nervous about this test, but obviously she was. "Relax, Rebecca. You are going to do fine."

"I'll try." She inhaled and let out a deep breath. "Ready."

Ben smiled, took a seat and looked at his watch. "Then you may…begin."

There was no hesitation as her fingers hit the keyboard and she began typing. The paper she was transcribing from was a copy of one of the practice sheets he'd given her earlier and he knew she'd used it the week before. He was sure she'd do well. He watched her for several minutes before checking his watch again. "Stop."

Rebecca immediately raised her hands from the keyboard as he came over and pulled the sheet of paper from the typewriter. "That was three minutes. Looks like you did pretty well on word count. I'll check that and your accuracy. Won't take but a few minutes."

Rebecca sat still as he went over her paper. Ben knew she was getting better, but she didn't know how fast she should be typing by now. She'd done very well on speed. He searched for mistakes and he found she'd done as well on the actual typing as he thought she had.

After only a few minutes, he smiled at her. "You've really improved since I checked last. You only misspelled one word and you averaged thirty-five words per minute. That's very good for how long you've been at it, Rebecca."

"What speed should I be typing to be able to get a good position typing?"

"You'd be able to get one now. But if you can get your speed up to forty to forty-five words per minute, you could get an even better-paying position. Or maybe even teach typing at the Y one day."

"Really?"

She smiled and her expression told him she'd never thought of teaching before, but the Y was always looking for people to teach classes. "Yes, really. Keep practicing to build up your speed and accuracy. I think you were a little nervous tonight, this being your first real test. I'll have you take another one next week, and I think I'm safe in saying you'll do even better then."

Rebecca's smile grew. "I'm certainly going to try. Thank you, Ben."

"I'm not doing anything—you're the one who is working hard and you've done really well."

As he watched a delicate pink creep up Rebecca's cheeks, he became more determined than ever to make sure she realized she could do this and would continue to improve over time.

"Thank you most for your encouragement, Ben. It means a lot to me."

"You're welcome, but I'm just telling you the truth. How about your math? Did you get your problems done for tomorrow night's class?"

"Not yet. I'll work on them in the morning, but I think I'll be able to do them."

Ben was glad to hear the confidence in her voice. "I'm sure you will. How did the grocery shopping with your mother go?"

"Very well. I didn't realize how much went into planning and ordering and arranging for deliveries before today. And Mama commands such respect when she walks into a store! I was so proud of her. I hope to garner that same kind of admiration one day."

There was an expression in her eyes that tunneled its way into his heart. Had she been treated in a way that made her think she was unworthy of respect in the past? He hoped not. "I'm sure you'll be shown the same kind of regard shown to your mother."

"Oh, I…" She shook her head and he had a feeling she'd said more than she intended to him. She changed the subject. "Thank you for offering to teach Jenny to ice-skate. I think I'd better go check on her and Mama. She's so excited—it will probably take an extra hour or so to get her settled down for the night."

"I'm looking forward to it." And he was. "Do either of you have ice skates?"

Rebecca shook her head. "No. That's something I must remedy by Saturday, thank you for reminding me. I wonder… Maybe Mama has some in the attic."

"She might."

"I think I'll go ask her." Rebecca straightened up her work area and got to her feet.

"All right. You have a good evening." Ben waited for her to leave the room and then headed downstairs. If she wasn't going to join the others, he didn't much want to, either. It wasn't quite the same with so few boarders at the moment.

And perhaps it was a good thing she didn't head into the parlor. He had no intention of letting his feelings for her get out of hand but there was no denying that he looked forward to being around her and her daughter more each day.

The next morning Rebecca, her mother and Jenny went shopping for housewarming gifts. A clerk at Macy's showed them all sizes and shapes of brass bowls. Finally, they decided on the two they liked best. Both were the same size and shape but had just enough difference in the pattern that they felt sure each couple would love them.

They arranged for them to be gift wrapped and delivered to Heaton House, and then Rebecca and her mother let Jenny browse to her heart's content. She led them upstairs and back down, looking at one thing after another—children's toys, of course, but also jewelry, gloves and handbags. And she loved the china, pottery and glass departments, too. In fact there didn't seem to be anything about Macy's that Jenny didn't like. Rebecca couldn't blame her—she could browse there all day, too.

But when her mother suggested they lunch at a nearby café, they both readily agreed. This kind of outing was something she and Jenny had never done before being reunited with her family, and it was such a joy to see her daughter so happy.

They took the trolley home and went straight to the attic to look for skates.

"I'm sure they're here somewhere," her mother said as they rummaged through different boxes and trunks. "We brought everything we didn't sell from home and—"

"I found them!" Rebecca began pulling out skates from the trunk she'd opened and her mother and Jenny rushed over to help.

"I think these might still fit me." Rebecca put one of the wood-and-metal skates under her shoe and belted it on, feeling as if she'd just found buried treasure. "They do!"

"Are these yours, too, Mama?" Jenny asked, pulling out a much smaller pair. "Did you wear them when you were little like me?"

Rebecca took them from her daughter and glanced at her mother. "Oh, Mama, you kept them, too?"

"I couldn't bear to get rid of them. Any of them. It'd be like saying we'd never find you…and I could not accept that."

Rebecca fought to speak around a knot of unshed tears as she hugged her mother. "I'm so thankful you didn't give up on me."

Her mother patted her back. "So am I, Becca. So am I."

"Me too! I wouldn't have a Granma, if you gave up!" Jenny squeezed in between the two women, hugging them both and lightening the mood so that the unshed tears turned to chuckles. She took the small skates from Rebecca. "Do you think these will fit me, Mama?"

"Let's see. I was probably about your age when I first wore them." Rebecca and her mother attached the skates to Jenny's shoes and they fit perfectly.

"Thank you for saving them, Mama. I like the idea of Jenny using my old skates."

"So do I."

"Oh, I can't wait till Saturday," Jenny said. "I'm really going to learn to skate!"

"Yes, you really are." Rebecca hugged her daughter.

"Let's dig a little longer," her mother said. "I must have an old pair in there, too. If my granddaughter is going to learn how to skate, I might as well tag along and see if I remember how."

Once they'd found her mother's skates, Rebecca inspected them. "They all seem pretty dull. Do you think we should have them sharpened before Saturday?"

"Perhaps," her mother said. "I'll telephone Michael and ask him where to take them. I think I'm looking forward to Saturday as much as Jenny is."

"So am I." Rebecca said as they took the skates back downstairs.

By dinnertime the skates were as clean as they could get them and Jenny was beyond excited. Usually quiet at the dinner table, she couldn't wait to tell Ben her news.

"I have skates, Mr. Ben!"

"You do?"

"Yes, they're the ones Mama used when she was little like me. And they fit!"

"That's wonderful, Jenny."

"Uh-huh. We cleaned them all up but Mama says they need to be sharpened, right, Mama?"

"That's right."

"And I forgot to telephone Michael to see where to take them."

"No need to telephone him, Mrs. Heaton. There's a shop I pass on the way to the college. I can take them in tomorrow and have them sharpened."

"Are you sure you don't mind, Ben?" Mrs. Heaton asked.

"Of course not. Mine could use some sharpening, too," he answered. Ben grinned and winked at Jenny. "I want them in good shape for Saturday. We don't want to be tripping over our own feet, do we, Jenny?"

She giggled and shook her head. "I don't think so."

Did Ben have any idea how much Jenny cared for him, Rebecca wondered?

"We need to pray the cold weather holds and we don't get a sudden warm-up," Matt said. "But from what I can see from my building, all the city lakes seem to be frozen solid. And the red balls signaling safe skating are up and easy to spot."

"We'll put you in charge of letting us know if they're up tomorrow, then," Rebecca's mother said. "If they are, surely the lake will be fine on Saturday."

Rebecca certainly hoped so. Jenny would be heartbroken if they had to call it off. But then again, she was sure her daughter would take things in stride. She'd been disenchanted more than once in her short lifetime. And because of that, Rebecca sent up a silent prayer that she wouldn't be disappointed this time.

Once dinner was over and her mother had Jenny under her wing, Rebecca hurried upstairs to freshen up for class. When she came back down, Ben was waiting for her, talking to Jenny and her mother. He helped her on with her coat as she said, "Thank you, Ben. You be good for Granma, Jenny."

"I will, Mama."

Rebecca bent down and gave her daughter a hug. "I love you."

"I love you, too."

"At least the wind isn't howling tonight," her mother said. "The walk to the trolley stop should be a bit easier."

"And that's a blessing." Rebecca gave her mother a kiss on the cheek. "Thank you, Mama. See you later."

Ben opened the door and they hurried out so as not to let in too much cold air. Rebecca took the arm he offered as they made their way to the trolley stop.

They didn't have to wait long and this time the trip seemed shorter since she'd made it once before. When they walked into Ben's class, many of the women smiled at her and she found an empty seat by Sarah. The young woman gave her a shy smile and Rebecca returned it.

Hopefully she'd get to know her and the others better over the next few weeks. There was a time in her life when Rebecca might have judged some of the women in this class, but no more. How many of them would look down on her if they knew her past?

She turned in her homework along with the others

this time and then concentrated on the math problems on the blackboard. Just as last time, Ben had everyone's attention and kept it through the class. That he gave of his time here, when he probably didn't need the money—and she was sure it wasn't much, perhaps he did it for free—spoke volumes of the character of the man.

When class ended Sarah turned to her. "It's good to see you here again…Rebecca, isn't it? How do you like Mr. Roth's class?"

"Yes, Rebecca is right. I'm enjoying it a lot. It's easy to learn from a teacher who loves what he's doing, isn't it?"

"It is," Sarah said. "And Mr. Roth is so kind to all of us. I look forward to the classes."

"Yes, I've found that I do, too. Mr. Roth said some of you live in the tenements. I used to, also."

"Oh? Where?"

Rebecca told her the address and they found they'd lived on the same street only not in the same building. "I want to get out so badly. And I need to…I—"

Several others who'd met Rebecca on Tuesday came up just then and Rebecca wished they'd have waited a few minutes longer. She wanted to know more about why Sarah sounded so desperate.

But the moment was lost and soon Sarah and the others were on their way out of class. She'd heard enough to know some women actually lived at the YWCA, while others came only for the classes. Surely she'd sort them all out soon. And maybe Sarah would open up to her before too long.

As the last woman left class, Ben smiled at her. "I

saw you speaking to Sarah and the others. Thank you for making an effort to get to know them."

"They all seem very nice and I look forward to getting to know them better."

He helped her on with her coat and took her arm as they headed down the stairs and out to the street. It was cold, but with no wind it wasn't bad at all.

As they neared the café, Rebecca's pulse suddenly sped up. Would Ben suggest they stop for hot chocolate again? Hope that he might warred with fear that he wouldn't—and confusion on what she should say if he did.

His steps slowed. "Want to stop for hot chocolate?"

Oh, yes, she did. But she didn't dare. She might begin weaving those dreams she'd fought against last time and she dared not let herself do that.

"Thank you. I'd like to, but it's been a long day and—"

"I understand."

Did he? The expression in his eyes made her wonder. Had she hurt his feelings? She certainly hoped not.

"There's our trolley now," he said.

Ben picked up his pace and Rebecca had no choice but to keep up. There was a tone in his voice she'd never heard before and it sounded a lot like disappointment. Even if he was disappointed, he couldn't possibly be more so than she was. She'd wanted to say yes, but she had a feeling Ben was already becoming too important to her. Rebecca strengthened her resolve. She couldn't let any man take hold of her heart again. It would only lead to heartache and she'd had more than enough of that in her life.

She settled back in her seat, but her chest felt tight and she didn't know what to say. Apparently, neither did Ben.

Chapter Seven

Ben had never felt awkward around Rebecca—until now. He didn't quite know what to say, so he didn't say anything. And neither did she.

The trolley stopped and he offered her his arm, which she took, but there was no laughter this time as they hurried down the walk to Heaton House. When they entered the house, he helped Rebecca off with her coat and did receive a smile for his efforts.

"Thank you, Ben," she said, before heading to the parlor, where they could hear the boarders had gathered.

After he said hello to everyone, he'd had every intention of going straight to his room where he hoped to shore up his weakened defenses. But Mrs. Heaton had hot chocolate waiting for them again and he followed Rebecca into the parlor and accepted a cup from his landlady.

Rebecca took her cup and went to sit by Julia while he stood in front of the fireplace, seeing the flame but not feeling its warmth. It was nothing like standing there with Rebecca a few nights ago. He took a sip of the warm liquid, but it didn't seem quite as sweet, either.

"Did Jenny give you any problem going to bed, Mama?" Rebecca asked.

"None at all. But she is very excited about Saturday. It wouldn't surprise me if she's still awake when you go up."

Ben turned to face the group. He couldn't help but smile that Jenny was still thrilled about learning to skate.

"I probably should go see if she is," Rebecca said. Then she clapped a hand on her cheek. "Oh, I forgot! I'll run up and get our skates, if you're still willing to take them to be sharpened, Ben?"

Her smile shot straight to his heart and his mood lightened. It was then that Ben knew he was in trouble. If this woman could change his disposition with a smile, she was beginning to mean way too much to him.

"Of course I am."

"I'll go get them then." Rebecca put her cup down and hurried out of the room.

"Anyone else need me to take their skates in?" Ben asked.

"No, mine are fine," Julia answered.

"I think mine are, too," Millicent said.

"I'm going to have to buy a pair on my way home tomorrow," Mathew said.

"You do know *how* to skate, don't you?" Millicent asked, raising an eyebrow at the man.

"I do, Millie. I just didn't bring skates with me

when I moved here. Never thought I'd need them. I'm sure looking forward to this outing," Mathew said.

Uh-oh, Millicent hated having her name shortened. Ben watched to see what kind of comeback she had for Mathew, but Mrs. Heaton spoke before she had a chance to say anything more.

"I do hope Kathleen and Luke and John and Elizabeth can join us," Mrs. Heaton said.

"Oh, I hope so, too," Julia said. "I've missed them all so much."

Rebecca returned just then with a bag containing the skates and handed it to Ben. "Jenny was asleep when I checked on her and she had the sweetest smile on her face. I'm sure she was dreaming about skating for the first time."

Their fingers brushed when Ben took the bag from her. An electric current sped up his arm and Rebecca quickly jerked her hand away. Had she felt it, too? "I'm looking forward to teaching her."

He took one last sip of his hot chocolate and said, "I'm heading for bed. See you all tomorrow."

But Rebecca followed him out of the room. "Ben, if you know how much it will be to have the skates sharpened, I can pay you now."

"No need. It won't be much." He saw a look of determination on her face and quickly added, "You can pay me when I bring them home."

Only then did she seem to relax. "All right. Good night."

"Good night."

Ben hurried downstairs to his room and set the bag by the door so as not to forget it the next day. He dropped down into his easy chair and let out a big sigh. Things still seemed strained between him and Rebecca, and Ben knew exactly the moment it had happened. He should have known better than to ask if she wanted to stop for hot chocolate again.

Just because she had the night it was so very cold didn't mean she wanted to make a habit of it—even if he liked the idea. And it was all for the best anyway. He had no business spending more time with her. She took up way too many of his thoughts lately as it was. He was attracted to her and there was no denying it. But he wasn't about to act on it.

She'd only refused to stop for hot chocolate this evening—but in that moment, it'd felt like a rejection of him. It had come on strong and swift. Had it been because of all he'd told her the other night?

He'd never shared any of his past before and although he'd felt glad that he did until this evening, he wasn't so sure about it now.

Surely that hadn't been her reason for not wanting to spend more time in his company tonight. Rebecca had been very encouraging about it and had treated him the same afterward and ever since. Maybe he was putting too much emphasis on her not wanting to stop at the café tonight.

Ben sighed in frustration and ran his fingers through his hair. All he really knew right now was that he had to be careful not to let himself care too much for this woman. But he feared he was on a slippery slope where his feelings for her were concerned.

He needed to take a step back and reinforce the fact they all they could ever be was friends. Only how could he step back when they lived in the same house and her daughter already claimed a place in his heart?

How did he keep her mother from doing the same thing?

Kathleen and Luke's housewarming was a great success the next night. Their small house was filled to the brim with people who wanted to warm their home with love.

It was wonderful to have everyone together again and Rebecca loved seeing her mother so happy to be with them all once more.

Kathleen's sister Colleen was there with her beau and her boys, whom Jenny followed around from the moment they arrived. Colin and Brody seemed quite happy with her company, as well. They were all very well behaved, and were content to settle at the kitchen table with their dessert and a jigsaw puzzle Colleen had brought with her.

Michael and Violet, along with Elizabeth and John, were there, rounding out the matches made at Heaton House and they all looked as happy as Kathleen and Luke. And everyone seemed sure Colleen and her beau, Officer O'Malley, would be engaged any day now. Rebecca tried not to feel envious, but it wasn't easy.

She tried to concentrate on how happy she was for them all and not think about how she longed to have what they did. She stayed close to those single boarders at Heaton House who she thought might feel the way she did. As far as she knew, Julia didn't have a beau; nor did Millicent, although she'd often wondered about her and Mathew. Could they be the next couple coming out of Heaton House?

"I don't think I'll ever have a home of my own unless I buy one for myself," Julia whispered. "And I believe I may have to move away to do that."

"Are you really thinking of going out west, Julia?"

"I am. Mama and Papa don't want me talking about it, and I understand their concern, but I truly want to see more of this country than New York City. They won't keep me from going—they know I'm independent and have a mind of my own. Perhaps they'll join me one day. Or maybe I'll come back."

"I certainly can understand the call of adventure." Rebecca said. And she did. She only hoped Julia's call had a better outcome than hers had. But Julia was a grown woman, not a starry-eyed youth, and she'd given a lot of thought to what she wanted to do. "I wish you the very best and will pray you have a grand adventure."

"Thank you, Rebecca. I've heard it's not uncommon for a woman to own property out west and I would so love to have a place of my own. I've been thinking of moving to Oklahoma where Mrs. Heaton's cousin is, or out to New Mexico. But one of the women I used to work with moved to Galveston, and it sounds really nice, too. With the port there, I'm sure I could get a job."

"Oh, Julia, please don't move until Mother gets more boarders. You were her first and she would miss you so much," Rebecca said.

Julia chuckled. "Oh, I'm not that close to moving yet. I have to decide where I'll go first. I'm sure

Heaton House will be full once more before I do anything."

Rebecca breathed a sigh of relief for her mother's sake. These boarders were family to her and so far they'd all stayed nearby. For one of them to move so far away would probably concern her mother as much as it did Julia's parents.

Millicent joined them. "Am I the only one who is envious of Kathleen, Elizabeth and Violet? Not to mention Colleen. I certainly hope your mother brings in a few new male boarders, Rebecca. I'd like to fall in love with one."

Julia raised an eyebrow. "Aren't you sweet on one already? What about Matt?"

"Mathew? He doesn't approve of anything about me. He thinks I'm much too independent, wanting to have my own photography business, and that I should have no interest at all in the women's movement. He wants a woman who agrees with him on every level and that's not me. No. Mathew and I are not matchmaking material. At all."

"I think you may be protesting a bit much," Julia said.

"No, I'm not." Millicent shook her head.

"Well, if Mathew really feels that way, he probably isn't the man for you," Rebecca said.

"Rebecca's right about that," Julia agreed.

"I know," Millicent said.

But her gaze sought the man in question and Julia and Rebecca exchanged glances. It appeared hearing their mutual agreement was the last thing Millicent wanted to hear.

Rebecca took some comfort in knowing she wasn't the only one who longed for true love. But she was almost certain the other two women had more chance of finding it than she did.

"I think I'll go check on the children." Rebecca turned and wove her way through the others to the kitchen.

She heard laughter, not just children's giggling, but a deep male laugh joining in. She reached the kitchen and pulled up short, totally surprised to find Ben talking to Jenny, Colin and Brody. Rebecca quickly backed around the corner of the doorway, peeking in to watch for a few minutes as his back was to her and he blocked the children's view of her.

They were all listening raptly to him as he told them how he'd first learned to skate. "It wasn't easy. I didn't have an adult to teach me, but a boy two years older than I was took me under his wing after some of the other boys from school teased me about not being able to skate. He took me to practice until I could fly across the lake on my own just as well as he did."

"You can fly across a lake?" Jenny asked.

Ben chuckled. "It kind of feels like flying when you can skate without falling down. But you just have to fall down and learn to get back up in the beginning."

"I want to fly across the lake!" Jenny said.

"So do I," Colin added.

"Me, too!" Brody's voice was full of excitement.

"Well, hopefully you'll all be able to one day. Just don't get too impatient and don't give up."

"What happened after you learned? Did those boys still make fun of you?" Colin asked.

"Not for long. Once my friend decided I'd learned to skate as well as he did, we went back to the lake where that group hung out. As usual, they teased me before I ever got my skates on. But then I got out on the ice and skated across the lake, through the middle of it and around again. They never teased me after that."

"And you're going to teach me to skate like that, aren't you, Mr. Ben?" Jenny asked.

"I sure am, Jenny."

"I can skate," Colin said proudly. "And I'm going to teach Brody."

"That's wonderful, Colin," Ben said. "I look forward to skating with you boys."

He moved just then and she could see the expressions on their faces. The man should have children. He was a born teacher and had a heart for little ones.

Jenny spotted her first. "Mama! Mr. Ben was talking to us about skating. I can't wait until tomorrow!"

Rebecca crossed the room and gave her a hug. "I know you can't. I just thought I'd check on you, but I see you're all in good hands." She smiled at Ben. "I think we're all going to have a wonderful time tomorrow."

His answering smile warmed her heart. "I think so, too."

Everyone gathered in the foyer the next afternoon—all the present boarders and the couples who'd once lived there. Michael and Violet had entrusted baby

Marcus to their maid, Hilda, for the day, but she'd come to stay at Heaton House to visit with her sisters, Gretchen and Maida.

Everyone was excited, but no one more than Jenny. She was jumping from one foot to the other and her eyes shone with excitement. Ben hoped the day went as she dreamed it would.

It was a beautiful day. Cold but sunny, and the light on the snow that had fallen late the night before made everything sparkle. He'd gone out right after breakfast to check the ice and had spotted the red ball at Central Park and several smaller lakes. He'd gone back to Heaton House to tell everyone the party was on.

The omnibus Mrs. Heaton had ordered arrived, and Ben and the other men helped carry the blankets and baskets she'd put together for them. Once they were ready to go, everyone gathered their skates and headed outside to pile into the bus. They stopped to pick up Colleen and her boys and Ben grinned as he watched excitement grow as the three children chattered amongst themselves.

He didn't know exactly how he'd ended up sitting by Rebecca, but she welcomed him with a warm smile and he began to hope that whatever the awkwardness was between them only a few days before had vanished.

"Jenny is beyond excited," Rebecca said. "I thought she'd never go to sleep last night. All she talked about was how you are going to teach her to fly across the lake."

Ben chuckled. "Well, there must still be some kid left in me, because I thought I'd never go to sleep last night, either." He wasn't about to tell her it was because he'd been thinking about how pretty she had looked at Luke and Kathleen's when she'd joined him and the children in the kitchen.

She'd had on a deep blue gown that looked wonderful with her blue eyes and that reddish-blond hair. And she looked beautiful now as she nodded. "I must admit it took me a while to go to sleep last night, too."

"Even your mother seems excited." Ben nodded toward Mrs. Heaton, who was talking to Violet.

"She is. It's been a very long time since she's skated. I do hope she doesn't fall."

"So do I," Ben said. Or anyone else. It'd been his idea to come today, after all. He sent up a prayer that they'd all return to Heaton House in one piece, then turned his attention back to Rebecca. Her cheeks were rosy from the cold and her eyes were sparkling with excitement. She looked lovely and he hoped he'd get a chance to skate with her before the day was over.

Chapter Eight

As they neared Central Park, traffic picked up and it became apparent they weren't the only ones wanting to take advantage of the beautiful day and the iced-over lake.

Ben was glad the omnibus stopped at a place where there were benches near the lake. He and the other men helped unload the blankets and snacks Mrs. Heaton had thought to bring.

It didn't take long for everyone to skate up and Ben helped Jenny with hers while Rebecca put hers on. They watched other skaters for a few moments and then Ben turned to Jenny.

"Are you ready?"

"Oh, yes!" the child said.

"Good. Let me go warm up and get a feel of the ice first, then we'll begin."

Jenny grinned and nodded as if to say *hurry up*!

He stepped out onto the ice and began skating, praying he wouldn't fall on his face in front of Jenny and Rebecca. It'd been a while since he'd skated, but he knew it would come back to him and it did. He skated out a ways and back, gliding across the ice, feeling as if he were flying as he'd tried to describe the night before. Then he turned and went back to get Jenny.

"Want to join us?" he asked Rebecca.

She shook her head. "Not until you teach Jenny how to stand up on ice and I get out there and make sure I still can skate."

He chuckled. "It'll come back to you. In the meantime, let's see if we can keep you standing, Miss Jenny." He held out his hand and Jenny slipped her small one into it, her eyes shining with excitement. The trust she showed him had Ben praying that she didn't get hurt today.

He walked her out to the side of the pond and then pulled her out in front of him, bending down and placing his hands on her rib cage. "We're going to slide for a few minutes so you can get the feel of the ice and then I'm going to teach you how to stand up on it by yourself and then how to walk on it, okay?"

Jenny nodded as they moved across the ice for a few yards, turned and came back to the edge where they'd begun.

By then Rebecca had her skates on and had come out the edge of the lake to meet them. "How did you like being on the ice, Jenny?"

"I love it, Mama!"

Rebecca smiled, then motioned to Ben to come nearer as she leaned toward him. He bent down while she whispered in his ear, "Jenny is excited, but I think I'm just plain afraid."

"I'll be glad to go out on the ice with you the first time. Jenny will need to rest in a bit."

"I'll see if I can get up my courage while you're with her. If not, I may have to take you up on your offer."

Ben bent down toward Jenny. "You ready?"

"Uh-huh. Let's go."

He laughed as he led her back out onto the lake and then got on his knees, his hands on her waist. "Now stand as still as you can and then I'm going to let go. If you fall, I'll help you get up."

She stood and let out a deep breath. He took one hand away and then the other and grinned at her. "You are standing on ice. All by yourself."

"Can I move now?" she asked.

"You can't try to skate yet. Just try to take a small step forward and then another. I'm right here with you."

Jenny nodded and took that first step. And then another. And then she fell.

"Oops!" She grinned at him and was up before he could give her a hand. The child was nothing if not determined.

It only took a couple more tries before she was taking small but confident steps. He slid alongside her, but he could tell from the expression on her face, she wanted to do it herself.

"You're doing great, Jenny. Let's go back nearer the bank and I'll show you how to work your heel and toes. Then we'll try to let you actually skate, but it might take several times before you feel like you're flying."

She smiled up at him. "Will you come with me?"

"I sure will, if your mother agrees," he said as they reached the bank where Rebecca stood watching them.

"We're going to do a few lessons on heel and toe placement—want to practice with us?" Ben asked.

"I probably should," Rebecca said, stepping out onto the ice.

"Take a deep breath, Mama. And just stand for a minute," Jenny instructed.

"Yes, ma'am," Rebecca said.

He couldn't contain his smile as she took the instructions from Jenny.

They both looked up at him.

"Now what?"

"Heels." He stood and showed them how to move their heels together, slide them apart and repeat it. They both followed his lead perfectly.

"Okay. Now, let's do our toes. Like this." Ben brought the big toes of his skates together, sliding them apart and repeating it, and watched as Rebecca and Jenny did the same. They did both exercises over and over again. Finally he looked down at Jenny. "Ready for your first skate?"

"I thought I'd never get to!" She put both hands on her hips and stood still on the ice.

Ben and Rebecca both laughed. "I think she might be a born skater."

"Well, I don't think she got it from me, but perhaps from Mama." Rebecca pointed across the way to where her mother was skating with Michael.

"I'm sure you'll surprise yourself once you get started."

Jenny tugged on Ben's hand. "Are we going skating now, Mr. Ben?"

"We are." He turned to Rebecca. "You coming with us?"

"I think I'll watch for now. I might join you soon."

Ben chuckled. He'd have to make sure she got on that ice and skated before the day was over. He kept his arm around Jenny and bent down, barely moving on the ice while he coached the child on how to slide, stop and turn over and over again until he felt confident she knew what to do.

Then he took her hand and they slowly made it back to the bank together. By then Mrs. Heaton was standing by Rebecca's side watching.

"Did you see, Granma?" Jenny asked. "I skated!"

"I did see. You did wonderful."

"You didn't do too bad yourself, Mama," Rebecca said. "I haven't been out yet and have to admit I'm a little nervous."

"No need to be. You skated very well back home."

Rebecca turned to Jenny. "I think you take after your grandma, Jenny. Are you tired?"

Jenny nodded. "A little. And hungry, too."

Rebecca's mother smiled and turned to Jenny. "Jenny, Uncle Michael went to get some hot chocolate from that stand over there." She pointed across the way. "Let's go help him bring it back. And I have the cookies Gretchen made this morning. Maybe Ben can take your mama out on the ice and get her past her skittishness. She hasn't skated yet."

"Oh, I don't want to take up more of Ben's—"

"You aren't taking up my time," Ben said. "I'm giving it to you."

"Go on, Mama. Mr. Ben will hold you up!" Jenny said, waving as she and Mrs. Heaton walked away.

"Jenny's right. I promise I won't let you fall." Ben grinned at Rebecca and held out a hand. When she hesitated, he whispered, "If we go while they're gone, no one will see if you do fall."

Her raised eyebrow and the spark in her eye told him she'd take his challenge.

"All right. Let's go." She took his hand and they headed back out on the ice.

Rebecca felt the color rise up her neck and flood her cheeks as she took hold of Ben's gloved hand. It felt warm and strong and—

"Relax, Rebecca, you can do this. Just take a deep breath and glide with me." He put his right hand on her waist and took her right hand with his left, holding her lightly but firmly as they stepped onto the ice.

Her heart began to slam against her chest as Ben slowly pulled her around with him.

"Take a deep breath and skate," Ben said in her ear.

His nearness had her taking that deep breath and releasing it, trying to get her pulse to slow down. He was only helping her skate, much as he'd done with her daughter. He wasn't holding her close for any other reason.

Rebecca forced her thoughts away from how nice he smelled and how warm it felt to be so close to him and tried to concentrate on moving her feet. At first she didn't even realize she was skating faster, keeping up with Ben. When it dawned on her, she looked up to find him grinning down at her.

"See, you haven't forgotten." Ben let go of her waist but held her hand and they began skating in the opposite direction.

Rebecca felt freer than she had in a very long time, gliding across the ice with the rush of air hitting her face. She *could* skate. And she could do it by herself. They reached the edge of the ice and she pulled her hand from Ben's. "I think I'll try it on my own now. But thank you. I'm not sure I would have gotten up enough nerve to try if you hadn't helped."

"You're welcome, I enjoyed it. Looks like Jenny is through with her hot chocolate. I'll take her out again."

Jenny ran up to them. "I saw you, Mama. You skate really good."

"Thank you, Jenny. I'm going out by myself this time, but Mr. Ben says he's going to take you out again."

Jenny grinned from ear to ear. "He says I have to practice if I want to skate by myself."

"And he's right. I'll be watching."

They were already back on the ice by then and Rebecca's heart twinged—with what, she didn't know. If onlys? Or what-ifs? Her daughter longed for a father, and Ben...should be one. Tall and tiny, they slid on the ice together, making Rebecca long for a future she couldn't have.

She turned and took off, skating from memory now, willing away thoughts of the past and dreams of the future, leaving only the moment. She skated around the lake, thinking about nothing but how good it felt to glide across the ice and enjoy the beautiful frozen landscape.

From behind her, she heard Jenny say, "Look, Mr. Ben, Mama is flying!" Rebecca turned too quickly, lost her balance and in trying to catch herself, she came down hard—twisting her ankle in the process. Pain, hot and sharp, shot up her left leg.

She heard a frantic "Mama!"

"I'm all right, Jenny. Don't worry," she called out.

But before she could try to get up and show her daughter she was, strong arms reached down to help her. She caught her breath at the pain the movement caused.

"Are you all right, Rebecca?" Ben asked gently.

"I think I twisted my ankle."

"Can you put any weight on it?"

Putting most of her weight on her good foot, Rebecca tried to stand, but as she put her other foot down and tried to stand on both feet, her leg buckled beneath her. She caught her breath at the pain. Ben kept her from falling once more and held her against his side.

"Looks like at the very least you have a bad sprain, and it could be broken. I know movement is going to hurt, but take a deep breath. I've got to get you off the ice and we need a doctor to look at you. Can you put your left arm around my neck?"

"I think so." She bit her bottom lip and slid her arm around his neck while Ben lifted her quickly and began skating over the ice. Once at the bank, Michael held his arms out to take her. But Ben shook his head and said, “No need to jostle her any more than necessary. I’ll carry her.”

Michael nodded. “All right. Mother’s got a hack waiting. She and Jenny are already in it. He’ll take you home and the rest of us will be right behind you.”

“Good. She needs to see a doctor as quickly as possible—I think it’s a sprain, but it could be a break.”

The two men exchanged a glance.

“I’m here, you know,” Rebecca said. “And I realize it might be painful to set, but it’s painful now, so I can handle it. And don’t mention *break* around Jenny. I don’t want to worry her needlessly.” Rebecca closed her eyes against a wave of nausea. “Please.”

“Don’t worry, Rebecca. We won’t frighten Jenny,” Ben answered.

They reached the hack and he gently settled her on the seat across from her mother and Jenny, and yanked off his skates while he explained to the two of them that they thought it was just a sprain.

“Are you hurting bad, Mama?” Jenny asked, her eyes full of fear.

“It hurts some, but I’m going to be fine, Jenny.”

“And we’ll see that she is, dear. Don’t worry,” her mother added, pulling Jenny close.

Ben gently took off Rebecca’s skates and asked, “May I unlace your boot? I’m afraid the swelling will make it much harder if we wait until we get back to Heaton House.”

Rebecca nodded and held her breath at the pain that engulfed her as he worked to ease her foot from her boot. “I’m sorry, I know it hurts. Let me settle your legs on the seat while you lean against me for support."

Rebecca really had no choice in the matter as Ben gently eased her foot onto the seat. He told the driver to take off and the motion threw her up against him. His arm settled round her to steady her and as she leaned against his strong arm, his warmth gave her comfort. She closed her eyes, ignoring the searing pain shooting through her ankle.

Once back at Heaton House, Ben was allowed to do what few men had ever done and that was to go up to the second floor. After he'd set Rebecca on her bed, Mrs. Heaton quickly thanked him and told him he could go back downstairs.

"Yes, ma'am." He turned to leave the room but was stopped by Rebecca's voice.

"Thank you for coming to get me, Ben. And for teaching my Jenny how to skate today." Rebecca reached out and pulled her daughter, who was hovering by her bed, into a hug.

Jenny smiled at him. "Yes, and thank you for picking up Mama, too, Mr. Ben."

"You're both very welcome. And while Jenny did wonderfully today, I think we may need a few more lessons before she flies like you did today, Rebecca. I hope to see you later after the doctor examines that ankle of yours."

The pain in Rebecca's eyes had him wanting to do something—anything—to take it away, but right now the best thing he could do was to let her mother make her as comfortable as she could. He turned and headed back downstairs.

Not long after he joined the others in the parlor, the doctor arrived and was shown to Rebecca's room. Ben tried not to show how concerned he was. If he did, there was no telling what the others would make of it. He had a feeling they'd been twittering about him rushing over to her the minute he'd seen Rebecca go down on the ice.

Gretchen brought them hot chocolate and cookies and they all took turns warming themselves in front of the fire and oohing and aahing over baby Marcus as they waited to hear what the doctor had to say about Rebecca.

Ben sipped his hot chocolate, trying not to remember back to the night he and Rebecca had stopped in at the café on the way home from class. Then all he could think of was that he should have stayed with her instead of letting her take off across the ice by herself. But she'd been doing fine and he was happy for her, until she'd taken that fall.

However, while falling was normal in ice-skating, most didn't end up with the need to see a doctor. Ben prayed Rebecca's ankle wasn't broken. She'd felt light as a feather when he lifted her into his arms and he'd liked the feel of holding her, perhaps more than he should.

They heard murmuring and steps on the staircase just before Jenny came running into the room as her grandmother showed the doctor out.

"Mama is going to be okay! She just can't..." She

turned to look at Mrs. Heaton, who came into the room. "Can't what, Granma?"

"She can't put any weight on that ankle for a week or so, and she'll be in some pain, but she should heal fairly quickly. No break, just a very bad sprain. He gave her some medicine to help with the discomfort and she's already dozed off."

Ben let out a relieved sigh and grinned at Jenny. She ran into his arms and hugged him. "Thank you for getting to Mama so fast, Mr. Ben. She said we'll go skating again just as soon as she's up to it."

"That's good to hear, Jenny. Best thing for a fall is to get back on the ice and try again."

And he was going to make sure Rebecca did get back on it soon as she was able to. Only next time, he'd make sure he was right there with her. He'd loved skating across the ice with her, holding her steady and matching steps with her.

She'd looked beautiful, her cheeks flushed, her blue eyes sparkling and her lovely mouth turned up in a smile. He knew it was due to the brisk air and the fun of being on the ice, but just for a moment he allowed himself to think she was happy because she was skating with him.

Chapter Nine

Rebecca hated missing church the next day, but when she'd tried to put weight on her foot first thing that morning and use the crutches the doctor had sent over, the best she could do was an awkward hobble just to get to the bathroom.

So she'd stayed under the care of Gretchen and Maida and sent Jenny with her mother and the others to church. Before they came home, though, Gretchen helped her get dressed. She was *not* going to stay in bed all day.

Once she'd been confined to bed for the evening the night before, her mother had helped her freshen up and get into a gown before Gretchen brought dinner up for her and Jenny. Her daughter hadn't wanted to leave her side in case she needed anything.

While they ate, Jenny entertained Rebecca with tales of how she felt trying to learn to skate and how wonderful Mr. Ben was when he hurried to pick up Rebecca.

"He saw you wobble and took off even before you fell, Mama."

"He did? No wonder he got there before I realized what happened."

"He must be very strong to pick you up without falling and skate back with you."

"Yes, he must be…"

Soon after they'd finished their meal, Millicent and Julia had stopped in to see how she was feeling while her mother got Jenny ready for bed. It was comforting to hear her mother talk to Jenny much like she had to Rebecca when she was that age. Knowing that she was here for them gave Rebecca immense comfort. She'd always wondered who would take care of Jenny, if she weren't able to. She'd even had nightmares about something happening to her and Jenny having no one to take her place. Thank the good Lord above, she never had to worry about that again.

Still, Rebecca wanted to be up and around as soon as possible. By the time the others were due home from church, she'd practiced enough that she hoped, with some help, she might manage to get downstairs and have Sunday dinner with everyone.

She was sitting on the settee in front of the fireplace in her room when Jenny burst through the door, Mrs. Heaton right behind her "You're up, Mama! How do you feel?"

"I am up and I'm not hurting quite as much as yesterday. Thank you for asking. How was church?"

"It was good. We asked everyone to pray for you to get better soon. And Granma says you might feel like eating with us—if you'd like to, and we can get you downstairs."

"I'd like that very much."

"Good," her mother said. "Ben, she's ready to come join us."

"Wonderful," Rebecca heard him say before she actually saw him. He smiled when he entered the room. "I'm here to help you do just that, Rebecca."

Rebecca tried to ignore the sudden fluttery feeling in her tummy and stood with the aid of her crutches. "I think I can manage on my own if—"

"No, dear," her mother said in no uncertain terms. "Ben is going to carry you down and I'll bring your crutches. We aren't taking a chance on you falling and ending up hurt worse."

"But—"

"Rebecca, dear…" Her mother held that hand up and sliced it through the air and Rebecca knew full well that meant no more arguing. "Please."

Giving in to her mother on this seemed the least she could do after all she'd put her through in the past. "All right."

That was all she had a chance to say before Ben's arm came around her to steady her while her mother took her crutches. Then he scooped her into his arms as though she weighed nothing. "Are you ready? I'll try not to jostle you too much."

"I am. And thank you." Rebecca slid her arms around his neck as he walked through the door and to the landing. Ben tightened his hold on her before taking the first step down. "I'm sorry to be so much trouble."

Ben glanced at her quickly before turning his attention to the steps in front of him. "You aren't any trouble, Rebecca. Besides, I feel it's partly my fault you fell. I should have stayed with you, knowing you were a bit nervous at the start."

"I wanted to try on my own, remember?"

"But I shouldn't have let you."

She chuckled. "I don't think I gave you a choice."

He grinned. "I shouldn't have given in to you."

Rebecca had a feeling they could go on like that for a while. And she would have enjoyed it. "Still, thank you for helping me."

"You're welcome." They were safely down the stairs and he turned to her. "But, truly, it's been my pleasure."

Rebecca felt color flood her face and she felt all jittery inside as she said, "You can put me down now and I'll try my crutches."

He gave her a doubtful look.

"Please. I have to do as much as I can on my own.'

Ben sighed and eased her to her feet, holding her at the waist to steady her, which did nothing for her flutters.

Her mother handed her the crutches and, stepping away from Ben's touch, Rebecca hobbled into the dining room. She could feel that Ben was right behind her, following as closely as he could until she reached the chair her mother directed her to so she'd be able to sit sideways and not worry about her ankle being hit. Her mother took the crutches while she eased down onto the chair, and Ben scooted it as close as possible to the table before taking his own seat.

Once Gretchen and Maida had served them a meal of roast chicken, scalloped potatoes and creamed peas, Rebecca's mother turned to Ben, "Will you say the blessing, please?"

"I'll be glad to. Please pray with me. Dear Lord, we thank You for today and we thank You for each other. We thank You that Rebecca is feeling a little better today and ask You to give her complete and quick healing of her ankle. We thank You for this food we're about to eat and most of all we thank You for Your plan for our salvation through Your precious Son and our Savior, Jesus Christ. It's in His name we pray, amen."

Rebecca was touched that he'd prayed for her, and that everyone seemed happy she'd joined them. "Thank you for your prayer, Ben, and all of you for your concern yesterday. And Mama, thank you for having my favorite meal."

"You're welcome, dear." her mother said. "I'm very thankful you didn't break your ankle. Michael and Violet said to tell you they'd be checking in on you later today and Kathleen and Elizabeth said to tell you they are praying. They'll be checking in on you, too."

"That's nice. I am sorry if I cut everyone's fun short yesterday."

"It was getting time to quit anyway, Rebecca," Julia said. "We're just sorry you sprained your ankle. Other than that, it was a wonderful day. I hope we get to go several more times this winter."

"So do I!" Jenny turned to Rebecca. "We will, won't we, Mama?"

"I hope so. I was having a great time until I fell. I'd like to go again."

"I don't think you have to worry, ladies. The lakes

are frozen solid. Unless we have an unusual warm-up, we'll be skating for a while," Ben said.

"I'm so glad." Jenny let out a huge sigh that had them all chuckling.

"So am I, Jenny," Ben said. "I want to see you fly like your mama did yesterday. Just don't want you to fall as hard as she did, so a few more lessons are in store."

"Are you saying I need lessons, Ben?" Rebecca arched an eyebrow.

He grinned and shook his head. "No, ma'am. I wasn't saying that at all. Any of us could have fallen like you did. It is ice, after all."

The expression in his eyes had Rebecca's pulse surging and her heart pounding.

Everyone began to scoot their chairs out, but Rebecca found she didn't have the leverage she needed to move hers. Ben was by her side in only a minute. He bent down to whisper in her ear as he scooted her chair out. "You aren't very good at asking for help, are you, Rebecca?"

"Why, I asked for your help in catching Jenny the day she flew down the banister."

"You did. But that was for the safety of your child. You don't ask for yourself."

"I suppose I did get used to doing things on my own."

"That is understandable when you were on your own. But you have people more than happy to help you now."

And he was one of them in so many ways. But the more he helped the more she began to see him as the hero her daughter did. And she knew better. She didn't believe in heroes anymore.

There was an unsettled look in Rebecca's eyes, as if she were troubled about something. Maybe he'd upset her by telling her she wasn't very good at asking for help. But he wanted her to know that he was there for her and Jenny and—

His gaze caught hers once more. Ben had a feeling that wasn't something she wanted to hear and he was sure it wasn't something he should say—not until he'd thought about his motivations, and he didn't want to think about them now.

"Are you staying downstairs awhile? Or do you want to go back to your room?"

"I'd like to stay down, but I have to admit, I'm a little tired. If I go rest now, maybe I'll feel better when visitors start to come. But I could do that in the little parlor so that you don't have to carry me up just now."

"Rebecca, I don't mind."

"I know. But back there, I can watch Jenny play and visitors can come there to see me. It will be easier on everyone."

"There's no need for you to go to the back parlor," her mother said. "And Jenny can play anywhere. Take her to the front parlor, Ben, and—"

"Mama, that's a good idea. But I am going to use my crutches to get to the parlor. It's just across the way."

"But—"

"Mama, if I can't make it, I'll stop and Ben can

help me." She turned to him and smiled. "Right, Ben?"

"Right." He smiled down at her. Maybe she was coming to her senses, but he had a feeling she was just appeasing her mother. "I'll make sure she doesn't fall, Mrs. Heaton."

"Thank you."

She handed the crutches to Rebecca and Ben helped her to stand. Once she put the crutches under her arms, she took off with Ben right behind her and Jenny following him.

She did wobble a bit, but she made it over to the nearest sofa and managed to sit down. However, as she laid her crutches to the side, she looked a little pale and Ben was pretty sure she'd tired herself out. "Are you all right? You should probably get your foot up."

"I am and I will. Thank you." She settled back against the sofa and he brought over a footstool and helped her get her bad foot up on it.

Ben wasn't sure what to do next except be nearby in case she wanted to go back to her room or needed help getting around. But he had a feeling that if he just sat and waited until then, she'd be shooing him out of the room.

"Why don't we play a game of charades to entertain Rebecca?" Millicent said. "Ben and Mathew against me and Julia. What do you think, Rebecca?"

"I'd enjoy it."

"Then let's do it," Ben said.

For the next hour, they had Rebecca, her mother and Jenny laughing at their attempts to outdo each other. It seemed to be just the distraction Rebecca needed until Michael and Violet showed up with baby Marcus. Violet handed the baby to Rebecca while she and her husband joined the game.

Rebecca smiled as Jenny sat close to her and began to talk to the baby. Jenny needed a sibling…and a father. And he—whoa! Where were his thoughts leading? He wasn't going there. Not now. A little rattled by his thoughts, Ben forced his attention back to the game.

Kathleen and Luke came over and then John and Elizabeth showed up not long after. They all stayed for afternoon tea and Rebecca seemed to be enjoying herself, but Ben saw her wince a time or two. He hoped her ankle wasn't hurting too bad.

"What do you think, Ben?" Michael asked, pulling his thoughts away from Rebecca.

"I'm sorry, I must have been woolgathering. What are we talking about?"

The grin Michael gave him had Ben wondering if he knew what he'd been woolgathering about.

"We're discussing the upcoming baseball season," John answered.

They'd enjoyed going to the games last season and Ben hoped they'd be going again this year. They discussed their team's chances until Marcus got fussy and Violet decided they needed to go home.

That seemed to be a signal for everyone to leave and for Rebecca's sake, he was glad. She'd been shifting her foot on the ottoman and he wondered if she was in pain.

Once everyone donned their jackets, they said their goodbyes to Rebecca.

"Thank you all for coming to check on me," Rebecca said.

"You'd do the same for us," Kathleen said. "You take it easy, you hear?"

"I will."

Mrs. Heaton and Jenny, along with the other boarders, went to see them out and once they all left, Rebecca let out a big sigh. Ben had a feeling they might have overstayed their welcome.

Expecting her to deny she was tired, he ambled over to her and asked, "You ready to go upstairs?"

She looked up at him with a small smile. "You know, I believe I am." She took up the crutches beside her and managed to stand, but her steps out of the room were on the wobbly side. Ben stayed as close as he thought she'd allow until they got to the staircase.

"You know, if I hold on to the railing I think I can make it and—"

"Don't even say it, Rebecca. If I let you go up by yourself, your mother will—"

"Be very upset," Mrs. Heaton said from behind him. "Jenny and I will bring the crutches, Ben. Will you please carry my daughter to her room?"

"Yes, ma'am."

Rebecca shook her head but didn't argue with her mother. Ben quickly lifted her into his arms and she put hers around his neck. He took care to get her up the stairs and to her room. "Where do you want me to put you?"

"I'm not a sack of potatoes, you know. The settee will be fine."

Ben chuckled at the vision she conjured up. "Now you know I don't think of you that way, Rebecca. If so, I'd dump you on that settee…instead of setting you down ever so gently." He lowered her with care as she slid her arms from around his neck.

"Thank you, Ben."

"You're welcome. Try to get some rest, okay?"

At her nod, he backed off to make room for Jenny to scramble up beside her mother. "Granma said you might like a nap. Want me to get you a blanket, Mama?"

"Thank you, dear, but I'm fine for now. Do you want to take a nap?"

Jenny shook her head. "Gretchen said I could help make dessert for tonight, if you said it was all right. But if you want me to stay with you, I will."

Even Ben could see the hope in the child's eyes.

"Oh, of course you may help Gretchen. I'm just going to rest a bit. You run on down and help her."

Jenny hugged her mother's neck and kissed her cheek.

"I'll go with you, Jenny. Maybe I can talk Gretchen out of a cup of coffee to take downstairs with me. I have some papers to grade."

She took his hand and waved to her mother. "Bye, Mama."

Jenny gave his hand a tug and he picked her up. "Come on, I'll carry you down like I did your mama."

These two females had a grip on his heart and he didn't have a clue what to do about it. None, whatsoever.

Chapter Ten

That evening Rebecca decided to take supper in her room so that Ben wouldn't come up and carry her down once again. She hadn't realized how strong he was until he'd picked her up and carried her down for Sunday dinner. Nor had she noticed how really blue his eyes were.

Truth be told, she'd liked the feel of being in his arms and she needed to find a way to get downstairs by herself before her mother insisted he carry her down again. So she used her crutches and hobbled around in her room during supper, hoping to get a little steadier on the unwieldy things.

Her mother came up with Jenny after the meal and brought a piece of the cake she'd help Gretchen with.

"This is very good, Jenny. You're going to be an excellent cook if you keep helping in the kitchen."

"Thank you, Mama. Mr. Ben said the same thing." Jenny glowed at the compliment. "He wanted to bring you down for supper, but Granma told him you decided to stay upstairs. He looked kind of sad."

"I think he was, Jenny," her grandmother said, before turning to Rebecca. "I telephoned the contractor and told him to wait a couple of days to start work, dear. I don't want you up here having to listen to them tear down walls and put up new ones. It's going to get pretty loud when they do."

"Oh, Mama, you didn't have to do that. I'm sure I can make it downstairs in the morning." She hoped.

"No. You'd have to get up and moving earlier than usual so Ben or Matt could help you down before they leave for work and right now you need to rest all you can so that ankle will heal. Wednesday will be soon enough for them to start work."

"Then, thank you, Mama. I'm sure I'll be able to get downstairs sometime tomorrow." But she was relieved that she wouldn't have to listen to all the construction noise the next morning.

"We'll see," her mother said. She helped Jenny get bathed and ready for bed and once she'd heard her prayers and kissed her good-night, she came back and helped Rebecca get ready for bed. Then she tucked her in much as she had when she was a child.

"It's so good to be here and know Jenny is being taken care of, Mama. Thank you."

"You're welcome. But truly, thank you for coming back to us and letting me enjoy being your mother and Jenny's grandma. I can't begin to tell you what joy you two have brought back into my life." She kissed Rebecca on the cheek. "Good night, dear. I hope you rest easy."

"Good night, Mama. I love you."

"I love you, too, dear."

"And I love you both," Jenny shouted from her room. "Night!"

Both women chuckled as they assured the child they loved her, too. "She has ears like you, Rebecca," her mother whispered.

"It appears so," Rebecca whispered back. "Something to keep in mind at all times."

Her mother nodded as she walked out the door.

Rebecca settled down in bed and grinned as she heard Jenny's gentle breathing from her room. She was already fast asleep.

Rebecca whispered her prayers and closed her eyes, willing herself to go to sleep and quit wondering if Ben had really been disappointed that she'd decided to take supper in her room. And there was no denying that she hoped he had been.

The next morning, Maida brought breakfast up to her while her mother got Jenny dressed to go downstairs. Midmorning, she was back to help Rebecca get dressed and settled on the settee. Her ankle was black-and-blue but the pain had eased somewhat and she was determined to do what she could on her own.

Her mother and Jenny joined her upstairs for lunch and then after they'd gone back down, Rebecca began using the crutches. She even managed to make it out into the hall by herself and then to the top of the stairs. But the thought of trying to make it down the stairs as she looked at the foyer below made her a bit queasy. *Maybe not today.*

She hobbled back to her room and put her foot up while her thoughts returned to Ben and how much she'd come to respect and admire him. And how much her daughter cared for him.

She hadn't encouraged it, but neither had she done anything to keep Jenny from making him her hero. And was there any way to stop the feeling of a child longing for a father figure in her life? Especially for one who'd saved her from getting badly injured?

Rebecca sighed. How did one stop thinking of a man as a hero when all he did was keep acting more heroic? How did one stop growing feelings for him when he not only acted the hero but also treated her child as special as she did herself? Oh! Where did those thoughts come from? She had to stop thinking about Ben!

Rebecca reached for her Bible on the table beside her and opened it. Her gaze fell on Psalm 22, verse 19: "But be not thou far from me, O Lord: O my strength, haste thee to help me."

Rebecca bowed her head. "Oh, Lord, please, help me. I'm afraid I could fall in love with Ben. And it will only lead to heartbreak for me and for Jenny. I must think of her more even than me. Please stop these growing feelings I'm having for Ben. He is such a good man, but he'd never want the likes of me. I know You've forgiven me, Lord. But I'm not sure any man could. And I don't know what to do. Please help me. In Jesus' name I pray, amen."

Rebecca sighed and read a while longer. Centering her thoughts on the Bible and letting the Word comfort her gave her peace until she heard Jenny's footsteps running up the stairs.

Her daughter burst into the room, her face flushed

and happy. She'd evidently been helping in the kitchen again for there was flour on her cheeks and all over the small apron her mother had found for her.

Rebecca chuckled. "Oh, my, I think you must have had a great time. What did you make for dessert tonight?"

"I can't tell you. Granma said it's a surprise."

"All right. I suppose we should start getting ready for dinner?"

"Uh-huh."

Rebecca's mother and Maida came in then to help them do just that. "Ben will be up to help you downstairs, dear."

Rebecca only nodded. Hopefully tomorrow, she'd be able to put a bit of weight on her foot, but she had a feeling she wouldn't be going to class that night. There were stairs there, too, and she could just imagine the ladies' reaction to seeing Ben carrying her to class. No. She wouldn't be going back to the Y until she could maneuver stairs by herself.

But when the knock on her door came, she couldn't stop the sudden jolt of her heart as her mother went to let Ben in. His smile sent her pulse racing and she tried to ignore it as she smiled back.

This was Ben, a boarder in her mother's home, a hero to her daughter and her teacher. He was a good man who helped others however he could and she needed to realize that right now he was only here to help her get down to dinner.

"You ready?" he asked.

"Yes, I—"

He scooped her up before she could say anything

more and she landed against his chest, her heart slamming against her ribs.

"We'll take your crutches, dear," her mother said. "Come on Jenny."

Jenny followed her grandmother out of the room while Ben carried Rebecca across her room. "How was your day? You didn't overdo things, did you?"

"No. Actually I stayed in my room all day, but I did try to get a little better with my crutches."

"Hopefully, you won't need them too much longer." Ben strode through the doorway and to the landing, but he paused before heading down the stairs. "Put your arms around my neck so I don't jostle you on the way down."

Rebecca did as he requested. Surprised at the pain under her arms, she let out a small moan.

"What's wrong?" The concern in his eyes warmed her heart.

"I think the crutches have made my arms sore."

"Oh, I'm sorry. They might be too tall for you. I'll look at them and see if anything can be done to make them more comfortable."

"Don't worry, Ben. Like you said, hopefully I won't need them much longer."

Instead of putting her down once they got to the bottom of the stairs, Ben carried her into the dining room and set her in her chair, pushing it up to where she could eat comfortably.

Her mother announced that dinner was ready and everyone hurried to take their seats, all asking how she felt or how her day had gone.

It was good to be downstairs again. Even if she did miss the warmth of Ben's arms.

Rebecca used her crutches to get into the parlor after dinner and Ben could tell they were too long. But they had no adjustment mechanism to them and the only way to shorten them was to saw them down.

"I think there's a saw in the storage room on the ground floor," Rebecca's mother said, sending both Ben and Matt on the hunt for it.

She was right. There was a small saw there, and with Matt's help he was able to trim down about an inch on each one. They hurried back up to see if it was enough and Rebecca's smile was all he needed to know that it had at least helped.

"Thank you! This is much better." She hobbled around the room with them and to Ben's thinking, she was handling them much easier than before.

"I'm glad it worked."

"So am I. Maybe by tomorrow evening I'll be getting around better. I hate to miss class and get behind."

Ben hated for her to have to. He'd gladly carry her to the trolley stops and up the stairs, but he knew letting him carry her downstairs and up here at Heaton House was about all she was willing to let him do. Besides, it would be a bit awkward to carry her into the classroom.

"I hate for you to miss, too." He liked her company going and coming from class. Liked getting to know her better. Had wondered if she might want to stop for hot chocolate again—if he got up enough nerve to ask her. He'd have to wait for another time. He could relieve her worry about getting behind, though. "How about I leave you the work you'd be doing in class, so you can keep up?"

"Oh, thank you, Ben. That will help a lot." The relief on her face was apparent.

"Don't worry about getting behind, I'll make sure you don't."

She seemed to relax after that and enjoy the company of the other boarders for a while.

"Will you play some music for us, Miss Julia?" Jenny asked.

"I'll be delighted to." Julia got up and went over to the piano and pulled out the bench. "Want to come sit by me?"

"Oh, yes, thank you!" Jenny hurried over and took a seat beside her. "What are you going to play?"

Ben sat down in the chair adjacent to the end of the sofa Rebecca was sitting on. He told himself it was just in case she needed him, but it was where he could have a clear view of her while she watched Jenny having such fun with Julia.

That she loved her child was evident to anyone in the room. Whatever pain she might be dealing with seemed to be forgotten as her smile grew when Jenny began to sing along with everyone. Julia played several popular songs and Jenny proved to be a quick learner.

"How do you know the words to those songs, Jenny?" Rebecca asked as she applauded her daughter.

"Sometimes I hear everyone singing when I'm in bed, before I go to sleep," Jenny said.

"Well, you know some of them better than I do, I believe," Rebecca said.

Jenny's smile had to warm her mother's heart—it warmed Ben's.

"I like to sing, Mama."

"I'm glad. But it is getting late and I suppose we'd better go get you ready for bed."

"I'll do it, dear. You know it's my pleasure. Come on, Jenny, dear."

Rebecca seemed a bit disturbed as Jenny followed her mother out of the room. "Your mother is right, you know. It would be hard for you to get her ready for bed."

"I know. I just feel I'm shrugging my responsibility."

"Oh, Rebecca. Think of it as giving your mother a great deal of pleasure, instead. She's been happier than any of us can remember since you and Jenny have come to live here."

"Ben is right, Rebecca," Julia said. "Not that she ever wore her feelings on her sleeve and she always seemed to enjoy her boarders, but there was always something that seemed to be missing and now it isn't. I don't know how else to explain it."

"Thank you, Ben and Julia. It's just that it's only been the two of us for so long and I don't want Jenny to think—"

"Jenny knows you love her, Rebecca. But I do think she's very glad to have more family around now."

"Yes, of course she is. I'm being silly. Thank you all for being so happy for us."

Gretchen came in with tea and coffee just then and talk turned to the upcoming housewarming party for John and Elizabeth. They'd found a place not far from Gramercy Park in a nice neighborhood.

"Have any of you seen it?" Ben asked.

"Not yet," Julia answered. "Have you?"

"I helped move some of their things over. It's very nice, although they aren't in the neighborhood Elizabeth's father would have preferred. But she and John are determined to live pretty much like they've been living here. Elizabeth has never had any desire to live life as her wealth would allow and John says he wouldn't know how."

Everyone chuckled. "Neither would we," Millicent said.

"I'm sure it's nice to know you could, though, if you wanted to," Julia commented.

"Perhaps. But then having a lot of money can bring its own set of problems. Glad I don't have to worry about that," Matt said.

"Living here feels like I'm wealthy, after living in the tenements." Rebecca released a sigh. "I don't think I appreciated my upbringing until I moved away. I—"

She suddenly stopped midsentence and Ben wondered what she'd been about to say. She gave a slight shake of her head and he felt sure she wasn't going to continue.

He quickly filled the gap in conversation. "Well,

on a teacher's salary, having too much wealth is something I certainly will never have to worry about."

"I don't think that's anything any of us will have to worry about," Millicent said.

"Or lose any sleep over," Julia said. "I think I'll call it a night."

"Yes, I'd better get up there and see how Mama and Jenny are doing." She got up with the help of her crutches and began to walk toward the doorway.

"I might as well go, too." Millicent yawned.

"Ben, you're going to carry Rebecca up, aren't you?" Julia asked as the two women started toward the foyer.

"I am."

"Then hand me your crutches, Rebecca, and I'll take them upstairs with me. I'll leave them at your door."

Rebecca hesitated for only a minute. "I suppose that's a good idea."

Ben put his hand at Rebecca's waist to steady her while she handed her crutches to Julia, then he lifted her into his arms. She slipped her arms around his neck and he smiled at her.

"I'm sure you'll be almost as glad as I will be when I can manage the stairs by myself."

"I really don't mind, Rebecca." At all.

Julia and Millicent were already upstairs by the time Ben reached the first step. He only just now realized how he'd been looking forward to having Rebecca in his arms once more.

He shifted her and her arms around his neck tightened. His gaze moved from her eyes to her lips and he heard the catch in her breath before he looked into her eyes again. Could she tell what he was thinking? That he wanted nothing more in that instant than to kiss her?

Chapter Eleven

Rebecca caught her breath at the expression in Ben's gaze as it moved from her eyes to her mouth, and she found she couldn't resist taking a glimpse of *his* finely chiseled lips. She looked back up and into his eyes, then quickly turned away and concentrated on not stealing a glance at him again as he carried her up the rest of the stairs to her room. But she couldn't ignore the rapid beat of her heart.

"My crutches are here. You can put me down now." Rebecca sounded breathless to her own ears.

Ben kept his arm around her waist until she had her crutches under her arms and then he opened her door. "I hope cutting these down helps and you won't be so sore tomorrow."

"I can already tell it has. Thank you. Good night, Ben." She allowed herself to glance at him and found him studying her as if he wanted to know what she was thinking. Well—she'd like to know the same about him. But she didn't ask.

And neither did he. "Good night, Rebecca. Sleep well."

She gave a brief nod and entered her room. Ben pulled the door shut behind her and Rebecca let out a pent-up breath. She'd enjoyed being in his arms way too much.

Her mother must be reading to Jenny, for she was nowhere around and Rebecca was relieved. She needed time alone to…stop thinking of what it might be like to be kissed by Ben.

Rebecca leaned against the door and willed herself to breathe slowly. There would be no kissing Benjamin Roth—no matter how much she'd wanted to in that brief moment. She forced thoughts of the handsome teacher out of her mind and hobbled across her room.

Dropping down on the settee, she began to unlace the boot on her good foot and silently prayed. *Dear Lord, please help my ankle to strengthen so that I don't have to put added work on Mama and so that Ben won't have to keep carrying me up and down the stairs. Please keep me from reading too much into a glance. Just because I was thinking about kissing him doesn't mean his thoughts are of the same kind. In Jesus' name I pray, amen.*

She'd barely finished praying when her mother came into her room. "Oh, good, you're here, dear. I've just run your bath. I'll help you get into it."

Rebecca took a long soak while her mother went to ask Gretchen to make some hot chocolate—the kind with a hint of cinnamon that Rebecca had loved as a child. When she returned, she helped her out of the tub and into her nightclothes.

Rebecca used her crutches to get to bed, and her mother fluffed up the pillows so she could sit up. By then, Gretchen was there with their drinks. Between the bath and the chocolate, Rebecca finally began to relax. "Thank you for your help, Mama. With Jenny and me."

"Oh, Rebecca. I love having you here *to* help. I know not being able to get around on your own bothers you but you'll be out and about like normal soon."

"I suppose I am a little too independent at times, but—"

"There's no need to explain to me, dear. I understand why you are. But not all men are like Jenny's father. Yours wasn't, Michael isn't, and one day you'll find—"

"Mama, I don't let myself think about that. What man would want a woman who…"

"The one who will love the wonderful woman you've become and accept you as you are."

"I'm not sure that man exists."

"Oh, Rebecca, dear. I'm sure—"

"No, Mama." Rebecca sliced her hand through the air, much like her mother did when she wanted to hear no more. "I've come to accept that I'll be raising Jenny alone. I can't waste time dreaming about something that has little or no chance of happening."

Her mother sighed, gathered up the cups and picked up the tray Gretchen had left. Then she kissed Rebecca on the cheek. "I hope you'll change your mind one day, dear. Sleep well."

"You too, Mama." Rebecca watched her mother leave the room and then turned out her bedside light. In the quiet, she listened until she could hear Jenny's breathing. She said her prayers, thanking the Lord for her many blessings and asking Him to keep her from dreaming impossible dreams—especially after the…moment…with Ben, and then the conversation with her mother. She couldn't let herself begin to think all that was possible. Couldn't take the chance, ever again.

But as she closed her eyes and began to drift off to sleep she couldn't keep out the thought of how wonderful it had felt to be held in Ben's arms for those brief moments. A lone tear escaped and slid down her cheek. Rebecca brushed at it impatiently and closed her mind to dreams that could never be.

The next day, after breakfast, Rebecca was more determined than ever to make it downstairs. One way or another.

She could put a little weight on her foot but not much. Still, when lunchtime came and her mother and Jenny brought up a tray, Rebecca announced that she was going to go downstairs that afternoon.

"Rebecca dear, it's only going to be for a few more days. I should have come up and helped you get ready before Ben and Matt left so one of them could bring you down. Please don't try this," her mother said as Rebecca managed to get to the top of the stairs.

"I'm sure I can do it, Mama. You and Jenny take my crutches down and I'll hold on to the railing and hop down. Please, let me try."

"I don't think I have any choice, do I?"

Rebecca grinned at her mother. "Not really."

"Come on, Jenny. Maybe we can break her fall at the end of the stairs," her mother said. "Please, be careful, Rebecca."

"I will."

She grabbed hold of the banister and, raising her bad foot, she step-hopped, from one step to another on the good one, stopping midway to catch her breath. It was more difficult than she'd thought it might be.

"Are you all right?" her mother asked.

"I am. I just need to rest a moment."

"Mama, could you scoot on your bottom to get down?" Jenny ran up the stairs and sat down on the step beneath her and used her arms to help her move down to the next step. "Like this?"

"That might work." Rebecca held on to the handrail and eased herself into a sitting position. Then she followed her daughter's example and scooted to the bottom step, releasing a sigh at the end. "Thank you, Jenny!"

"You're welcome, Mama."

Rebecca gave Jenny a hug and then released a deep breath. Grinning, she took the crutches her mother handed her.

"You did it, dear!"

"You can go up the same way, Mama," Jenny said.

"And I suppose you know this, because?"

Her daughter smiled that sweet smile of hers. "I do it sometimes."

"Uh-huh. I thought that might be the case. Want to go play while I practice my typing?"

Jenny nodded. "But can I help Granma and Gretchen later? She said I could, if it is all right with you."

Rebecca looked at her mother. "Is it all right? Gretchen really doesn't mind?"

"Gretchen is loving it. And so am I. Jenny is going to be a fine cook one of these days."

"Well, then, you may help in the kitchen when they begin preparations. But mind your manners."

"I will, Mama."

"If you have time later, and feel up to it, I'd like you to take a look at the books, Rebecca," her mother said. "Get an idea how Michael and I've been doing them, and see if it makes any sense to you."

"I'd love to. Why don't I practice awhile, and then when Jenny goes to help in the kitchen, I'll go to your study?"

"That sounds like a good idea. I'm going up to take stock of the linens. I think we'll need to buy more before we get new boarders. Remember the workers will be pounding away upstairs tomorrow."

"Another reason for me to make it down the stairs."

Her mother chuckled and shook her head. "I suppose I can't argue with you there."

Rebecca hugged her and hobbled down the hall to the small parlor. Jenny was already there playing with the doll she'd received for Christmas. Rebecca was quite happy she'd made it downstairs under on her own steam. And it felt good to be typing again, although she felt she'd lost some speed and promptly went about building it back up. She was just finishing when Gretchen appeared at the door.

"Are you ready to come help, Miss Jenny?" Gretchen asked.

"Yes. May I go now, Mama?" She looked at Rebecca for permission to leave, and at her nod she quickly put her doll up and skipped out of the room.

Rebecca neatened up her workspace and grabbed her crutches. They were much easier to use since Ben cut them down, but still, she'd be so relieved to be rid of them. She hobbled out of the room and heard familiar voices in the hall.

"Rebecca is going to be so glad to see the two of you. Let me go tell her you're here," she heard her mother say.

"No need, Mama," Rebecca called out. "I'm on my way." She hurried her gait as best she could to find both Kathleen and Elizabeth in the foyer.

"We just had to come see how you are doing," Kathleen said.

"Oh, how sweet of you. I've been missing the two of you!" Rebecca said. "I'm better than I was on Sunday. But impatient to be able to get rid of these crutches."

"I can certainly understand how you would be," Elizabeth said.

"Why don't the three of you go to the parlor and I'll make us some tea?" Rebecca's mother suggested.

"That sounds wonderful, Mrs. Heaton," Kathleen said. "And that way Rebecca can get that foot up for a while."

Rebecca made her way into the parlor and over to the nearest sofa, then she sank down with a sigh.

Kathleen sat at the other end, but Elizabeth stood in the doorway.

"Not easy to use, are they?" Elizabeth asked. "I broke my foot when I was young and I so hated not being able to do things as normal. Kathleen and I have been thinking about how hard that would be on you and… We hope you don't mind, but we brought you a gift."

"A present? Whatever for?" Rebecca said.

"For having to endure those awful crutches," Kathleen said.

Elizabeth hurried back to the foyer and returned with an oddly wrapped package, which she handed to Rebecca. "We thought you might need this once you're able to put a little more weight on your foot."

"What is it?"

"Open it and see," Elizabeth said.

Rebecca tore the paper off to find a beautiful cane, with a white porcelain handle, decorated with pink flowers. "Oh, it's lovely, but you shouldn't have."

Elizabeth placed a hand on each hip. "And why not? John and I want you at our housewarming on Friday and I'm hoping you won't need to use those old crutches. But one way or another—even if you have to be carried—we want you there. And besides, a cane is always in fashion."

"That's true and this one is beautiful. Thank you both so much. I love it and can't wait to try it out. And I *will* be at your housewarming, Elizabeth—one way or another."

But she sent up a prayer that she could use that cane by Friday. As it was, she was already wondering if she'd make it up the stairs by herself that evening. And if she couldn't make it up the stairs, Ben would have to carry her…and she'd be thinking of kissing him all over again. As she was doing now. Her pulse raced at the very thought.

Chapter Twelve

Dinner that evening was quite lively as Jenny told everyone how she taught her mother to scoot down the stairs.

"Only a child would come up with that idea. I'm glad it worked for you, Rebecca," Julia said.

"I'm relieved you weren't hurt. I'll be glad to bring you down before I go to work tomorrow," Ben said. "I don't have an early class."

"Oh, Ben, I'd be so grateful if you can manage that," Rebecca's mother said. "I know it wasn't as easy as it sounds for Rebecca. And it was very hard to watch."

"I was fine, Mama."

"I know. But…"

"I'll bring you down when you're ready in the morning," Ben said as if that was all there was to it.

And Rebecca didn't know what to say. She felt frustrated and relieved all at the same time.

Ben left right after dinner, and Rebecca joined the others in the parlor because Jenny wanted to play charades with them. She was very good at it and everyone wanted her on their team.

But once her mother went to bathe Jenny and put her to bed, Rebecca hobbled back to the small parlor and, true to his word, Ben had left the class lesson with a note that he'd check it when he got home.

Rebecca sat down at the round table to work out the math problems and looked at the clock. She should have headed to the small parlor a bit earlier so she'd have time to scoot up the stairs before Ben got back and while her mother was occupied with Jenny.

Of course, she couldn't do that. It would appear as if she were avoiding having Ben help her—which was exactly the reason she'd be doing it. She was sure he was helping out of the kindness of his heart and she didn't want to hurt him.

She kept telling herself she should dread the fact that Ben would have to carry her upstairs once more. But her heart beat faster just thinking about being in his arms again.

She gave herself a shake and went to work. After half an hour or so, she'd finished and felt confident she'd get a good grade. She left the paper out and made her way down the hall to her mother's study. The ledger was on her desk and Rebecca sat down to look it over.

The bookkeeping system seemed simple and straightforward and was easy to understand. She could see right away that while her mother did make some money with Heaton House, she watched her pennies quite well. She seemed to be able to run Heaton House without getting into her own savings and after going shopping with her, Rebecca realized it was because she was an excellent businesswoman. She hoped to learn more from her.

"Rebecca dear, you don't have to do that now," her mother said as she came into the room. "My goodness, you've had a long day today. Why don't you sit in one of the easy chairs and I'll go fetch us a cup of tea. Ben should be home anytime now and he can take you upstairs. I suppose we could ask Matt, but—"

"Oh, no. I don't think Millicent would like that, Mama." And well, if she *had* to be carried up, it might as well be by someone she was used to.

"Oh, I'm sure she'd understand."

"Perhaps, but I'll take you up on the offer of tea and we can visit awhile."

"Good. I'll be right back."

Her mother left the room and Rebecca got up from behind the desk and made it over to the nearest chair flanking the fireplace. She put her foot up on the footstool, leaned back and closed her eyes.

But not for long. She heard the front door close and was sure it must be Ben coming home. Then solid footsteps sounded in the hall and her pulse began to ripple through her veins. She sighed and shook her head. This had to stop.

She heard him pass the study but, instead of calling him, she closed her eyes again and tried to will her pulse to slow down—all to no avail as she heard his footsteps coming back. "Rebecca? Did I wake you?"

She opened her eyes to see him enter the room, his expression filled with concern.

"No. I—"

"I thought you'd be in the little parlor."

"After I finished in there, I came in to have a look at Mama's books. I'd been going to earlier in the day, but never got to it. You can check my work, if you'd like. It's on the table, but I'll stay here if you don't mind."

"Not at all. You look tired. Do you want me to carry you up now?"

Her heart slammed against her chest. Oh yes, she did. "No, I'm fine. Mama is bringing tea."

He nodded. "I'll go check out your math and be right back."

"Okay." Maybe she'd have time to quit reacting like a love-struck adolescent. Frustrated with herself, Rebecca sent up a silent prayer. *Dear Lord, please let me get over this attraction, or whatever it is I feel for Ben. Please.*

He'd only been gone a few minutes before her mother returned with a tray. "Did I hear Ben?"

"Yes, he's checking my work. He'll be back."

"Good. I brought an extra cup just in case." She poured Rebecca and herself a cup and they'd barely taken a sip when Ben entered the room once more.

His smile took in both of them before his gaze came to rest on Rebecca. "You only missed one problem, Rebecca. I worked it out for you so you could see where you made the mistake, but you can look at it tomorrow."

"Thank you. I will."

Ben turned to her mother. "Mrs. Heaton, do you have enough of that tea for me to have a cup?"

"I certainly do. Please take a seat. I'll sit here at

my desk," Rebecca's mother said. She handed Ben a cup after he took the seat on the other side of the fireplace from Rebecca.

"Thank you." Ben took a sip and looked at Rebecca. "Several women asked about you in class tonight and Sarah and Molly asked if they might come by to see you. I wasn't sure if I should say yes, but I didn't want them to think you wouldn't want to see them and—"

"Oh, I'd love to visit with them," Rebecca said.

"I'm glad, because I told them yes and gave them the address. I do hope I didn't overstep my—"

"Of course, they'll be welcome here," Rebecca's mother said.

"I know they will, Mrs. Heaton, and I appreciate it. I'm not sure if they'll come or just wanted to see if they could, though."

"Well, if they don't make it, hopefully I'll get to see them on Thursday," Rebecca said. Surely she'd be able to get around on her cane by Thursday.

"Do you think you'll be able to go to class by then?" Ben looked doubtful.

"I hope so. I think the Epsom salts are helping and I can put a little more weight on my foot."

She stood with her crutches to show them, but after a long day, her foot wasn't as strong as she'd thought it would be and she winced as a twinge of pain shot up her leg. She quickly sat back down.

"No scooting up the stairs for you tonight, dear," her mother said. "If you're finished with your tea, I'm sure Ben won't mind carrying you up."

"It will be my pleasure," Ben stood quickly.

And, fight as she might against it, Rebecca had a feeling it would be hers, too.

Rebecca's mother grabbed her crutches. "I'll take these to your room and check on Jenny, dear."

Rebecca sighed and nodded. "Thank you, Mama."

Her mother hurried out of the room as Ben scooped Rebecca up in his arms, headed out the door and down the hall. "I can tell you're frustrated that you can't get up the stairs by yourself yet. But I do think you may have done too much today. Earlier, Jenny said Kathleen and Elizabeth came by for a visit this afternoon."

"They did, but visiting with them didn't tire me out. It was good to see them. They brought me the most beautiful cane for when I can put a little more weight on my foot. And Kathleen told me she expects me to be at the housewarming on Friday, one way or another."

Ben chuckled as he paused at the bottom of the staircase. "Oh, I'll see to it you are."

If he had to carry her most of the night, he'd make sure she was there. As if he minded. As if he hadn't been thinking of her all day. He'd even cut class a few minutes early this evening to get back to Heaton House and see how she was. He hadn't had a chance to talk to her alone, except for those few minutes in her mother's study, until now.

"How is your ankle feeling?" He looked her in the eye, trying to avoid the draw of his gaze to her lips. But the expression in her eyes had him holding his breath.

She broke eye contact and looked ahead. "It's a bit sore this evening, but better than yesterday. I'm going to soak it in Epsom salts again tonight. It seemed to help last night."

"Just don't try to rush things. Jenny wants you to be able to skate again and if you don't give your ankle time to heal completely, that might not be possible this year."

She did look at him then—with an arched eyebrow and a slight smile on those lips he was trying so hard not to look at. "Yes, doctor."

He smiled and kept moving. But at the top of the staircase, he paused, his heart beating so hard he wondered if she could hear it, feel it even.

"Are you all right? I know it's not easy carrying me up these stairs night after night."

Ben laughed. At least she didn't know that it was the highlight of his day. "You're light as a feather. It's no hardship at all."

"Oh? You paused and I thought you were having to catch your breath."

Oh, he'd caught his breath all right, but it had nothing to do with it being hard to carry her. In fact, he wished her room were on the third floor so he could hold her longer.

"Perhaps it's your beauty that takes my breath away, my lady." He spoke the truth but in a way that made her giggle.

"Oh, I'm sure. You just don't want to admit that near the top of those stairs I feel a bit heavy, do you?" There was a sparkle in her eyes as she smiled at him and he couldn't keep his gaze from taking in those lips once more. Did she have any idea how much he wanted to kiss her? He hurried his pace to her door. "You are not heavy in the least. And you—"

Ben broke off—what was he thinking? He couldn't finish that sentence. He couldn't tell her she *was* beautiful and there were times she did take his breath away and he wanted nothing more than to kiss her. Right now.

He set her down gently, holding on to her until she got her crutches under her arms and looked up at him.

"Thank you, Ben. I do appreciate you helping me up the stairs. Hopefully, you won't feel you have to much longer."

"For your sake, I hope your ankle keeps getting stronger, but for mine—I think I'll miss the opportunity I've had to help you."

"You help in all kinds of ways, Ben."

"I'm glad to help in any way I can." There was something about this woman that had him dreaming about things he'd given up hoping for. Something that brought her to mind much too often during the day. He needed to distance himself from her and, yet, that was the very last thing he wanted to do. He leaned across her and opened her door.

"Thank you."

He didn't dare kiss her, but he couldn't resist tucking an errant curl around her ear. "You're welcome. I hope you sleep well, Rebecca."

"I hope you do, too, Ben. Good night." She entered her room and turned back to him with a smile.

"Good night. I'll get the door." Once she was well inside her room, Ben closed the door behind her and released a huge sigh. *Dear Lord, I'm not sure what's happening here, but please help me to figure it out soon. And to keep whatever it is I am feeling to myself until I do.*

He hurried to the landing and down the stairs, his insides churning. He was glad there was no one in the parlor, for he didn't feel like speaking to anyone.

Yet, knowing he'd never be able to sleep, he decided to take a walk. Maybe a bit of fresh air would do him a world of good. He let himself out quietly and took the steps two at a time. Striding down the street, he couldn't get thoughts of Rebecca out of his mind.

It had taken all the willpower he had not to kiss her tonight. And if he had given in to the temptation? How would she have taken it? Would she have slapped him? Or let him know in no uncertain terms that he'd crossed a line?

His growing feelings could lead to heartbreak and that was the last thing he needed. He enjoyed her company and that of her daughter. He didn't want to ruin it. Besides, she was his landlady's daughter and if things were awkward between them, he'd feel he had to leave and this was home to him.

He must strengthen his resolve to tamp down his attraction to Rebecca. But it wasn't going to be easy. Each time she came into a room, she sent his pulse galloping like a racehorse at a county fair, and when she smiled at him, his heart tightened as if squeezed by a vise—both reactions that could spell trouble. He'd lived at Heaton House for several years now and while he found the women boarders attractive, he wasn't attracted to them. They were like family to him. But Rebecca…was a different story altogether.

Ben walked around Gramercy Park three times, trying to put Rebecca out of his mind, but by the time he let himself back in Heaton House, he knew he'd failed completely in that endeavor.

Chapter Thirteen

The workers began tearing down walls on the third floor the next day, and the noise was enough to make Rebecca try to crawl downstairs, but Ben had come to get her that morning. And there was no way she could deny that she enjoyed the feel of being in his arms much more than scooting downstairs.

And as Ben would have had to carry her up the stairs at the Y, she decided she'd wait until the next week to attend class. He'd assured her he didn't mind, but two floors was a lot of stairs. Not to mention that she was sure someone from class would see him carrying her and could just imagine what kind of reception she'd receive from the other women.

She continued to fight the feelings being in Ben's arms brought, trying to ignore the racing of her pulse, the hammering of her heart, until he carried her back up that night and it started all over again. She'd never felt more cared for or protected than she did in Ben Roth's arms. Ever.

But she couldn't dwell on those feelings. Ben was

helping her as best he could but that didn't mean he was as attracted to her as she was to him. And if he knew of her past…well, she couldn't let herself even think of what his reaction might be.

So she strived harder each day to put thoughts of Ben out of her mind, and she used her cane as much as possible. By Friday morning, she was confident she'd make it to Elizabeth and John's housewarming without her crutches.

She also had visitors that afternoon. She and Jenny were in the front parlor, trying to ignore the noise from the third floor, when her mother came in followed by Sarah and Molly.

"You have guests, dear. These young ladies said Ben had told them about your accident and they wanted to see how you're doing."

"Sarah, Molly, how nice to see you both! And how sweet of you to come to see me. Please come in and sit down."

While she still wondered if they might only be curious about where Ben lived, they were very nice to her mother and Jenny and truly seemed concerned about her.

"Mr. Roth told us how you sprained your ankle and couldn't come to class," Sarah said. "Is there anything we can do to help you stay up with the lessons?"

"We can help with your homework, if you'd like."

"Oh, that's very nice of you both, but I've been managing to keep up, with Mr. Roth's help." Rebecca didn't think she should refer to him as just Ben in front of them, at least not yet.

They stayed for tea and she found out a little more

about them. Molly wanted to find a good job so that she could help her family move out of the cramped quarters they lived in. And Sarah…Rebecca felt there was something on her mind, but she wasn't ready to confide anything other than that she needed to be able to take care of herself.

When they took their leave, Rebecca invited them to come back anytime. She was more determined than ever to befriend these young women and see if she could help them in some way.

It was time to get ready for Elizabeth and John's housewarming and her mother made sure the workers left early so that everyone could dress for the party without worrying about running into them.

Ben seemed to show up at just the right time to carry her upstairs so that she could get ready for the party. Her mother helped Jenny get dressed while Rebecca washed up and managed to change into one of her favorite dinner gowns—a green velvet her mother had bought her for Christmas.

Jenny and her mother took her cane down and told Ben she was ready to come back down. He must have been in the parlor because it was only a minute or two before he knocked on her door. He truly was the most thoughtful man she'd ever met. And he looked quite handsome all dressed up for the party.

"You look lovely tonight," he said as crossed the room and lifted her into his arms.

"Thank you. You look very nice yourself."

"I'm glad we don't have to do this every night, but it's nice to see everyone all dressed up."

The others were putting on their wraps when they

arrived downstairs and between her cane and Ben's steadying her, she managed to put on her own. She grinned up at him. "I feel like I'm making progress. I dressed myself tonight!"

"That can only mean one thing," Ben whispered in her ear.

"What is that?"

"I'll only have the pleasure of helping you up and down the stairs for a short while. I think I'll make the most of it." He scooped her up into his arms once more as everyone made their way out to the two hacks waiting for them.

"But Ben, I can—"

"Let's save your energy for the party. You'll have more fun if you aren't tired out when we get there."

She couldn't argue with his logic and, besides, she felt a little sad he wouldn't be carrying her much longer. No matter how often she told herself she'd be glad when she could maneuver the stairs on her own once more—she knew she'd never forget the feeling of being in Ben's arms.

Elizabeth and John welcomed them all into their home and it was even nicer than Rebecca thought it would be. It was a bit larger than Kathleen and Luke's and it was furnished beautifully.

"Aunt Bea helped me. She insisted that I take some of the family heirlooms—now that she and Papa are married and he's selling the house in Boston, she wanted to make sure I got what I wanted from my childhood home."

"Oh, that was very nice of her," Rebecca said.

"Yes, it was. The parlor suite was a wedding gift from them, but the dining room furniture was my mother's. Two of the bedroom sets came from home. And some of the knickknacks were my favorites, but I didn't want too many for I want John and I to be able to add the things we love."

"Your home is lovely, Elizabeth," Rebecca's mother said.

The couple seemed thrilled with the brass bowl they'd all gone in on for them.

"I love it," Elizabeth said. "It's gorgeous and will look great with a fern in it in the front window."

Rebecca did the tour of the downstairs—the parlor, a small study, the kitchen and dining room—but elected to see the upstairs when she could make it under her own steam.

"Jenny and I will describe everything to you later, dear," her mother said.

"Thank you. I look forward to hearing all about it." Rebecca watched as Jenny took her grandmother's hand and headed upstairs with her.

"I'll keep you company," Ben said from behind her. "I saw the upstairs when I helped them move. Why don't you take a seat in the parlor and rest your ankle while they're gone?"

"All right, I think I will, although it's not bothering me too much and the cane helps immensely."

Ben took her arm and gave her what support he could and she found it much easier to maneuver around with his help. He made sure she was settled comfortably in one of the easy chairs and pulled a nearby footstool close so that she could elevate her foot.

"You're making good progress and if you're up to it by Tuesday, I'm sure I can help you maneuver the stairs at the Y."

"I hope so. I'd like to get to know Sarah and Molly better. They came by to see me this afternoon."

"They did?"

"Yes. And I asked them back anytime. I have a feeling Sarah would like to talk to someone, but maybe not with Molly around."

"You could be right. But I'm very glad they came to see you. I wasn't sure they would."

"I didn't think they would, either. But I'm glad they did. I'll feel more comfortable around them in class now and, hopefully, they'll feel more comfortable around me, should they need someone to talk to."

Everyone began to drift back downstairs then, and Rebecca felt like a special guest, as Elizabeth insisted she stay put and the party would come to her. Her aunt's maid, who was helping that night, brought her a plate of food and soon everyone had joined her in the parlor.

Rebecca was pleased to see how happy Elizabeth's aunt and father seemed to be and wished her mother had found someone special to share her life with. If it could happen to Bea Watson, surely it could happen for her mother one day.

The party was still going strong when Rebecca began to tire and wish she were home. Suddenly Ben was by her side as if he could read her mind. "You look tired. Your mother suggested we call a hack to take her and Jenny and you home. It should be here any moment now. I'll go, too, so that—"

"Ben, I'm sure I can manage the stairs—"

"Not tonight, Rebecca. Please. I'd feel terrible if you couldn't and I wasn't there."

She knew from his tone he wasn't going to change his mind—funny how she'd begun to recognize that about him in the short time she'd been living at Heaton House.

She nodded and stood with the aid of her cane. When Ben offered his arm to help her out to the hack, she took it, wanting to show him how well she could do. But she was thankful for his arm to lean on, as all the practicing she'd done during the day had tired her out.

He must have sensed it because when they got back to Heaton House, he helped her out of the hack and carried her to the house.

"Ben, I can walk."

"I felt you bobble when we came out of John and Elizabeth's. You can't make it up the stairs and I have a feeling that's where you want to go, isn't it?"

"Well, yes, but—"

"No need to exhaust yourself. I'm sure you'll feel stronger tomorrow if you don't push it today."

"He's right you know, dear," her mother added from behind.

"Let Mr. Ben carry you, Mama. I'll bring your cane," Jenny said with a yawn.

Her daughter was sleepy and it would be easier on everyone if she just let Ben carry her from here. "All right."

"Thank you." Ben flashed her a grin.

Jenny and her mother rushed up the steps and

opened the front door, waiting for Ben to bring her in. Once he did, her mother shut the door behind them and then she and Jenny hurried on upstairs.

But Ben seemed in no real hurry as he followed them inside and upstairs. They passed Jenny's room on the way to hers, and Rebecca heard her daughter giggling as her mother helped her get ready for bed.

Evidently, so did Ben as he chuckled. "I love the sound of Jenny's laughter. It never fails to make me smile."

"She's certainly a joy to me."

They arrived at her door, which her mother must have opened and, instead of putting her down outside her room, Ben paused before saying, "I don't see your crutches or cane—where do you want me to set you?"

"The settee will be fine. Mama will bring me my cane in a minute."

Ben nodded as he strode across the room and gently deposited her on the settee in front of the fireplace. He hesitated for a moment, then said, "It looks as if you won't be needing me much longer. I think I'm going to—"

"Oh, there you are," Rebecca's mother said as she came into the room, Jenny right behind her. "Jenny wanted to kiss you good-night."

Jenny ran to Rebecca and threw her arms around her and when Rebecca looked up at Ben, the expression in his eyes melted her heart. Was that…could it be…longing in his expression as he looked down at them?

Ben tamped down the yearning that had washed over him and turned to go. "I'll let you get everyone settled, Mrs. Heaton. And I'll be up in the morning to bring you down to breakfast, Rebecca."

They each thanked him and said good-night and he hurried out of the room and down the stairs. The others had returned and gathered in the parlor to talk over the evening. He debated whether to join them or go on downstairs, but he knew that if he were by himself there'd be nothing to keep him from thinking of Rebecca and Jenny and how very much he'd wished—no! He couldn't get carried away with his thoughts or his longings.

Rebecca would be managing those stairs on her own within a week and he'd no longer be needed to help her. His heart squeezed at the thought, and yet he'd be almost relieved when she didn't. For he'd never felt more alive than when he held her in his arms. He couldn't deny that his feelings for Rebecca were growing and that was a problem. For he was still determined never to risk losing his heart again—not to the point where he faced rejection. If Rebecca rebuffed him, what would happen to the relationship they had? He shook his head and pasted on a smile as he entered the parlor.

"Oh, good! Another man," Matt said. "Come join us, Ben. I feel outnumbered with these two women."

Ben chuckled and joined them, hoping to keep his thoughts off the woman upstairs.

"I thought you'd all have gone to bed by now," he said.

"No, we've been talking over the party and wondering who Mrs. Heaton might add as boarders next,"

Julia said. "I say a man, but Matt and Millicent think a woman. What do you think?"

"I haven't given it any thought, really. But I imagine she's got room for a couple more men at least and perhaps a couple more women, too. Once she puts that sign out, I think she'll have a full house within a week."

"Do you?" Millicent said. "I hope so."

"Yes, so do I," Julia said.

"At least there are more of you upstairs," Matt said. "With just Ben and me down below, it gets mighty quiet at times. And we can hear laughter up on your floor and wonder what's going on."

"Oh, you cannot," Millicent said. "You're teasing."

"No, he's not," Ben said. "But it has to be really quiet for us to hear anything."

"You can't actually hear what we say, can you?" Julia asked.

"Why, do you talk about us?" Matt asked.

"If we did, we wouldn't tell you and since you had to ask, I'll assume you can't hear all that much."

Matt laughed. "I'll never tell."

"Mathew Sterling! You—"

"Calm down, Millicent," Ben said. "We can't hear you talking on your floor. Just a burst of laughter now and again. Matt is just teasing you."

"As always," Millicent said. Then she yawned. "I'm tired and am going up. See you all tomorrow."

"Wait for me, I'm going, too." Julia headed out of the parlor right behind her.

"You sure had her going for a while, Matt. She

really thought we could hear what they said up in their rooms."

Matt chuckled. "I know. And I shouldn't tease her like that. She's just so…naive at times. And so pretty when she gets all worked up over something."

"Hmm. Are you attracted to her?" Ben asked.

"Might be. Like you're attracted to Rebecca."

"I never said—"

"You don't have to, my friend. But don't worry. I don't think she has any idea you might be."

"Well, if I were, it's not something I'll be acting on. I'm not going down that road again."

"Same here. Millie and I are like oil and water. It'd never work."

They both headed downstairs to their rooms. Ben entered his and flung himself into his easy chair. So much for getting Rebecca out of his mind.

Chapter Fourteen

Rebecca wanted to get back to her classes at the Y and was more determined than ever to be able to manage the stairs there the next week.

Over the weekend, she practiced with her cane and was getting around very well, except by the evening she couldn't deny she was very tired and with her mother and Ben watching, she'd bobbled a tad while attempting to go up by herself and they'd rushed to help.

Ben scooped her up and carried her the rest of the way to her room, while her mother took her cane.

"I'm beginning to wonder if you just have an aversion to my carrying you, Rebecca," Ben said. "You know I don't mind."

"Ben, I do not have a distaste to you carrying me." In fact, it was just the opposite. "I just—"

"Are a bit too—"

"Independent?"

"At times, maybe."

Her tummy did a dive at the grin he gave her. "Perhaps. But as my mother will tell you, I've always had an independent streak and while it's gotten me into trouble on more than one occasion, and after…well, suffice it to say, I might carry it a bit too far at times, but I'm not about to give my independence up totally."

"Oh, I'd never suggest that you do. But it *would* be nice if you'd accept help when you need it once in a while."

Had she come across as ungrateful? For that was the last thing she wanted to do. "Oh, Ben, I'm sorry if I've given you the impression that I'm unappreciative, for I am ever so thankful for your help. I just feel I'm taking advantage of you." And she enjoying being in his arms entirely too much.

He stopped midway up the stairs and shook his head before capturing her gaze with his. "You are not taking advantage of me. If I were getting tired of this or didn't want to help you, don't you think I'd have left it to Matt to get you up the stairs? It's not as if I'm the only male around to help. But I didn't want Matt helping you. I wanted to."

Rebecca's heart thudded against her ribs as his gaze shifted from her eyes to her lips, drawing her gaze to his once more. He dipped his head and—

"Rebecca dear, I've left your cane just outside the door. I'm going to run Jenny's bath," her mother called from up above.

Ben cleared his throat and continued up the stairs.

"Thank you, Mama." Rebecca barely got the words out and she sounded breathless even to her own ears, as if she'd run up the stairs instead of being carried by Ben.

What would have happened if her mother hadn't interrupted just then? Would Ben have kissed her as she'd thought he might? Wanted him to? Would she have kissed him back?

He lowered her to her feet and held her with one arm around her waist as he handed her the cane. "Can you make it from here?"

"I think so." She had to.

But she caught her breath and held it when Ben reached out and tucked an errant curl around her ear once again, grazing her cheek in the process.

Then he opened the door for her. "Good night and sweet dreams."

"Good night, Ben." She hoped she didn't dream, for lately they had been sweet and all about him, leaving her longing once again for the impossible.

Ben turned and took the stairs two steps at a time. He'd really come close to kissing Rebecca tonight and if not for her mother's interruption, he would have—and most likely ruined the delicate relationship he and Rebecca seemed to have formed.

He knew in his heart that she wasn't ready for a deeper friendship than what they had now and neither was he. Until recently he'd thought he never would be, but his actions and how he felt when he was around her were affecting him in a way he'd never experienced before.

But there was too much at stake to give in to his longing to kiss her before he'd considered all the risks involved in doing so. And for now they seemed insurmountable. So he'd better concentrate on being her friend instead of how much he wished he'd kissed her delectable lips.

On Sunday, Rebecca had been happy to make it to church with everyone, and on Monday all the hammering and sawing on the third floor continued, but at least they weren't knocking down walls.

Rebecca would have loved to see what was taking place up there. However, it was all she could do to maneuver the stairs from the second floor to the first and back up again. She felt sure she'd be able to make it to class on Tuesday night. At least she hoped so and she wasn't going to push it by climbing another flight of stairs just yet.

The night before, she'd managed to make it upstairs holding on to Ben's arm as a practice run and had done very well except for missing him carrying her up. She told herself it was much better this way—that the longing to have him kiss her would eventually subside if she wasn't in his arms each night, only she wasn't sure she believed it.

That morning, she practiced her typing in the small parlor while Jenny played. Then after lunch and a bit of a rest, Jenny went to help out in the kitchen.

Since her mother had gone to visit Violet and baby Marcus, and her daughter was enjoying herself, Rebecca took that time to learn more about how her mother kept the books so that when she began doing them there would be a smooth transition. Once her ankle was totally healed she looked forward to helping with the shopping and taking inventory of everything. She couldn't wait to get back to it.

When her mother came in right before teatime, she sounded more than a little excited as she hurried down the hall calling her name. "Rebecca?"

"What is it, Mama? Is something wrong? I'm in your study."

"Oh, no, dear. Nothing is wrong, but you'll never guess who Violet has heard from!"

"Who?"

"Let me ask Gretchen to bring us some tea and I'll tell you all about it." Then she disappeared from view.

Rebecca closed the ledger and with her cane she eased her way around the desk to sit in one of the easy chairs, just as her mother came back into the room and sank down in the other chair flanking the fireplace.

"Now, tell me who Violet has heard from and why you're so excited about it."

"Why, it's Georgia Marshall. Remember her? She was a few years ahead of you and became a schoolteacher."

Rebecca did remember Georgia. She was a neighbor and they'd gotten along well, although they weren't what one would call close friends—not like she and Violet had been. "What did her letter say?"

"She's coming for a visit this weekend!"

"Oh? Did that come as a surprise to Violet and Michael?"

"Not really. She'd written them saying she was thinking about it, but Violet never mentioned it because she was afraid she'd change her mind. Evidently she's said she was coming before, only never did. But this time she says she's even contemplating moving here!"

"Really?"

Gretchen showed up with Jenny right behind her to give them both a hug. Jenny loved taking tea with them, although she always had more milk than tea in her cup. She sat down on the footstool between the two chairs and took the small cup and saucer Gretchen handed her. Rebecca's mother had found them at Macy's on one of their shopping trips and it was just the right size for her.

"Thank you, Gretchen," Jenny said, making Rebecca proud that her daughter had remembered her manners.

"You're quite welcome, Miss Jenny. I appreciate your help in the kitchen."

Jenny's smile was huge as she thanked the woman once more.

Once Gretchen had served their tea and left, Rebecca turned to her mother. "So, why has Georgia decided she might move here? Did she say?"

"From what I gathered, she's had a heartbreak of some kind, so she gave her notice at school for the end of the term and hopes to find work here. It shouldn't be hard. Perhaps Ben will know of a job opening for her."

"Perhaps." Rebecca tried to tamp down the small wave of anxiety that suddenly enveloped her. For what reason she wasn't sure, but it made her uncomfortable. "I'm sure we can ask him."

"She's told Violet she hopes I'll have a room available if she does move here. Said she didn't want to impose on Violet and Michael, especially as they are getting used to having baby Marcus around and she wants to pay her way. And she knows her parents will feel better if she lives at Heaton House than if she got a room somewhere else."

"Well, I can certainly understand that." And she could. It'd be nice to have someone she knew living here. Even if she wondered how Ben might take to her as they were both teachers and would have much in common. She tamped down the jittery feeling the thought gave her.

"Oh, and I put out the vacancy sign just a few minutes ago. We should have a full house again before long."

"More boarders, Granma?" Jenny asked excitedly.

"Yes, Jenny, dear. Any day now, I hope."

Jenny clapped her hands. "Oh, I'm glad!"

"So am I," Rebecca said. Her mother had paid cash for the home when she bought it, but she needed regular boarders to help keep Heaton House running and not deplete her savings. And so that those young women who needed a place to stay, even for a short while, would have one at a lower rent or even for free, depending on their circumstances.

Her mother's smile was contagious. "I'm glad you're both happy about more boarders. I wouldn't be adding any if you weren't. But Georgia is an old friend and I hope you'll both enjoy her company if she moves here. I asked Violet and Michael and Georgia to come to dinner on Saturday evening. That should give Ben time to check on job vacancies."

"I look forward to seeing Georgia again. And it will be good to have Michael and Violet over, too."

"And baby Marcus!" Jenny added.

Rebecca hugged her daughter close, reminding herself that it didn't matter how Georgia and Ben got along. What mattered was raising her daughter. She had no claim on Ben. He was only a very good friend who was there for her. There could be nothing more between them. The very thought twisted her heart deep inside for she knew that on her side, Ben had come to mean much more…

Ben hurried off the trolley and down the street toward Heaton House. From down the block, he could see the nice new sign hanging under the Heaton House sign that read Vacancies: Apply Within. A young woman approached from the other direction. She stopped and looked at the sign just as he got there.

"Hello, miss. I'm Benjamin Roth and I live at Heaton House. May I help you?"

"Why, yes, you can. Is there really a vacancy here?"

"There is."

"I'd like to apply then. My name is Emily Jordan. Do you know whom I'd see?"

"Yes, the landlady. I'm sure she's home now." Ben smiled and opened the door for her to enter, then followed her inside. He motioned to the parlor. "Please just go have a seat and I'll see if I can find Mrs. Heaton."

But before Ben turned down the hall, Mrs. Heaton came out of her study, followed by Rebecca and

Jenny. "Good afternoon, Ben." Mrs. Heaton smiled and looked at Miss Jordan. "Who is this young woman you have with you?"

"This is Miss Emily Jordan. I met her on the walk outside and she'd like to speak with you about renting a room."

"Oh, wonderful. Why don't you come to my study, Miss Jordan?" Mrs. Heaton said. "Other boarders will be here anytime now and we'll have more privacy there."

"Thank you, I'd be pleased to do so."

The women headed out of the room and as their footsteps told him they were out of hearing range, Ben looked over at Rebecca and Jenny, glad to have them to himself for even a few minutes. "How has your day gone? Have you managed with the cane all right?"

"It's been a good one, hasn't it, Jenny?"

Jenny nodded. "I got to help in the kitchen."

"Her favorite thing to do lately," Rebecca said. "And yes, I've managed with my cane better today. I think I'll be able to go to class tomorrow evening."

"Oh, I'm glad to hear it. I'll help you maneuver the stairs, should you need me to, you know."

"I do."

Ben smiled at Jenny. "With you in the kitchen helping out, I'm sure we have something very good for dessert, don't we?"

She smiled back at him and nodded. "But it's a surprise."

"Well, I look forward to finding out what it is."

"I think Jenny and I will go up and freshen up," Rebecca said. "That's where we were heading when you came in. You can see for yourself how I manage getting upstairs."

"I'll take you up on that offer. Just to make sure," he added with a grin.

Rebecca smiled and, with the help of her cane, she started toward the doorway.

By the time Ben reached her, Rebecca had already made it up the first few steps holding the railing and he watched until she got to the landing and glanced down at him.

"See?"

Her smile shot straight to his heart and it took him a moment to answer. "I do see. You did very well."

"Told you," she grinned down at him. "See you at dinner."

Ben just chuckled and watched until she got to the top and disappeared from view.

He was happy for her—no doubt about it. He wanted her healthy and able to get anywhere she needed to go. But at the same time, he felt a little twinge of sadness… It appeared his time of holding Rebecca in his arms had come to an end.

Chapter Fifteen

The next day was very busy. Two gentlemen came to apply for the room vacancies and by dinnertime, there were no more rooms to let. At least not that Rebecca's mother was letting out now.

"I think you'll all be pleased with the new boarders we have coming in," her mother announced at dinner. "There are two men and one woman who will be joining us."

"Wonderful, Mrs. Heaton. That was really fast," Millicent said.

"It appears Ben was right about putting out a sign, Mama," Rebecca said.

Ben grinned and nodded. "I didn't want to say 'I told you so.' But I'm glad it worked well."

"So am I, Ben," Rebecca's mother said.

"Tell us about them, Mrs. Heaton," Matt said. "It will be good to have our numbers going up, won't it?"

"It will. Mostly, though, it'll be good to see this table full again. The young woman is Emily Jordan—she is a window decorator at Macy's."

"Oh, that sounds like a fun job," Millicent said.

"It does, doesn't it?" Mrs. Heaton said. "She seems quit nice. And one of the men is Joseph Clark. He likes to be called Joe and he works in Michael's building. When Michael told him I had openings, he jumped at the chance to live here. I think you'll all like him. And then there's Stephen Adams. He's staying with the Johnsons down the street and saw the sign. He works at that new Siegel-Cooper department store. Should be interesting having two new people working for competing department stores."

Everyone chuckled.

"It certainly might be," Matt said.

"Should be quite fun," Julia added.

Rebecca was happy that everyone seemed excited about the new boarders and she hoped they all got along. But she had a feeling they would find a way to, for her mother's sake.

She felt very good that evening for she was going to class with Ben and while it was still quite cool out, the days weren't near as cold as they had been the first night she went to class. If the wind were blowing like that night, she would have felt she had to stay in. She was getting used to her cane, but a good stiff wind could knock her down. Ben had offered to call for a hack, but she'd insisted the trolley would be fine and she sent up a prayer that she would have no problem getting around.

But there was no need to worry, for once she'd kissed Jenny goodbye, Ben was there to help her on with her jacket and give her an arm as soon as they were outside. Between him and her cane, she felt quite steady and it felt wonderful to be out and about again.

The trolley posed a bit of a challenge, but with Ben's help she made it on.

"Your mother seems quite pleased with the boarders she's chosen," Ben said after they'd taken their seats.

Rebecca nodded. "I think she is. And she was so excited, she forgot to tell everyone that Michael and Violet would be bringing a guest for dinner this Saturday. A friend of the family is coming up for the weekend and will be staying with them. She wants to check out teaching positions for next year. She may be moving here. Mama thought you might know of some openings coming up."

"Oh? What kind of teacher is she?"

"I'm not sure, as I was away when she started teaching."

Ben nodded. "We have a lot of schools in the city and there are always openings come fall. I'll ask around and find out what I can."

"Thank you." That was Ben. Always ready to help anyone in need. And that's what she had to keep reminding herself. His carrying her upstairs was nothing personal for him—he'd have done the same for Millicent or Julia.

But would he be attracted to Georgia? They were both teachers and Rebecca remembered her as being quite pretty. Suddenly she felt a little queasy. The thought that Ben might be attracted to anyone didn't sit well with her at all.

They reached their stop and Ben stepped into the

aisle to make room for her to scoot out of the seat and steady herself with the cane. When she reached the door, he quickly moved around her and down the steps so he could help her. Only instead of waiting for her to maneuver the steps, his hands clasped her at the waist and he swung her to the walk.

"Easier and faster. I hope you didn't mind," he said, looking down at her with a grin.

Her racing pulse had her catching her breath as he steadied her and she shook her head.

"You ready?"

She took hold of his arm, let out a deep breath and found her voice. "I think so. And thank you. That was much faster and I'm sure the other riders were glad to get me out of the way."

They took off down the block, passing the café. It held good memories and Rebecca wished Ben would ask her if she wanted to stop for hot chocolate again on their way home this evening, but she was afraid to hope.

They entered the Y and she looked up at the stairs. She could do this. She had to do this. She took the first step and grabbed the handrail.

"I'll be right behind you. I'm not going to let you fall."

"I trust you won't."

"But if you get tired, let me know. We'll stop or I'll carry you the rest of the way."

The temptation to take him up on his offer was strong and swift. But it had nothing to do with her being tired and everything to do with being far more attracted to him than she should be. And she *had* to put all that out of her mind.

She could just imagine the looks on her classmates' faces should Ben carry her into the room. So instead, she sent up a silent prayer asking the Lord to take that temptation away, to help her get her attraction to Ben under control and give her the strength to manage the stairs under her own steam.

Ben's admiration for Rebecca rose with each step she climbed. The woman was independent to be sure. But he felt sure she would accept his help should she need it. However, he had a feeling she was determined not to require it here.

He didn't know who was more relieved to reach the classroom—Rebecca or him. Her breathing was a bit labored, showing him that it had been a real effort to climb the two flights of stairs, but she took a deep breath and entered the room with a smile.

"Rebecca! You're back," Sarah said. "Come sit by me."

Ben was glad the seat was near the front of the room as Rebecca made her way to it.

"How are you feeling?" Molly asked from the desk behind.

"I'm feeling much better. I hope to be able to get around by myself soon."

"Well, don't push it," Sarah said. "That's a lovely cane."

"It is and I'm thankful to the friends who bought it for me," Rebecca said.

Several of the others came up to tell her they were

happy to see her. Ben was sure he'd done the right thing by asking her to be a mentor, even though she hadn't had much opportunity to do so since spraining her ankle. Maybe now that they were beginning to know her, they would open up a bit more. He hoped so. She'd be a good example for them to look up to.

Hoping to get out fairly early, he began class right away and, as always, he was pleased with how prepared everyone was.

Rebecca had managed to keep up with the class very well and he was proud of her. And she seemed happy for everyone who came to the board to work a problem and got it right. Sarah seemed a little distracted when she took her turn at working a problem, but she finally managed to get the correct answer. She didn't seem herself, though, and Ben wondered if something was wrong.

He was glad she lingered behind to speak with Rebecca after class, while he was cleaning the board and answering questions from some of the others.

But Rebecca's expression showed concern when he joined them and Sarah suddenly stopped speaking.

"I'm sorry. I didn't mean to interrupt. I just got the impression you weren't feeling well tonight and wanted to make sure you're all right, Sarah."

Sarah's smile was tight but she said, "I am. Thank you for your concern, Mr. Roth."

She turned back to Rebecca. "Are you sure it will be all right if I drop by for a visit tomorrow after lunch?"

"Yes, and I look forward to visiting with you."

"I'll see you then. Good night." The young woman picked up her books and hurried out of the room.

"She seems—"

"She's not feeling well. Said she was a bit nauseated and had been for several days," Rebecca said.

"Oh…well, I hope she feels better soon. I'm sorry I interrupted your talk."

"It's fine. We were just setting up a time for her to visit." She stood and Ben helped her on with her coat. Then she took her cane from the back of the seat.

"Are you ready to make it down? Should I walk beside you or in front this time?" Ben asked.

"I think I'll be able to manage, but perhaps beside me might be best—I'd hate to knock you down the stairs should I fall."

"That's the point—I'd break your fall."

"And no telling what else," Rebecca said. "I'll go down slowly. Hopefully most everyone has gone down by now, and I won't hold anyone up."

"Doesn't matter if you do."

By then they were at the head of the stairs and Ben let Rebecca take the lead. It was slow going, but she made it down and they both released big sighs at the bottom.

"Why don't we stop and have some hot chocolate to give you a rest?" he asked.

"Thank you, that would be nice."

Ben was glad the café was just up the street, because Rebecca was beginning to look weary to him. And she must be, for he didn't know if she'd have agreed to stop otherwise. After all, the last time he'd suggested it, she'd turned him down. But she hadn't this time and he was glad to have her to himself, even if just for a bit.

Once they were seated at the same table by the window that they'd had before and given their order, he leaned back in his chair and looked at Rebecca. She had a little color in her cheeks now—probably from the stairs and the walk here. "Are you sure *you* feel all right?"

She smiled and nodded. "I'm fine. Just a little out of breath, but I feel excited that I managed two floors! I'm on the mend for certain. Perhaps tomorrow I'll go up and see what's being done on the third floor at Heaton House."

"Please don't overdo it."

"I won't. I promise."

"So how did the impending visit with Sarah come about?"

"I asked if everything was all right with her other than the nausea and she said she needed to talk to someone and I—"

"Volunteered."

"I had to. She looked so forlorn."

Ben smiled over at her. "You are your mother's daughter, you know."

"I'm glad I inherited some of her wonderful qualities, but I'm not sure I'll ever be the woman she is. I'm just thankful she's my mother."

"Yes, so am I. And I'm thankful you're Jenny's. She seems to be thriving."

"Jenny is such a blessing to me. I wish—"

She paused and Ben wanted to ask what she wished for, but the waiter brought their hot chocolate just then and he didn't want to appear pushy. If she wanted him to know, she'd tell him.

She took a sip and closed her eyes. "Mmm, this is wonderful. Thank you for suggesting we stop, Ben."

"You're welcome. I'm glad you agreed. It helps me to wind down a little after a full day. I visited the orphanage today. There are several young people who are graduating from high school this year and I try to help them decide what they want to do next, and if they want to go on to college, I look into seeing which one would fit them best and see what I can do about getting them in."

"That's a wonderful thing to do."

"No more than you agreeing to be a confidante to some of the young women in class."

"It feels good to be able to help others, especially after I've received so much." Rebecca blew on her cup and took another sip.

"It does. And there is a lot of need in this city. I think that's why I love being at Heaton House. I don't know anyone there who doesn't reach out to help in some way or another."

"That's true. I hope the new boarders fit in well."

"I'm sure they will. Your mother has a knack for finding people who do. She always has. I've never met anyone who wasn't drawn to her. And I think her boarders are better people for knowing her."

"Well, I'm not going to argue with you on that." Rebecca smiled across the table and then she swiftly changed the subject. "The lady at the orphanage…is she good at her job?"

"Mrs. Butler? She's wonderful. She's cared for

each child who's brought in and that's rare in this city of orphanages. As far as I know, none of the children in her care were ever sent out on the Orphan Trains. And she's taught others, so when she does retire, and I believe that might be soon, the change will be as easy as possible on the children."

"She sounds like a very admirable woman."

"She is. Mrs. Butler was the only mother figure I ever had until I moved to Heaton House. Now your mother pretty much fills that roll."

Rebecca smiled. "I'm glad. And speaking of home, I suppose we should be getting back so I can check in on Jenny. I think that may be our trolley coming now."

"Of course. Why don't I have the waiter call for a hack? It'd be much easier on you."

"No, I need to try to make it on my own, Ben. But that's very thoughtful of you."

He stood immediately, took some bills out of his pocket and paid the waiter who came forward. Rebecca made her way to the door and he opened it for her, thankful it wasn't near as cold and windy as it'd been the last time they'd been here.

Much as he wanted to pick her up and carry her onto the trolley, he stood behind her and let her use her cane and then followed her up the aisle only a short way to the first empty seat. He slid in beside her and smiled. "You did it. I think we'll be out skating again before you know it."

Rebecca shook her head. "I don't know. I must admit, I'm a little afraid to try again."

"I'll skate with you and I won't let you fall. And

you know, not all falls result in sprains or broken bones."

"I do, but still—"

"No need to worry about it now. It's supposed to start snowing tonight. If we get enough this week, maybe we can plan a sleighing party one night, instead. I'm sure Jenny would like to go."

"She'd love it and so would I. It's been a very long time since I went sleighing."

"Maybe this weekend would be a good time, with Michael and Violet and their guest coming over."

"It might be. I'll speak to Mama about it."

Rebecca was rather quiet after that and Ben put it down to her being tired. But as their trolley came to its stop near Heaton House, and he moved to let her out into the aisle, he knew she was determined to get down by herself. He could only trust that the Lord would nudge her to ask for help, should she need it. But would she listen?

Chapter Sixteen

When Sarah came to visit the next day, Rebecca took her to the small parlor and asked Gretchen to bring their tea there. Earlier, she'd told her mother about the visit and she'd offered to take Jenny to see baby Marcus so they wouldn't be interrupted.

If anything, the young woman appeared more stressed than she had the night before. Rebecca waited until Gretchen brought their tea and then asked, "Sarah, please tell me what's wrong. Are you ill?"

Sarah gave a brief shake of her head. "Not ill, not really. I…" She took a deep breath. "I have to tell someone, Rebecca and I'm not sure how to even get it out."

"But you need to." Rebecca had her own suspicions about what was troubling the young woman. "Sarah…are you expecting a child?"

Sarah covered her mouth and closed her yes. She nodded. "I am. And I'm not sure how to tell the baby's father. I'm afraid he'll be angry and—"

"It doesn't matter if he is or not. You must tell him, Sarah."

"I know. But what if he leaves me? What if my parents disown me? I—"

"Sarah, I can't tell you none of that will happen, but I can assure you that I'll be here for you if it does."

"You will?"

Rebecca nodded. "Yes. Tell the father first. Give him a chance to take responsibility. He might, you know."

"I'm not sure he will." Sarah's voice broke and she began to sob.

Rebecca hugged her and rocked her back and forth. "Then you'll have to tell your mother. And I'll go with you for that, if you need me to. But you don't know that you will. Not yet. Are you afraid of the young man? He wouldn't hurt you, would he? If so, I'll go—"

"No, he won't hurt me physically. But he might not want me anymore."

Rebecca's stomach clenched. She knew all too well that Sarah could be right, and remembering that kind of pain—being left by a man who she thought loved her, to fend for herself in a city she wasn't familiar with, sent tears flooding her eyes. She could remember her heart breaking and how desperately alone she'd felt. Being so ashamed she couldn't face her own family. Now she hurt for what this young woman might face.

"You'll get through it, Sarah. I promise. But don't assume the worst yet. It might all turn out far better than you expect. Come now, drink your tea. It'll do you good. I'm glad you told me."

"I didn't know who else to go to. Molly is a friend,

but—" she shook her head. "She can't really help. She warned me about this kind of thing and I didn't listen to her. Oh, how I wish I had."

"I understand." But Rebecca knew wishing couldn't change the facts and right now she had to help Sarah the best she could.

"There is always an extra room here if you need one." She patted the younger woman's hand. "If you need to talk to me, just tell the operator to ring through to Heaton House in Gramercy Park and ask for me."

For the first time since the evening before, some of the tension seemed to drain out of the young woman and she released a deep sigh. "Thank you, Rebecca. I can't tell you how much I appreciate you being willing to listen to me."

"You're welcome. When do you think you'll be able to talk to the baby's father?"

"I don't know. He's been working on the docks and it could be several days before I see him."

"I'll be praying for you, Sarah. And remember this. The Lord is always with you."

"But I've disappointed Him, so. I sinned and—"

"He will forgive you. You need to ask for Him to and let Him guide you through all this. He will."

Sarah closed her eyes and nodded. "I've taken up enough of your time today. I'd best be on my way."

"I'll see you at class tomorrow night."

Sarah nodded. "Yes, tomorrow night."

Rebecca saw her to the door and gave her another hug. Her heart hurt as she watched the young woman walk away and wished there was more she could do for her. But she knew full well that she was not in control. So she did the only thing she knew would help. She leaned against the door and whispered a prayer.

"Dear God, please be with Sarah right now. Let her know You are near. Please help her to tell those who must be told and I pray the father accepts his responsibility and stands by her. I pray she gives her mother a chance to be there for her and that she doesn't turn Sarah away. But mostly, I pray for her to turn to You to guide her. In Jesus' name, amen."

She went back to the parlor and poured herself another cup of tea before practicing her typing. Sarah's problems brought her past to the forefront, but she wasn't going to revisit it. Not now. She'd gotten through it all and she knew that Sarah would, too, with the Lord's help. However, she'd promised to be there for her and she meant to keep her word.

Dinner that evening was very enjoyable with everyone looking forward to the new boarders moving in. Rebecca had mentioned Ben's idea of the sleigh ride to her mother and she'd called Violet to see if they'd like to join them. Violet thought Georgia would love it and so they brought it up at dinner.

"Ben had the best idea for this weekend. Anyone up for an evening sleigh ride?" Rebecca asked.

"I'd love it," Julia answered. "Have we ever done that as a group?"

"Not since I've been here," Millicent said. "What fun. I want to go!"

"Well an old friend from Virginia is coming to visit Michael and Violet for the weekend and we thought it'd be a nice treat for Jenny and Georgia and us all," Mrs. Heaton informed them.

"I'm in," Matt said. "I'm sure a night ride will be quite different. I've heard about them, but never been on one."

The group was more than a little enthusiastic about it, so plans were put in place.

"I'll reserve us an omnibus," Ben said.

Jenny was beyond excited and Rebecca found herself looking forward to the outing a great deal. It would be Jenny's first sleigh ride.

She'd mentioned to Ben and her mother that she wished to speak with them about Sarah after she put Jenny down for the night and she came downstairs to find them both waiting in her mother's study .

Had Ben not asked her to be a confidante to the woman, she might not have included him, but he had and she knew he cared. As for her mother—if things didn't work out for Sarah, she might well need a place to stay.

Her mother poured her a cup of tea once she'd taken a seat and she took it gratefully. She'd had Sarah's troubles on her mind all evening, but she didn't even know how to begin to tell them about it.

"How was Sarah today? Was she feeling any better?" Ben asked.

Bless him for easing her into it. "No, not really. And she's not likely to feel much better for the next few months."

"Oh?"

Rebecca let out a deep breath. "Sarah has gotten herself into trouble. She's expecting a baby and she hasn't told the father. She's afraid that he won't…be there for her. And if that happens, she's terrified to tell her mother and—"

"I feared it might be something like that. It's not the first time it's happened to one of my students. And I've seen a young man hanging around waiting to walk Sarah home." Ben shook his head. "I'll be praying he does the right thing."

"If not, she'll have a place right here should she need it," her mother said.

"I knew you'd say that, Mama, and I've assured her she would. I just wanted you to be aware it might happen. I'm hoping she has a chance to speak to her young man before class tomorrow evening. Maybe it will all be settled then."

"I hope so," Ben said. "Thank you for being here for her, Rebecca. I knew some of these women needed someone to talk to and not everyone is willing to listen—even if they can't help."

"I'm glad I could be here for her." She prayed she'd been of some help. Sarah reminded her so much of herself and it brought back all the devastation and heartbreak of the past. So much so that she was having a hard time sitting here with Ben, knowing he really knew nothing of her life the last few years

And she didn't dare look at her mother, for she'd most likely see the heartache she'd put her through in her eyes.

"I—"

"You've done what you can for now, dear," her mother said. "I'm very proud of you for trying to help. And we'll be here for her if she needs us. I just pray the young man in question will stand by her."

"I did remind her that the Lord was there for her. And I believe she knows that He will get her through. I'm certainly praying she realizes it."

"I'll be praying the same," Ben said. "And if you need me to do anything in this process of helping—just let me know. As a teacher, I do have to be very careful of things and I can't begin to thank you enough for being willing to listen and advise Sarah from one woman to another. I feel totally inept at knowing what to say in this kind of situation."

That brought a chuckle from both Rebecca and her mother.

"I think most men would feel the same way, Ben," her mother said. "It's not easy to know what to say sometimes, even as a woman."

"It's very difficult to know you've disappointed loved ones and, most importantly, the Lord," Rebecca said. "Even when you know He and they have forgiven you—it sometimes remains hard to forgive oneself for inflicting pain on them."

Mrs. Heaton nodded. "But the Lord wants those He's forgiven to release that guilt they carry and forgive themselves. He wants them to get on with their lives and help others."

The love shining from her mother's eyes assured Rebecca that she wanted her to forgive herself and live her life fully. Her love was unconditional—she wanted the best for her daughter, just as Rebecca wanted the best for Jenny.

How could she not have known that from the very

beginning? The peace that washed over her came with the realization that her forgiveness from the Lord and from her mother was real. They weren't taking it back. Suddenly, Rebecca realized that she needed to live as if she were forgiven and quit letting guilt drag her back into her past.

She and her mother smiled at each other. No words were necessary. And while she might need to tell Ben about her past one day, this wasn't the time or the place.

Sarah wasn't in class on Thursday and Rebecca sat by Molly. "Have you seen Sarah this week? Is she still feeling bad?"

"I haven't seen or talked to her—I'm assuming that she isn't feeling well, since she's not here. I'll try to check on her tomorrow."

"Thanks, Molly. If she needs anything, will you let me know?"

"I will." Molly smiled at her and Rebecca felt she would contact her if need be.

She pulled one of the Heaton House cards from her purse. "You can stop by anytime or, if you prefer, you can telephone. Just ask for Heaton House."

Molly took the card. "I'll let you know what I find out."

Ben started class just then and there was no more time to speak. Rebecca tried to concentrate on the problems being worked out on the board, but it wasn't easy with wondering what was happening with Sarah and then worrying about when she should tell Ben about her past. He'd shared the most painful time in his life with her and for the sake of the growing friendship between them, she wanted to be as open with him as he'd been with her. Still, she didn't know quite how to go about it and prayed the Lord would let her know what to say and when to say it.

A soft snow was falling as they left the Y, the night was still and quiet and Rebecca quite enjoyed the walk to the café. Ben didn't even ask if she wanted to stop, but he'd ended class early and there was no need to stand outside to wait for their trolley when they could have a cup of hot chocolate and watch the snow fall from inside the café.

"It's beautiful out there, isn't it?" she asked after they gave their order.

"It is. I think we'll have a great weekend for our sleighing party."

"I hope so. Have you had a chance to find out about any teaching openings for Georgia?"

"Not yet. I've asked around at several high schools—the one I went to and one a friend of mine attended. They both said they wouldn't know until summer break or later. I'll check out some of the grade schools, tomorrow."

"That's all you can do for now."

"Seems we're trying to help others, but we need to wait on the Lord to let us know what to do next," Ben said.

"That's true. It's not always easy to do, is it?"

"No. It's not."

Ben took a sip from his cup and looked over the rim. "Is Jenny still excited about going sleigh riding?"

"Oh, yes. She can't wait. She's been very good

about not being able to skate as much as she wanted to because of my ankle, so I'm very glad we've planned the outing."

"You know, now that you can get around, maybe we could try going skating for an hour or so one afternoon. You wouldn't have to skate just yet, but you could watch. Perhaps by the time you're up to it, Jenny will be able to skate by herself."

"But, Ben, that takes up your free time and—"

"I wouldn't suggest it if I didn't want to do it, Rebecca. Besides, I promised Jenny I'd teach her and I don't intend to break my promise."

He was such an honorable man and Jenny was becoming fonder of him with each day. He always showed her special attention whenever he saw her. Rebecca wondered if it was wise to put her in a position to let her feelings grow for the man.

But what could she really do about it anyway? They all lived in the same home. Keeping her daughter from being around Ben was near impossible and, besides, it would look odd if she suddenly said no to something that'd been promised to Jenny and that she'd encouraged.

"I'd hate to have you break your promise. And I want Jenny to learn to skate with confidence. I hope one day to get mine back, as well."

"You will. I'll make sure of it, once your ankle has completely healed."

At the thought of skating with him again, Rebecca's pulse sped up. She'd felt confident and protected when she'd skated beside him. "That's kind of you."

"Not at all. I look forward to seeing you skate like you were before you fell."

His gaze met hers, causing her heart to do some kind of funny spiral dive. Whatever was she going to do about her growing feelings for this man?

Chapter Seventeen

By midmorning Friday, the remodeling was finished and there was a collective sigh of relief when the last worker took his leave.

"Now, no peeking," Rebecca's mother said to Gretchen and Maida. "There's still the decorating to do and I want you to be surprised. Furniture is being delivered this afternoon and once it's all set up and we've added the finishing touches, you'll be able to see what's been done."

"But don't you need our help?" Gretchen asked.

"I'll be helping, Mama," Rebecca said. "I can put more weight on my foot now, and I've been going up and down two flights of stairs at the Y. I've also snuck up a time or two to see the progress being made on the third floor. It's going to be beautiful."

Maida and Greta had been sharing a room at the top of the stairs while a curtain was hung to hide the work being done, but they'd promised not to peek and Rebecca was sure they were very excited to see it all finished.

Not only would there be a sitting room, but her mother was refreshing all the rooms. New wallpaper had been put up in each room and the new bedding she'd ordered had arrived just that morning.

Her mother would always keep several rooms open for temporary boarders, but there would now be a couple more rooms to let for regular boarders, although they would be smaller than those on the second floor. But so would the cost to rent one, for those just getting on their feet, and Miss Jordan would be the first to move into a new room.

The doorbell rang; the furniture her mother had ordered had arrived. Rebecca kept Jenny downstairs until her mother was satisfied with where the deliverymen put each piece and then they hurried up to help with the decorating.

It was a busy afternoon and Jenny had great fun putting knickknacks around while Rebecca and her mother hung pictures. The workers had hung the curtains in each room before they left and everything looked lovely.

The new sitting room was done in a flowered rose-and-green wallpaper, with a settee and four easy chairs in the same hues. There was also a writing desk in a corner of the room.

"Oh, Mama it's very pretty and I'm so glad Gretchen and Maida will have a place to relax at the end of the day."

"Of course, the girls who live up here can make use of it, too, but most of the time I'm sure they'll be down with the other boarders."

"May I come up sometimes, Granma?" Jenny asked.

"Of course, if it's all right with Maida and Gretchen. Which I'm sure it will be. They've taken quite a liking to you, young lady."

Jenny grinned from ear to ear. "I like them, too."

Rebecca was sure the two women had probably already promised Jenny she could visit them.

Once the sitting room was done, they went on to put new bedding in Gretchen and Maida's rooms and then they called the two women up to see the transformation.

"Oh, oh! It's beautiful! Mrs. Heaton, thank you! I—" Gretchen broke off and brought up her apron to wipe her eyes.

"I don't know what to say. This is more than we ever imagined," Maida said, wiping her own eyes.

"It's all well deserved, my dears. I couldn't do without you two—although I realize I won't have you forever—you'll both be getting married one of these days. But however long I have you with me, I want you to be comfortable here."

Rebecca's own eyes teared up as the two women hugged her mother and then even her and Jenny.

"There's no doubt that we'll be comfortable here. And it will take some really wonderful men to persuade either of us to move away!" Gretchen said.

"We certainly haven't met them yet," Maida added emphatically.

Rebecca chuckled along with her mother. "Well, we're glad we'll have you with us for a while."

"You surely left the other rooms for us to help with, didn't you, Mrs. Heaton?" Gretchen asked. "Dinner is in the oven and will be fine while we get them done."

"With all of us helping, we'll finish in no time," Rebecca said.

"No, dear. You've done plenty for one day. I want you to be able to enjoy the weekend. Why don't you go take a break and make sure nothing burns in the kitchen."

Rebecca knew there was no arguing with her mother and she had to admit that while it felt wonderful to be able to do something to help, she did feel a little winded. "All right. I'll go have a cup of tea and watch the oven."

"It'll be fine, Miss Rebecca. It's roast chicken and I just put it in," Gretchen said.

"Do you want to come with me, Jenny?"

Jenny hesitated long enough that Rebecca realized she'd rather be up here where all the fun was. "It's all right if you want to stay here."

"Oh, thank you, Mama! I do want to help."

"That's good. I won't feel so bad about not helping, if you stay."

"Just be very careful maneuvering those stairs," her mother said. "Perhaps I should make sure you get down safely."

"No, Mama, there's no need for you to do that. I will make it down fine."

She could tell her mother was concerned, but she appreciated that she only nodded and let her go. There was sometimes a fine line between knowing when to mother and when not to, and her mother was trying very hard to find that balance. Rebecca suddenly realized she'd have to do the same when Jenny became an adult.

At dinner that evening, the talk was all about the sleigh ride planned for the next evening and the impending arrival of the new boarders. They'd be moving in the next week and everyone seemed quite excited about having a full house once more. Ben would be glad for everyone's sake, but he'd actually come to like their small group since Rebecca and Jenny had moved in and he hoped new people wouldn't disrupt things as they were.

"I am glad they aren't moving in this weekend," Rebecca said quietly to him. "Mama looks tuckered out tonight from putting on all the final touches upstairs and getting the downstairs rooms ready for the new male boarders."

Ben looked closely at Mrs. Heaton. She did look a bit fatigued but happy. "Perhaps she's just tired from all she did today and after a good night's sleep she'll be rested tomorrow."

"I hope so. I know she's looking forward to having Michael, Violet, baby Marcus and Georgia over for dinner and the outing tomorrow evening, but I hope it isn't all too much for her."

"I think she'll be fine. She looks very happy tonight, probably because she's got it all done. And I think she's excited about the new boarders. Pleased as I am with things like they are, I can see where the others might enjoy having more boarders around."

"You aren't looking forward to it?" Rebecca asked.

"Oh, I'm sure it'll be nice to have others around. It's just that I've enjoyed getting to know you and Jenny and I don't feel a real need to have more people at the table. But I know everyone else does and I'll adjust." He grinned at her and then nodded in Jenny's direction. "Your daughter looks sleepy this evening."

Rebecca looked over to see that Jenny was having a hard time keeping her eyes open. "She's had a busy day. Nothing could keep her from helping get the upstairs ready for Gretchen and Maida and the new boarders. I'm hoping her busy day has curbed some of the excitement for tomorrow so that she'll be able to get a good night's sleep."

"I don't think you need to worry about that."

Rebecca chuckled. "I don't think so. I hope she makes it through the rest of the meal."

Maida brought dessert in and Ben chuckled as Jenny sat up straight in her chair and forked a piece of the buttermilk pie the maid put in front of her. "I think she will, but I don't think she'll go much past this dessert."

"I'll take her up soon as we finish here."

"Oh, I forgot." Ben took a folded piece of paper from his pocket. "Here is a list of schools that might have openings come next year. I thought you could give it to your friend tomorrow."

"Thank you, Ben. She's coming here for dinner tomorrow night—you could give it to her then."

He shrugged and stuffed the paper back in his pocket. "All right. I'll give it to her and I'll be glad to answer any questions she has about who to contact to check about them after she goes back home."

"That's very nice of you, Ben."

"That's what I hear." He smiled down at her. Always the nice guy—but never the sweetheart. Now, where did that thought come from? He wasn't looking to be anyone's love interest. But the way his chest tightened when Rebecca returned his smile had him wondering if he was being completely honest with himself.

As soon as everyone finished their dessert, Rebecca excused herself and her daughter. "I think it's time I take Jenny upstairs and get her ready for bed, or she's going to fall asleep at the table."

"I think I must have worked her too hard," Mrs. Heaton said.

"No, Granma, I had fun. But I am kind of sleepy." Jenny yawned, needing no encouragement to go with Rebecca. "I can't wait until tomorrow."

"Well, the quicker we get you ready for bed, the faster tomorrow will be here."

Ben watched as the two made it out of the room and headed for the stairs. He was sure Rebecca was glad she could get her daughter ready for bed herself again, but he felt a decided twinge of melancholy that she didn't need him to help her up the stairs any longer.

New snow had fallen during the night and part of the day, making a perfect evening for sleighing. It was cold but not windy, and wearing their warmest coats, hats and muffs, and armed with plenty of blankets, the group would be fine.

Rebecca felt almost as excited as Jenny by the time Michael, Violet and Georgia arrived with baby Marcus. He'd be staying in with Gretchen and Maida, who were preparing a late supper for them instead of dinner. It was a good thing they'd all decided to go earlier in the evening, for excitement was running high at Heaton House.

Georgia looked almost the same as Rebecca remembered her. She was very pretty with dark brown hair and deep green eyes. Everyone was nice to her, including Ben, but there wasn't much time to converse as the omnibus arrived to take them to Central Park only moments after they arrived.

The ride to the park was very jolly and excitement grew when they caught sight of the large sleigh Ben had reserved, ready and waiting for all fourteen of them. It looked kind of like an omnibus transformed into a sleigh.

Laughing, they all piled in and took seats around the sides of the sleigh. Ben had stayed close to Rebecca—probably because he feared she might slip and fall, but she couldn't say she was upset at his watchfulness of her. Especially when Georgia was looking at him in an interested way.

But when Ben took a seat next to her, Rebecca felt herself relax. Jenny was on the other side of her, and her mother sat beside her granddaughter, wanting to see Jenny's reaction to it all. Michael and Violet, along with Georgia, sat across from them and the others took the seats that were left.

Everyone had a good view of the snowy landscape and with lanterns lit all around the sleigh, they could easily see others out enjoying the evening. Central Park took on a totally different look at night after a snow. The moon was bright and trees and bushes stood out against the starlit night.

"Oh, it's so pretty, Mama," Jenny said, her eyes sparkling.

"It is, isn't it?"

"Do you remember sleighing in Ashland, Becca?" Michael asked.

"I do, but it's been such a long time. I remember Mama used to make cocoa in a pot, after Papa lit a fire, and we'd skate on the pond." Rebecca hadn't let herself go down memory lane much in the past few years. It'd been too heartrending, feeling that she could never go home again.

But now home was here and she felt as if she had a new beginning in all kinds of ways. She might never have what she longed for, but she had a life that was so very much better than it had been six months earlier. She sent up a silent prayer of thanksgiving that the Lord had delivered her out of the mess she'd made of her life, reunited her with her family and given her a new beginning—of sorts. Because of her own bad judgment, she'd made decisions that had made what she'd dreamed of back then impossible forever, but at least she was with her family again and she'd made good friends.

The driver put the sleigh in motion, his horses' bells jingled and there was shared laughter as they took off. Rebecca forced her thoughts to the present to see Jenny's eyes light up as she took in the scenery and felt the cold air on her cheeks. It was invigorating and Rebecca gathered her daughter in a hug, happy that she was having such a good time.

"I'd forgotten how much fun this is," Ben said. "We should try sledding soon, while we have the snow."

"I think there are some sleds in the attic," Rebecca's mother said. "We can check."

"Oh, could we go, Mama?" Jenny asked.

Ben's gaze met Rebecca's and she knew there was no way she'd refuse, looking into two pairs of eyes that begged her to say yes.

"I suppose we could go tomorrow afternoon after church and Sunday dinner, *if* the weather holds."

Jenny rewarded her with a kiss on her cheek and Ben's smile warmed her heart to almost melting. The expression in his eyes had her pulse rushing through her veins. She really needed to distance herself from this man, or her heart might be hurt worse than Jenny's if anything happened to damage their growing friendship.

But how was she going to do that when she accepted every suggestion the man came up with for them to be together?

Chapter Eighteen

Ben enjoyed watching Jenny and Rebecca as the sleigh rounded each bend and a new view or others out for a ride came into vision. It was the perfect evening for it and he almost hated to see it come to a finish.

But as everything must end, so did the sleigh ride. They headed back to Heaton House, where supper was served almost immediately. It was a good thing, because the cold night air and all the excitement seemed to have made Jenny sleepy again. They'd all barely finished their supper of clam chowder, hot biscuits and cobbler before Rebecca excused herself to go put Jenny to bed.

But she promised she'd be down as soon as she did and so Ben joined the others in the parlor. Georgia seemed nice and he struck up a conversation with her. "Miss Marshall, Rebecca told me you're thinking of moving here and she asked me to find out what I could about openings for teachers in the area."

"How nice of her and of you, Mr. Roth."

"Please, call me Ben. We don't stand on formalities at Heaton House."

"Well, then, Ben. But only if you call me Georgia."

"Georgia it is. I told Rebecca I'd be glad to answer any questions you might have. She wasn't sure if you'd want to teach the lower grades or high school. That would help narrow down the schools to check into."

"I've been teaching first grade in Ashland, but I'm qualified to teach high school, also. I'll take whatever I can find."

He pulled the list he'd made out of his pocket and handed it to her. "This is what I have so far, but I'm sure there will be more openings after this term ends and I'll be able to add a few names to that list."

"That will be wonderful. Again, I thank you so much."

"You're quite welcome."

Ben looked up just as Rebecca entered the room. She seemed a bit…perturbed? But what could she possibly be upset about? She appeared undecided, maybe, as if she wasn't sure whom to join—him and her friend, or any of the others grouped in small clusters in the room. He smiled and motioned to her and for a moment he'd thought she wouldn't join them, but then she smiled and headed their way.

"Rebecca, I've just been taking to Georgia about the list I made."

"Thanks so much for enlisting Ben's help for me, Rebecca. I'll contact these people on Monday. I took several days off so that I could look into everything. If things work out, I hope to move here come summer." She smiled at Rebecca. "I've told your mother I hope she has an extra room then."

"You never know," Ben said. "They seem to fill up fast around here."

"That's what Violet told me. I'd better make up my mind soon. Perhaps I could pay a deposit and ask her to keep one for me." Georgia turned. "I'll just go speak to her about it."

With that she was off and Ben was relieved that he had a moment alone with Rebecca. "Do you think your mother will hold a room for her?"

"I'm sure she will. Mama and Georgia's mother are old friends. You two seemed to be in deep conversation. You must have a lot in common."

"I don't know about that. We didn't talk about anything but job openings. If you mean we're both teachers, there is that, but not all teachers are alike, you know." He grinned at her and was rewarded with a small smile.

She sounded almost…what? Jealous? No, of course not. What was he thinking? What was he wishing?

Rebecca didn't know what had come over her, but when she entered the parlor and saw Ben speaking to Georgia, her friend listening to his every word, she'd felt something very akin to…jealousy. And she had no right to feel that way. No reason at all…except that she didn't like seeing them together. She didn't like it one bit.

O dear Lord, please help me. I think I'm falling in love with Ben and there's no way he'd ever return my feelings. Not if he knew everything and—

"Rebecca? Are you all right?" Ben asked, his gaze full of concern.

"I am. Just woolgathering, I suppose." Rebecca looked across the room to see her mother, Violet and Georgia coming their way.

"Rebecca, dear, I'm going to show Georgia and Violet the updates we've made upstairs. Do you want to come?"

Rebecca shook her head. "I'll stay down here for now. I think one more trip up to my room will be about all I want to manage tonight."

"That's a wise decision," her mother said. "We'll be back down in a bit."

Once they left the room, Ben turned to her. "Is your ankle giving you problems?"

"Not too much, just a twinge once in a while."

"You know that if you need help, I'll be glad to carry you up."

Her heart turned warm and mushy at his offer. He couldn't possibly know how badly she'd like to take him up on his offer. But being in his arms was the last thing she needed right now. "Thank you. But I'll be fine. I'll just take it easy. I must work to strengthen my ankle, you know."

"I do. I just don't want you to injure it again. Should we put off the sledding trip tomorrow?"

"I don't think so. I'm sure it'll be stronger after a good night's sleep. And if it isn't, I'll just watch you and Jenny. I'd hate to disappoint her now she's looking forward to it."

"So would I. But we'll see how you feel tomorrow."

Gretchen came in then with hot chocolate and they

settled down with the others to enjoy it. But Rebecca couldn't stop thinking that she'd never been shown such concern by any other man. However, she dared not let herself read too much into it because Ben was just as kind and considerate to others.

He'd enlisted her to enroll at the Y and to be there to help his students. He'd helped her catch up with the others and he'd gone out of his way to get her mother a typewriter so Rebecca could practice and build up her speed here at home. Not to mention how kind and caring he'd been to carry her upstairs and down for days.

And he'd tried to find school openings for Georgia just as *she'd* asked him to. And then she felt upset when he gave the list to her friend just as *she'd* told him to? The truth was, she was just plain jealous seeing them together and wondering if they might be attracted to each other!

O dear Lord, please keep me from falling in love with Ben. My heart has been broken once...and...I don't want to go through that kind of heartbreak ever again. Please help me.

Rebecca was still out of sorts with herself the next day as she and the others went to church. She'd tossed and turned most of the night, longing for things to be different and asking the Lord to help her accept that she'd never have what she wanted most.

But as she listened to the sermon taken from Isaiah, to fear not—God was there. She was reminded, once again, that the Lord was with her, always had been. He'd seen her through her darkest hours. It was as if He were letting her know He'd heard her prayers. She sighed and began to relax. No matter what happened, He would see her through.

By the time the last hymn was sung and the closing prayer said, Rebecca felt at peace. And she remained that way, for Violet and Michael were taking Georgia out for Sunday dinner, and while she told herself once again that she had absolutely no reason to feel jealous of Georgia, she was a bit relieved that Georgia wouldn't be joining them for Sunday dinner.

It was nice to have only the regular boarders at the table, especially with the new ones arriving the next day. When Rebecca's mother asked Ben to say the blessing before the meal, he asked that they all try to help the new boarders fit in and that together they would all be a blessing to her mother, just as she was to her boarders.

Rebecca felt the sting of tears at the back of her eyes when she saw her mother wipe her eyes.

Because it would be the last outing before new boarders joined them, they all went sledding that afternoon. Rebecca decided not to chance twisting her ankle again and chose to sit with her mother and watch as Ben and Jenny slid together.

The laughter they shared rang in the cold crisp air and she smiled, knowing her daughter was having a great time.

"Ben is such a good man, isn't he?" her mother asked.

"Yes, he is."

"You know, dear, the Lord has a plan for your life.

And when the time comes that you fall in love again, I hope it is with someone like Ben."

Rebecca's heart did a twist and dive at her mother's words. Did she have any idea that Rebecca was already wrestling with her feelings for Ben? "Oh, Mama, what man—"

"The man the Lord brings into your life will love you for who you are, not for your past, but for your future, Rebecca. I realize it will take a special man to convince you of that. But I know the Lord has a plan in mind for you. Just trust that He'll let you know what it is—in His time.

"I know He does. But I'm not sure His plan for me includes my falling in love. If so, I think He may have to hit me over the head with something to make me realize it."

"Oh, I have no doubt He'll get your attention when the time comes."

Rebecca hoped so, for as Ben and Jenny made their way back to where she and her mother sat, his smile made her catch her breath and for just that moment she let herself hope that Ben might be in that plan.

They'd only been back at Heaton House long enough to change for supper and gather in the parlor—with Jenny going to help in the kitchen as usual—when a knock came on the door.

Rebecca hurried to answer it to find Sarah and Molly both standing there. Sarah had a small carpetbag in her hand. "Oh, Rebecca, I'm so glad you came to the door."

"So am I," Molly said. "I had a hard time talking her into coming here."

"Come in, please. Follow me to the back parlor and we'll find out what we can do for you, Sarah."

Rebecca hurried them out of the foyer before the other boarders came out and asked questions. Once they were in the parlor, she turned to them. "Please, take a seat and tell me what's happened."

"I told Shaun about the baby." Sarah shook her head and closed her eyes. "He…was upset and I haven't heard from him in two days."

"Oh, Sarah, I'm so sorry." Rebecca reached over and gathered her hands in her own. "And then…did you tell your mother?"

The younger woman nodded, tears flowing down her cheeks. "This afternoon. She told me I'd brought shame on the family and said I need to get out of her sight. Then she ran to her room crying."

Sarah began to sob and Rebecca wrapped her arms around her. "Oh, Sarah, I'm sure she didn't mean it. She loves you. She's just hurting right now. But you have a place to stay. Molly can let your mother know where you are—because she's bound to worry and I'm sure she'll change her mind."

Sarah shook her head once more. "I'm not so sure, but I do thank you for offering me a place to stay for now. I don't know what I'm going to do."

"You don't have to make up your mind right now, child," Rebecca's mother said from the doorway. "Come, we'll show you to a room, and you and your friend can have supper with us or I'll have something sent up to you."

"Oh, I don't think I could eat anything," Sarah said.

"And I need to be getting home," Molly said. "I just wanted to make sure she got here safely. But I'll come check on you, Sarah, I promise."

"Thank you, Molly." Sarah picked up her bag.

"I'll see Molly out and then come upstairs," Rebecca said.

Her mother put an arm around Sarah's shoulders, "Come this way, dear. It's going to be all right. You'll see."

Rebecca hoped her mother was right. But at least they would do what they could to help Sarah and if she knew her mother as well as she thought she did, Rebecca was certain she'd do all she could to reunite Sarah with her mother.

"Thank you so much for getting her here, Molly."

"Oh, thank you for taking her in. She knew you would, still, she was hesitant to come, but I insisted."

"I'm glad you did. You come over anytime and see her, all right?"

"Yes, ma'am. I will. I'm going to have a talk with Shaun, too. I think he's just scared. At least I hope that's all it is."

"Yes, so do I. Do you have money for the trolley?"

"I do. Thank you."

"You're welcome. Good night, Molly." Rebecca shut the door and turned to see Ben coming down the hall. He must have just come up from downstairs.

"Was that Molly I saw just leaving?"

"Yes." Rebecca lowered her voice. "She brought Sarah over. Mama is getting her settled upstairs. I'm going to check on her but will fill you in after supper."

Ben nodded, but his brow was furrowed and she knew he was as concerned about Sarah as she was. She hurried up the stairs, praying all the way for things to work out for the young woman.

She met her mother on the landing.

"I think Sarah wants a little time to herself, dear. She started crying when she saw her room—said it was too nice and she couldn't pay anything right now. I told her about our temporaries and ran her a bath. Said I'd have a tray sent up and you'd come up to see her later."

"Are you sure we should leave her be, Mama?"

"Yes. Let's go down and have supper and we'll check on her in a little while. Do you have her home address? I think I'd like to pay her mother a visit."

"Ben might have it. If not, I'm sure he can get it for you."

Her mother nodded. "Good. And Rebecca, I can't begin to tell you how proud I am of you. Of what I heard you say to her in the parlor."

"I only advised her with what I wish I'd done and known, Mama."

"I know, dear." They'd reached the foyer and her mother turned to hug her. "I know. I'd better tell Gretchen we're ready for supper. Will you call the others in?"

"I will. Mama?"

"Yes, dear?"

"I love you."

"I love you, too." Then her mother gave a short nod and headed toward the kitchen.

Rebecca entered the parlor. "Mama says supper is ready."

Everyone moved toward the dining room and took their places just as Gretchen came in with their first course of turtle soup.

After Matt said the blessing, Millicent asked, "Did one of the new boarders arrive?"

"We have a new temporary boarder," Rebecca's mother said. "She's one of Ben's students and she needs a place to stay for a bit."

"Oh, will she be joining us for supper?" Julia took the basket of rolls, chose one and passed it on.

"Not tonight. She's rather tired and will take supper in her room. You'll all get to meet her tomorrow, I'm sure."

Rebecca tried to pay attention to the dinner conversation, but her thoughts were on Sarah and how she must be feeling. When Jenny began to yawn, she immediately saw an opportunity to get away to check on the young woman.

"I think Jenny's weekend has caught up with her. I'm going to put her to bed early tonight. I'll be back down in a bit." She glanced at Ben and, from his slight nod, she knew he'd be waiting to hear what she had to tell him about Sarah when she came back down.

Chapter Nineteen

Ben joined the others in the parlor while he waited for Rebecca to come back. Evidently things hadn't turned out well for Sarah after she'd told her young man about the baby, or she wouldn't be here now.

He could only imagine how she must be feeling right now. The news about Sarah had managed to push thoughts of the conversation he'd had with Mrs. Butler from his mind. But as he waited, it all came back to him and he still wasn't sure whether or not to believe what she'd told him. He wasn't ready to process any of it yet.

He tried to pay attention to the conversations going on around him, but it was near impossible with his thoughts flitting from his conversation that afternoon to Sarah and all that she was dealing with. He'd nearly decided Rebecca wasn't coming back down when he heard footsteps on the stairs. He went out to meet her and found both Rebecca and her mother on their way down.

"Let's go to Mama's study," Rebecca suggested. "We'll fill you in there."

Ben followed them down the hall and took a seat once both women had sat down. "How is she?"

"She's better now than when she arrived," Rebecca said. "Evidently, her young man is running scared and her mother is furious with her. Told her to get out of her sight."

"Oh, I'm sorry to hear that."

"I'm sure she didn't mean it," Mrs. Heaton said. "But I'm going to find out for sure and do some plain talking while I'm at it."

"Do you have her address?" Rebecca turned to Ben.

"I'm sure it's in my files. I'll find it for you. I can't tell you how glad I am you're giving her a place to stay. What would she have done if not for you two?" Ben shook his head.

"But she is here now, Ben. And you could have brought her here at any time, should you have needed to," Mrs. Heaton said.

"I know you would have taken her in, Mrs. Heaton. But—" He shook his head. "As a teacher of young woman at the Y, I've had to be very careful not to give any of them the wrong impression. Had I been the one to bring her here, where I live, there might have been talk and she'd have more to deal with than she does already."

"I can see how that might happen. But that wouldn't be your fault, Ben, only the fault of those who have nothing better to do than stir up trouble."

"There might still be, if word gets around she's

here," Rebecca said. "But we can't be worrying about it."

"That's true. This *is* the best possible place for her right now."

"It is," Rebecca said. "And Molly and I will nip any gossip in the bud should we hear any, but I really don't think that's going to happen."

"I wish I knew where that young man lived. I'd—"

"No, Ben. You might make things worse," Rebecca said. "Molly said she was going to speak to him. All we really can do now is be here for Sarah and pray and wait. The Lord knows what is needed and He'll give her the answer…in His time."

"Would you two like some tea? I think I'll have Gretchen make a pot," Mrs. Heaton said.

"I would, thank you, Mama," Rebecca said.

"And I'd love to have a cup, also, Mrs. Heaton."

"Coming up."

Mrs. Heaton left the room and Ben looked over at Rebecca. "I can't thank you enough for being available when Sarah needed to talk."

"Oh, Ben, I'm glad I was too. There's no need to thank me." Rebecca smiled at him, sending his pulse shooting through his veins as she continued, "You're the one who convinced me to help if I could. And I'm glad you did. At least she's here at Heaton House tonight instead of wandering the streets. Would she have tried to seek shelter at the Y?"

"I don't know. Perhaps. But I'm still glad she came here."

"So am I."

They both sighed and then Ben said, "I, ah, wanted

to tell you…I had a call from Mrs. Butler at the orphanage today."

"Oh? Is someone there needing your help?"

"Not this time. She had a telegram from a woman claiming to be my aunt and she asked Mrs. Butler to arrange a meeting."

"Oh, Ben. Your aunt? What…how do you feel about all of this?"

"I honestly don't know. On one hand, I want to know if she truly is my aunt and if she can answer the questions I have about my mother. And why she's coming *instead* of my mother. Then, on the other hand, I—" He shrugged. "I'm not sure how I feel, Rebecca."

"I'll be praying it goes well. When is she coming?"

"She'll be there tomorrow."

"Tomorrow? Oh, that is soon."

"Yes, I—"

"I'm sorry it took so long," Mrs. Heaton said, coming into the room with a loaded tray and interrupting what Ben had been about to say. He rose to take it from her. "I sent Gretchen up with a pot of tea for Sarah. I thought it might help her sleep."

"That was nice of you, Mama. Hopefully it will." Rebecca glanced at Ben and, from the expression in her eyes, he had a feeling she wanted to apologize for her mother's timing.

He smiled at her to let her know he wasn't upset at the interruption, but he wasn't going to say more in Mrs. Heaton's company. For some reason, Rebecca was the only one he felt comfortable talking to about his past.

She was the only one he'd ever told about being abandoned by his mother, and now he realized he'd waited all evening to share this latest news with her. He was comforted to know that she'd be praying it went well and that she'd be there to listen when he came home the next day. This woman was becoming more and more important to him with each passing day and he could no longer deny it. But what was he going to do about it?

The next day was more than busy at Heaton House with making sure the new boarders' rooms were all ready for them to move into that afternoon and checking in on Sarah from time to time. Rebecca prayed continually that Sarah's mother and the young man would come to their senses and be there for her—and, especially, that all went well for Ben.

Several of the boarders had made arrangements to have their things brought over that morning before they went to work, and Rebecca helped her mother, Gretchen and Maida get the boxes and carpetbags to the rooms they'd been assigned. It would be up to the boarders to unpack and put their personal effects where they wanted them.

Rebecca and her mother had prayed with Sarah that morning and she appeared to be in better spirits when she came down to lunch, although there was no doubting the sadness in her eyes. "I think I'll go for a walk."

"All right, dear. But remember my rules are that the young women living in my home cannot be out after dark without an escort or in a group."

"Yes, ma'am, I won't be gone that long."

Rebecca's mother went out to do a few errands shortly after Sarah left and Rebecca had a feeling one of them would be to pay a visit to Mrs. Jarvis. If anyone could help the woman change her mind, she knew it would be her mother. At the very least, she'd give Sarah's mother much to think about.

And, hopefully, Molly would be able to talk to Shaun and make him think long and hard about the responsibilities he needed to take hold of.

Her mother came back around teatime, and said she'd visited with Mrs. Jarvis, but she and Rebecca didn't speak any more about it until Jenny headed off to the kitchen with Gretchen as she usually did after tea.

Once they were alone, her mother let out a sigh. "I have no idea what Mrs. Jarvis will do. She did seem relieved to know Sarah was safe and not on the streets. And she cried when I told her she'd regret sending her daughter away if she didn't make an effort to mend their relationship." She took a sip of tea and shook her head. "She said she needed time. I know she's hurting, and that's understandable. But I think—I pray—she'll come around soon."

"You did what you could, Mama. Now we need to pray and give it over to the Lord."

"When did you get so wise, Rebecca?"

"I suppose, from watching and learning from you. And from making some wrong decisions in my life, but finally realizing that the Lord was with me, helping me through it all. And that I have a mother who loved me enough to come look for me, even though I didn't know it at the time. I pray Sarah's mama loves her that much, too."

Her mother wiped her eyes and stood up. "So do I. I suppose I'd better check and see how the dinner preparations are going—with four more people at the table now, I'm thinking I ought to hire someone else to help around here. I don't want to wear Gretchen and Maida out."

"I can help," Rebecca said.

"We'll both help, if needed, but we'll see how it goes. It won't hurt to bring someone else in. No matter what Gretchen and Maida say, they'll find husbands one day."

"I'm sure they will." Rebecca wished that was a dream she felt would come true for her, but—

The doorbell rang and her mother went to answer it. Miss Jordan was the first new boarder to show up.

"You wanted to check on how dinner is coming along, Mama. I'll be glad to take Miss Jordan up."

"Why that would be a big help, dear. Just follow Rebecca, Emily. Dinner is at seven this evening to give everyone time to get settled. There is no need to feel you must dress up—regular work clothes will suffice during the week. We do dress up a little more on the weekends, but your Sunday best will suffice."

"Thank you. I'm looking forward to getting to know everyone."

"And we're all looking forward to getting to know you. Go on up and settle in and when you are ready to come down, everyone meets in the parlor before dinner." With that, Rebecca's mother headed toward the kitchen.

"Come on, Emily. You'll feel at home here in no time." Rebecca led the way to Emily's room.

"I'm sure I will." She was delighted with her room and didn't seem to think it was small at all. "I've been thinking about this room ever since your mother showed it to me. It does remind me of my room at home and I love the colors."

"I'm glad you're happy with it. I'll just leave you to put your things up where you want them. Come down and join the others when you're ready."

Rebecca got downstairs just as Sarah came in, and she told her about the new boarder on the third floor. "Emily seems very nice and you'll meet her at dinner."

"I'm still feeling a bit queasy, Rebecca. Would it be all right to eat in my room again this evening? I—"

Her eyes were swimming with unshed tears and Rebecca didn't have the heart to tell her no. "Of course. I'll tell Mama and we'll have a tray sent up."

"Thank you, Rebecca."

"You're welcome." She hugged Sarah and turned to go. "I'll check on you later."

Her heart was heavy as she headed back downstairs.

When Ben arrived at the orphanage, he wasn't sure what to expect. Mrs. Butler greeted him and told him that the woman claiming to be his aunt was in her office.

"She does know the date your mother brought you here and the things your mother had packed for you—

even the wording of the note she left. I do believe she is who she says she is, Ben."

His chest tightened at the realization that he might actually have a family of his own.

Mrs. Butler showed him into her office, where a nicely dressed lady who appeared to be in her late forties sat in one of the easy chairs by the fireplace. She turned and smiled at him. She had dark blond hair and blue eyes, and if she was his aunt, it appeared he might have gotten his coloring from his mother.

"Ben, this is Laura Morgan, who I do believe is your aunt, and she'd like to speak with you about your mother. Mrs. Morgan, this is Benjamin Roth, one of the finest men I've ever known. I'll go make us a pot of tea and leave you two to talk in private for a bit."

"Thank you, Mrs. Butler." She left the room and Ben crossed over and took the woman's hand in his. "I'm eager to hear what you have to say, Mrs. Morgan. Are you really my aunt?"

"I am. And I'm so glad you agreed to see me, Ben…Mr. Roth," she said.

The expression in the woman's eyes warmed Ben, making him hope she was who she claimed to be. He took the other chair flanking the fireplace. "Please tell me what you know about me."

"First, I am sorry it is me who's come here and not your mother, but I must tell you that she passed away a few weeks ago and it was only when she was about to die that we learned about you."

Ben wasn't sure how to take the news that the woman who'd given birth to him had died without him ever knowing her. He felt very bad for her family and deeply saddened that he'd never had a chance to know his own mother, but—

"I realize all of this must come as a shock to you after so many years. Please believe me that I haven't come here to make you feel bad, or expect you to feel anything at all for my sister. But Loretta—that was your mother's name—did want me to give you this letter should I be able to locate you, and to let you know that giving you up was the most difficult thing she'd ever done." She handed him an envelope.

"But evidently not difficult enough that she came back to get me."

"No. And I'm sorry. I..."

Ben took the envelope. "No, none of this was your fault and I apologize for sounding so rude."

"I think you have every right to sound however you feel. I'd like to tell you how I know I am your aunt—"

"Please do," Ben said.

Mrs. Morgan sighed and nodded. "My sister's memory of that night was very clear and before she passed away she told me about the note she'd left asking the orphanage to take care of you and that your name was Benjamin. That she'd wrapped you in a blue-and-white-striped blanket and tucked a red rattle into the basket she placed you in. And she told me the time and the date she left you. I think Mrs. Butler will tell you that everything confirms that I am your aunt."

"Yes, she believes you are." Ben opened the letter. It was short and to the point.

Dear Son,
I called you Benjamin, but I don't know what name you might go by now—or if you'll ever even receive this letter. However, I feel I must let you know that I do regret giving you up. I felt I had no choice at the time, and still feel that way. I was convinced your life would be better without me in it back then. But now I find myself wondering if I did the right thing. It was truly the most difficult thing I've ever done. I also want you to know that you are heir to a small inheritance left me by my grandparents. I hope this gets into your hands and that my family will honor my wishes.
Please forgive me,
Your mother.

"She told you about the inheritance?"

Ben nodded.

"She'd told us her wishes and we could have seen that you got it, had she not written the letter, for she did tell us everything before she took her last breath."

"I don't want her money."

"But we want you to have it. It's the least we can do, Ben. I loved my sister, but I cannot condone her abandoning you. I wish we'd known about you from the beginning. But when she came back home to Boston, she never wanted to talk about what had happened while she was gone. When we asked questions, she always said that was in the past and she didn't want to revisit it." Her voice broke before she continued.

"I've never been able to have children of my own and would have adopted you myself, had I known. I—we—want to make sure you know that you *do* have family. My husband, Robert, and I, and my parents, want very much to be a part of your life, if you'll let us. But I realize it may take some time for you to decide."

She pulled a card out of her purse and handed it to him. "This is my home address and should you wish to telephone, you can tell the operator to ring the Robert Morgan residence at that address. And on the other side is your grandparents' information."

"Mrs.—Aunt Laura, I do appreciate, more than I can say, you coming to tell me all of this. I'm sure this has not been easy for you—"

"Oh, finding I do have a nephew is a joy to my heart, although the circumstances surrounding it brings us all heartache in one way or another."

"Thank you. Your words mean a lot to me. And I would like to meet my grandparents at some point, if you are sure they want to meet me."

"I am certain they want you in their lives just as I do."

"I will be in touch with you and with them then."

"Thank you, Ben. I hope before too very long."

Mrs. Butler came in with a tea tray and Ben spent the next half hour getting to know a little more about his family. He was still finding it hard to believe that he had one. When it was time to leave, Mrs. Butler took the tray away and left them to say their good-byes.

"I...may I hug you, Ben? I—" Tears flooded his

aunt's eyes as Ben blinked against the sting of them in his own. He stood and so did she. He gathered her in his arms and let her hug soothe the child within him and ease the sorrow that he'd never known his mother.

What Rebecca had said to him, about how his mother giving him up must have been the hardest thing she'd ever done, had proven to be true and he now thought he could finally begin to forgive his mother.

"I'll be in touch soon," he promised as he left.

Ben's thoughts were in turmoil as he made his way to Heaton House, which seemed to be in chaos as two of the new boarders had arrived at the same time.

Rebecca looked at him closely, but there was no time to speak about how things had gone with his meeting at the orphanage.

"Can we meet in the little parlor after you put Jenny down for the night?" he asked quickly.

"Of course. I should be there around nine."

He only nodded and then offered to show Mr. Adams and Mr. Clark to their rooms on the ground floor. As the two men followed him downstairs, Ben thought nine o'clock couldn't come too soon.

Chapter Twenty

Even though Ben was eager to talk to Rebecca and tell her about the meeting with his aunt, he found dinner with all the new boarders quite interesting.

Everyone seemed to be taking stock of one another to see how they fit, but he knew from experience it would take weeks before they all were totally comfortable with each other.

Except, for some reason, he'd felt at ease around Rebecca almost from the first. Otherwise, he'd never have tried so hard to get her to be a mentor to the young women at the Y. And then she'd helped him begin to forgive his mother even before he'd met his aunt and found out anything about her.

"You're a teacher, Mr. Roth?" The new boarder, Emily Jordan, broke into his thoughts. "Do you enjoy it?"

"Please, call me Ben. I'm sure Mrs. Heaton told you we don't stand on ceremony here. We all call each other by our given names. And, yes, I enjoy teaching very much. And you work for Macy's—is that right? That must be very interesting."

"Please call me Emily, then. It's never boring, that's for sure. I enjoy working at Macy's very much."

Joe Clark captured her attention then, and Ben glanced over at Rebecca, who was speaking with Steven Adams. He wasn't quite sure he liked the new seating arrangements, but at least she was close enough that he could still converse with her if her attentions weren't taken elsewhere. Matt didn't look thrilled, either. Millicent was listening to the conversation going on between Joe and Emily.

Ben had to grin at Jenny, who was trying to take it all in, looking from one to another of the new boarders and trying to listen to four or five conversations going on at the same time.

For the most part everyone seemed quite genial and once they found out that most nights the boarders gathered in the parlor after dinner to talk, play games or sing around the piano, the new people seemed quite happy to join them on their first night.

He stayed until he thought it must be time for Rebecca to return from putting Jenny to bed, and, after excusing himself, he ambled down the hall to the small parlor and took a seat in one of the easy chairs.

It was only then that Ben let himself think about the aunt he'd never known he had and what she'd told him. After all these years, he'd met a member of his family. And he didn't know how he felt about it. He placed his elbows on his knees and bent his head, running his fingers through his hair. *Dear Lord, I don't really know what to think about all this. For so long I've wondered why my mother left me, if she ever cared about me and—now I find she did. Although, I still don't understand how she could have left me. But I know so much more than I ever have before and I thank You for that. I—*

"Ben? Are you all right?" Rebecca asked from the doorway.

His heart warmed when she hurried over to take the chair next to him. "You look a bit bemused, I must say. Do you want to talk about it?"

He was glad she was there. "I do. But first, how is Sarah doing? She didn't come down to dinner."

"She wasn't feeling well, and I think meeting so many new people at once was more than she could deal with right now. I just checked on her after I got Jenny to bed. She's better this evening, but not really good. Mama had a talk with her mother today, although Sarah doesn't know that. We're praying Mrs. Jarvis will think about what not being in Sarah's life would mean to her and that she'll soften toward her daughter."

"I'll be praying that she does."

"I know you will, Ben. Now, tell me about your meeting. How did it go?"

"It actually went rather well. I met my aunt—Laura Morgan is her name. Apparently my mother passed away a few weeks ago after a long illness—"

"Oh, Ben. I'm so sorry."

Ben shrugged, "I never knew her, Rebecca. I'm sorry for my aunt and her family, but I truly don't know how I feel about her passing. I am glad to finally know who my mother was. And that, according to the letter she left for me, she loved me. She wrote that giving me up was, as you said, the most difficult thing she'd ever done. I'm thankful to know that."

"Oh, I am glad that you finally do know, Ben."

"So am I." Emotion threatened to overtake him and he cleared his throat. "My aunt also told me my mother did say she regretted giving me up, at the very end, when she told her family what had happened. My grandparents were shocked to find out about me, and they asked if I'd be willing to meet with them."

"What did you say?"

"That I'd be in touch soon. I feel I must meet them, get to know them." Ben pressed his thumb and forefinger to the bridge of his nose and shook his head. "I never thought I'd ever have family of my own."

"And now you do. I'm so happy for you, Ben. Your aunt…how was she?"

"She was very kind and I think they are all as stunned as I am to find this out after so many years. Evidently, my mother never let them know about me until she was about to die."

"I imagine it was hard for them to take it all in and to realize they never had the chance to know you."

"Yes, I'm sure it was. I do want to meet them, want find out more about my mother, but I—" He paused and didn't finish what he'd been about to say.

"You don't have to decide when right now. Do you have a way to contact them later? Is your aunt still in the city?"

"She was going back to Boston tonight. But, yes, she left me addresses for both her and my grandparents. I told her I would be in touch with them soon."

"Good. Then you can think it over and pray about it. I'm sure the Lord will guide you."

"He will. I just need to let Him. Right now I'm having a hard time not feeling guilty about not being able to grieve for the woman who gave birth to me. But I never knew her, Rebecca. I wish I had, but I didn't."

"Oh, Ben!" Rebecca reached out and covered one of his hands with one of her own. "That is no fault of yours. You feel sorry for her family. And obviously they feel remorse that they never knew you because she didn't let them. Neither they, nor you, are at fault here."

"I know. I just wish I could grieve for her. I wish—"

"Oh, Ben. Don't beat yourself up over this. I wish she'd kept you and loved you, as you deserve to be loved. I—" She stopped suddenly and the expression in her eyes touched his heart on many different levels.

She began to pull her hand away, but he clasped it with his own and looked into her eyes. "Thank you, Rebecca. No one has ever said anything like that to me and I can't begin to tell you how much it means to have you to talk to, to share all of this with. And even though my mother never came back for me, you were right. She seemed to believe she had no choice."

He could tell Rebecca was trying to hold back her tears and he took a deep breath. To know this woman cared about him… He stood and pulled her to her feet.

"You are very special to me, Rebecca." Ben looked down into her eyes and tipped her chin. "Thank you for being here for me."

He set out only to kiss her forehead, but one look at her lips and he couldn't resist bending down and touching his own to hers. The answering softness of them had him deepening the kiss and he pulled her farther into his arms.

Ben's kiss was all Rebecca had imagined and more, and she couldn't help but respond. But much as she never wanted it to end, she couldn't let it go on. She broke the kiss and took a step away, taking a deep breath and trying to calm her rapidly beating heart. She didn't know what to say. "I—I'd better go check on Jenny." She turned and only Ben's hand on her arm stopped her from running out of the room.

"Rebecca, I…I know I should apologize, but I enjoyed kissing you entirely too much to do so."

Oh, she didn't want an apology. She wanted another kiss. But once he knew the truth about her past, he wouldn't— "It's all right, Ben. I know you were just thanking me. You've had an emotional day and… I'm glad you shared with me. I want you to know I'm ready to listen anytime…" She was rambling, wanting to stay with him and run all at the same time.

He'd enjoyed the kiss, too. She knew it, felt it. But what did that mean? Did he feel the same kind of spark that she did? The kind that warmed her heart clear through and sent her pulse racing? Surely a kiss that affected her the way his did would have had an effect on him, too?

She had to tell him about her past. Now. This man had told her things she knew he'd never told anyone else. She owed it to him to be as honest with him as he'd been with her. She couldn't run again.

"There's something I need to tell you." She couldn't put it off any longer. Rebecca began to pace.

"What is it? Please sit down, Rebecca."

She nodded and sat down once more. Only then did Ben take his seat.

"Is something wrong? Are you upset with me for kissing you?"

She shook her head. "This isn't about that. It's just that there is something I need to tell you, and I should have told you when you first told me about your mother and if not then, certainly when we found out about Sarah."

"My mother and Sarah? What do they have to do with anything you should be telling me?"

Dear Lord, You've helped me through so much. Please help me find the words. "The reason I understand so well why your mother must have felt she had no choice, and how confused and hurt Sarah is feeling now is because I am not that different from either of them."

"What are you trying to say, Rebecca?"

"I left home in Ashland, Virginia over five years ago—ran away you might say—leaving my family to think I wanted to make it on my own in the city. But I really ran away to marry a man they disapproved of. He promised we'd marry as soon as we got to New York City." Rebecca took a shaky breath. There was no way to pretty it up. "And I thought we *did* marry—but the certificate meant nothing. It turned out to be fake, which I found out when he left me three months later."

"He left you? Just like that?" Ben jumped to his feet and began pacing, clenching and unclenching his fists.

"He did."

"Did he know you were…expecting his child?"

"No. I only found out a few weeks later. He left me with just enough money to live on for a few months—told me to go home to my mama."

The tears in her eyes were almost Ben's undoing as she continued.

"But I couldn't bring that shame on my family. Or thought I couldn't. Now I know my mother would have taken me in, but at the time I couldn't bring myself to go home. I gave Jenny and myself my grandmother's maiden name, and as time went on, I convinced myself I had done the right thing for all of us. Only it was so…"

"Difficult?"

Rebecca nodded as tears began to slide down her cheeks. She couldn't look at Ben. Didn't want to see the disappointment in his eyes. She brushed at her tears, stood up and began to pace again. "I took in washing and ironing and I managed, but barely. Still, I'd made the decision to run away with him on my own and I couldn't go back. Oh, Ben, I was so impulsive and rebellious. I don't excuse any of it. I did wrong."

"And with all of that, you kept your child. You didn't give her up."

"I couldn't. Jenny was all that kept me going until I

finally realized the Lord was watching over us, keeping us safe even where we lived. And that's why I know giving you away must have been the most difficult thing your mother ever did. And how I understand how badly Sarah is hurting right now. I pray her young man will stand up and become a man and this will turn out different for her. Right now she doesn't have the option of going home."

Ben jumped up and stopped her pacing with a hand on her arm, gently turning her toward him. "Oh, Rebecca, I am so sorry."

"No! I don't want your pity. I just wanted you to know the truth about my past and I know I don't deserve—" She broke off. She didn't know what to say. Didn't want to look in his eyes and see the disappointment in them. "I have to check on Jenny."

She pulled away and hurried out of the room and down the hall as fast as she could. A burst of laughter from the front parlor had her scurrying up the stairs as fast as her ankle would let her.

She entered her room, closed the door and leaned against it, sobbing. Her heart was beating so hard she could feel it to the tips of her fingers as she brushed at the tears streaming down her face. At least she had Ben's kiss to remember. For she was certain there would never be another. Not after tonight.

Ben watched Rebecca go, wanting to stop her, to pull her into his arms and kiss her pain away. But the time wasn't right. She'd only think he was being kind when that was the last thing he felt right now. He was furious.

What she'd told him didn't really surprise him. He'd wondered about it, but then pushed the thought away, not wanting to think she'd been taken advantage of in that way. Now he clenched his fists and unclenched them. If there was any way he could get hold of the cad who'd treated her in such an abominable way, he'd…

Dear Lord, help me here. I want to avenge what happened to Rebecca, but I don't even know who the man is or how to find him. And vengeance isn't mine, but Yours. Please help me to control this anger I feel. And thank You for bringing her and Jenny home to Heaton House.

He took the stairs down to his room, trying to make sense of the day. First he'd found he had family who wanted him in their lives, and then he'd found the woman he'd come to care so much for had suffered a heartbreak of her own, and all he wanted to do was take that pain away from her.

He wanted to make her see the woman he saw—one who might have made the wrong decision to trust a man who'd only used her, but who'd paid many times over for her actions. And yet, with the help of the Lord, she'd come through that shadow and back into the light. She was a woman ready and willing to help others, a wonderful mother and the kind of woman he—

The realization washed over him with certainty and he finally admitted it to himself. He was falling in love with Rebecca. And he didn't want to run from it, but only toward it.

Much as he hated the pain she'd gone through

being rejected by a man she thought loved her, he had to admit that he was relieved that she hadn't left a husband. Instead she'd kept her baby, made a living for them both and trusted the Lord to guide her. And become a strong, wonderful woman.

And yet, she still felt she didn't deserve to be loved. He was sure that was what she'd been about to say. And how very wrong she was. *O dear Lord, how do we convince her that she can have true love? That she can have a man who wants to honor her and love her and her child. One who will never forsake her. Please, will You help me?*

With all the new boarders trying to get used to the way things were done at Heaton House the next morning, Rebecca was glad she stayed busy explaining it all to them so that she didn't have to look at Ben and see the disappointment in his eyes. For she was sure her revelation of the night before had changed how he viewed her.

"You just help yourself to whatever you want from the sideboard and if any of you need a sack lunch to take to work, let Gretchen or Maida know and you can pick it up in the kitchen before you leave," she explained to Emily and the others as they made their way into the dining room.

"Really?" Emily asked. "Oh, how wonderful. Your mother had told me room and board, but I wasn't sure what all that included. Nor did I expect the kind of meals we've had. No wonder your sign doesn't stay out long, Mrs. Heaton."

"And it doesn't go up very often," Julia said. "If

four of our boarders hadn't gotten married within such a short time of each other, it wouldn't have gone up this time."

"Oh? Four? Did they fall in love here?" Emily asked.

"They did," Mrs. Heaton answered. "But I can assure you all that any matchmaking is done on your own. Much as everyone likes to tease me, I haven't been involved in any of that. Not that I'm opposed to helping things along once I see both parties might benefit from it. But I do not run a matchmaking service here."

"That's good to know, Mrs. Heaton. That you wouldn't mind to lend a helping hand," Ben said in a teasing manner that caught Rebecca's attention.

She glanced up to see his gaze on her and she caught her breath. There was no censure in his eyes as he smiled at her. He seemed to be looking at her in the same way he had yesterday morning—before she'd told him about her past. Was it possible they could still be friends after the kiss they'd shared and what he now knew about her?

She told herself to quit her dreaming, but Ben's gaze moved to her lips and her heart began to slam against her chest. Was he thinking about that kiss? She'd dreamed about it the night before and had thought of little else since waking.

Stop it. She couldn't afford to let herself care about him any more than she already did. In fact, she was going to have to find a way to distance herself from him or her heart would surely be broken. For, if she wasn't mistaken, she was only a heartbeat away from falling totally in love with the man.

She forced her thoughts back to the present as the boarders began to scoot back their chairs and get ready to go to work. In the rush of them gathering their things and picking up their lunch bags, Rebecca helped keep order and tried to put that kiss out of her mind.

"Sarah still not feeling well?" Ben asked her mother as Rebecca came back into the dining room.

"No. Poor dear. Maida took her up some tea and toast. Hopefully she'll feel better soon. I do wish her mother would realize how much she needs her."

"Yes, so do I," Ben said. "And for her young man to do the right thing. In the meantime they're both making this much more difficult for her than it should be. I'll be praying for her." He pulled out his pocket watch. "I suppose I'd better be getting off to work, myself. I'll see you all this afternoon. Have a good day."

"You too, Ben," her mother said.

"Bye, Mr. Ben," Jenny said, just as he left. "May I go play upstairs, Mama?"

"You may."

Ben's sympathies for what Sarah was going through touched Rebecca's heart, reminding her of what a truly wonderful man he was. They all knew this was as much Sarah's fault as it was her young man's, but no one realized it more than Sarah; of that Rebecca was certain.

"I do hope Sarah feels better soon. She's not eating enough and I worry about her," her mother said, as Rebecca poured them both a second cup of coffee.

"I know. So do I. I opened up to her about my similar situation this morning, Mama."

"Oh? That couldn't have been easy for you," her mother said.

"No, but I felt she needed to hear it. It seemed to help—to know that Jenny and I have a better life now and that there is hope for her and her child. She even smiled when I left the room and there was a little more color in her face. I don't know what else to do but pray for her, Mama."

"That is the best thing we can do, dear. The Lord knows what she needs and He's watching over her."

Rebecca nodded and took a sip of coffee. "I told Ben last night, too."

"Told Ben? About—"

"My past. The same thing I told Sarah this morning."

"What brought that on? I thought you didn't want anyone to know."

Rebecca shrugged. "I didn't. But he'd shared some of his past with me and I…felt it was time I told him. That's all."

"Rebecca, are you…do you care about Ben in a romantic way?"

"I'm afraid I do. But regardless of that, Ben has been a good friend and I felt the need to tell him."

"I see. Ben is a fine man, Rebecca."

"Yes, he is. Too good for—"

"Rebecca!" her mother sliced her hand through the air. "I'll not hear you talk like that. The Lord forgave you long ago. It's time you forgave yourself."

Chapter Twenty-One

Ben's thoughts were so much on Rebecca that day it was a wonder he'd been coherent at all in class. Thankfully it was a test day, so he didn't have to talk that much the whole day...and that left him plenty of time to think over the night before.

About the kiss and all Rebecca had told him. That had to have been very difficult for her and he was humbled that she'd opened up to him. But why had she decided to do so just then?

Was she was testing him to see what his reaction was? Oh, he didn't think she realized it, but he had a feeling she wanted him to know her past before he kissed her again. And that he'd better not even try to unless he could accept her for who she was.

Because she *had* responded to his kiss in a way that had him longing for another. Her lips had been soft and sweet and responsive. But then she'd drawn away and he'd seen the vulnerability in her eyes.

She'd barely spoken to him that morning and if

he wasn't mistaken, he was pretty sure Rebecca was going to try to distance herself from him.

Until recently, he'd thought he should do the same, but he couldn't bring himself to pull away from her. She simply meant too much to him. Still, he hadn't been able to let her know of his growing feelings for her—that fear of rejection had run deep.

But Rebecca had been the one who tried to convince him that his own mother loved him. And the look in her eyes when she told him she wished his mother had kept him, had loved him the way he deserved—his heart warmed to melting just thinking about the expression in her eyes.

Rebecca cared about him, he was sure she did, but Ben believed that, deep down, she didn't think any man would want her after what happened with Jenny. Well, he was going to convince her of just how mistaken she was. And how any man would be blessed to call her his wife.

It was time he admitted how much Rebecca and her daughter meant to him, and that if she would have him, he'd spend the rest of his life trying to show her just how much he cared for her.

He was going to set out to woo her. And if he had to enlist everyone he knew to help him, he'd do that, too. With the testing over for the day, he gathered his students' papers, stuffed them in his satchel and headed to Heaton House a little earlier than usual. By the time Ben arrived, he had the beginnings of a plan in mind.

However, he walked in on a very different scene than the day before. Mrs. Heaton, Rebecca and Molly were in the front parlor, talking animatedly and looking happier than he'd seen them in several days. Mrs. Heaton motioned for him to join them. "Come have some tea with us, Ben. We want to tell you the news."

"What is it? What's going on?"

"Oh, Ben, the most amazing thing," Rebecca said, her eyes shining. "Just an hour ago, Sarah's mother, Molly and Sarah's young man arrived wanting to see her. At first, we had a hard time talking her into coming down to see them, but finally, she agreed. And, oh, her young man—Shaun—rushed forward when he saw her, grabbed her hands and asked for her forgiveness. Then he went down on one knee and proposed to her. Told her that they could live with his parents until he got a better job and they could afford to be on their own."

"I think Molly finally got him to see what he was giving up by running," Rebecca's mother added.

"Oh, I knew he loved her. I've seen how he looks at her. I've seen them together. He was just frightened out of his wits," Molly said.

"What about her mother?" Ben looked at Rebecca.

Her eyes welled with tears, although they didn't fall. "Well, then her mother began to cry and asked Sarah to forgive her, too, telling them they could live with her until they got on their feet, also."

"Sarah gathered her things and they were going to speak with their minister and ask him to marry them right away," Mrs. Heaton said. "I told them they could use our parlor for the wedding, but they didn't want to put it off and I'm glad. I think they'll be fine now."

Mrs. Heaton wiped her tear-filled eyes. "The Lord answered our prayers faster than we ever dreamed."

"He does that sometimes." Ben prayed the Lord would answer his own prayer to be able to convince Rebecca of his love just as quickly.

Rebecca had debated most of the day whether to go to class that evening. She needed to distance herself from Ben until she could get her feelings for him under control. But how did one stop caring for someone as much as she cared for Ben?

How did she put thoughts of the kiss they'd shared out of her mind when the very thought of it sent her tummy topsy-turvy? And how did she get out of going to class without making Ben wonder why? He'd have more questions than she wanted to answer and she wasn't going to lie to him.

Her thoughts were scattered all during dinner, trying to be polite to the new boarders and avoid looking at Ben all at the same time.

Ben would treat her as kindly as he always did, of that she had no doubt. Still, she was more than certain he wouldn't be kissing her ever again. Her heart twisted at that thought, but she'd get through this new kind of heartache. She had to. And she had to make sure she was friendly to Ben. Her mother had gone through too much because of Rebecca's decisions in the past—after selling the family home in Virginia, she and Michael had come here to try to find her. And they'd stayed to search every lead, never giving up hope that she would be found, even as the years passed and they'd begun to wonder if she was even alive. During that time, her mother had opened up Heaton House to try and help other young women who needed a safe place to stay. A place where they could feel at home. Hoping no other families had to go through the pain of losing their daughter. Oh, what she'd put her mother through! And she wasn't going to bring tension of any kind to her home, not now—not ever.

So she freshened up right after dinner and told herself to try to act as normal as possible, but when she came back down to find Ben waiting for her, talking to her daughter, bringing a smile to Jenny's face, she wasn't sure that was possible.

What was normal? Acting the way she had before they kissed or now, when her heart swelled at the sight of him—thinking about what a wonderful father he'd be, what a loving husband he would make?

Oh, please, dear Lord, help me to keep my feelings for this man from showing. I don't want to make him feel uncomfortable and I don't want Jenny to be hurt because of my actions. I don't know what to do—or how to act. And I—

"Rebecca, there you are." Ben's smile seemed the same as always, warming her heart as usual. "Jenny and I were wondering if she should run up and see what was keeping you."

"I'm sorry. I must have been dillydallying. I hope we won't be late."

Ben pulled her jacket off the rack and held it out for her. "Not if we get going. We'll be fine. And you look lovely."

"Why…thank you." Rebecca felt her face flush at

his compliment and she tried to hide it by bending down and kissing Jenny. "You behave for Granma, you hear?"

"Yes, Mama. I will."

"She's always minds me, dear. You two have a nice evening."

Ben opened the door for her and Rebecca waved to her daughter and mother before hurrying out into the chilly night air. He took her arm and steered her toward the trolley stop. "No need to hurry. It isn't there yet. Besides, I can tell your ankle isn't completely healed as you've been favoring it lately."

The very fact that he'd noticed warmed her heart. Ben was the most compassionate man she'd ever known, but he was thoughtful of everyone, so she needn't read anything into it.

"It is getting better. Only later in the day it seems to give out once in a while. I should have brought my cane."

"No need. Remember, I'm here."

How could she forget? He pulled her hand through his arm and she did feel steadier as he matched his steps to hers.

The trolley arrived just as they reached their stop and on the way to the Y, they talked about how things had changed so quickly in Sarah's situation and how happy they were for her.

"I think Mama gave Sarah's mother a lot to think about, and Molly got Shaun to see what he'd be giving up and realize how much he loved Sarah. She was a great help to Sarah through all of this—even talking her into coming to Heaton House."

"Yes, and you helped more than you realize just by being there for her."

"I hope so. I did tell her about my situation before I was reunited with my family, but just this morning. I wish now I'd told her sooner." She paused, surprised that she'd confided in him again. What was it about this man that had her willing to open her heart to him?

"I'm sure confiding in Sarah helped her immensely, Rebecca. To know your situations were similar. And I'm thankful it turned out the way we'd all prayed for it to. I wish…you hadn't had to suffer such heartbreak on your own. You deserve so much better."

Rebecca's heart melted at his words. Did he really believe that? Or was he just trying to make her feel better? Suddenly, it dawned on her that either way, Ben cared about her—only as a friend she was sure, but her revelation of the night before had not pushed him away.

And if she could keep *her* feelings—which deepened with each passing day, each passing moment—from him and everyone else at Heaton House, perhaps they could remain friends. Oh, she prayed that would be the case.

Ben wasn't sure how to proceed with letting Rebecca know how he felt about her and there had been no time to line up any support in his effort to woo her. But when he'd seen interest in the two new male boarder's eyes at dinner, he'd made up his mind right then and there not to put his efforts off any longer.

His fear of losing Rebecca far exceeded his uncertainty of her rejection. For if he didn't try, he'd never know if she returned his feelings. And he must know how she felt about him.

He was so into his thoughts as they climbed the stairs at the Y that he didn't notice Molly waiting just outside his classroom. Her smile was wide and her eyes sparkled.

"Oh, Molly! I was hoping you'd be here," Rebecca said. "Can you tell us how Sarah is?"

"Oh, yes! She's deliriously happy. She and Shaun's minister married them this very evening. They were totally honest with him and he saw no reason to make them wait. So she is officially Mrs. Shaun Kelly now. She said to tell you and to thank you both for being there for her. Said they'd come calling soon as they could."

"Please tell her how happy we are for her," Rebecca said. "And that we *do* expect that visit."

"Will she come back to class, do you think?" Ben asked.

"I'm not sure. But they're moving in with her mother and she seems quite happy about it."

"Thank you for all your help in getting Shaun to step up and be a man, Molly," Ben said.

"I was glad to. I knew he loved her."

Several other women arrived and they ceased talking and made their way into class along with them. A few of the women asked Molly about Sarah and she just told them she was feeling better.

Evidently she was going to leave it there and see if Sarah made it back to class. If not, Ben was sure she'd let them all know Sarah was a married woman now. He sent up a silent prayer that the young couple would have a good marriage and a happy life and then got on with his class.

"Let's see what you've all learned this week." He knew what he had learned. He'd realized that he cared deeply for the woman sitting in the front row. And he couldn't wait to start convincing her of it. He'd watched Michael with Violet, Luke with Kathleen and John with Elizabeth. Surely he'd learned a little bit about how to pursue a woman.

By the time class was over, Ben still had no idea exactly how he was going to go about things, but he intended to take advantage of having Rebecca all to himself for just a bit longer tonight.

He cleaned the blackboard and put the class's homework in his satchel while Rebecca exchanged small talk with some of the women.

Once the others had taken their leave, he checked the time on his pocket watch and made sure he and Rebecca took the stairs slowly in order that their trolley would have come and gone by the time they neared the stop and they'd have no choice but to wait for the next. He could hire a hack to take them back, but the only way he'd do that was if she didn't agree to his plan.

They came out of the building and started down the street just in time to see their trolley pass by.

"Oh no—it looks as if we missed it, Ben. I'm sure it was because I'm still not walking as fast as usual. I'm sorry."

"I'm not," he answered truthfully. "It gives us time to have some hot cocoa. It won't be long until we'll be wanting ice cream instead. Unless you'd rather I procure a hack to take us home?"

"No, there's no need for that. If you'd like some cocoa, I'm happy to have a cup with you."

The tightness in his chest eased as he led her inside the café that had become his favorite simply because of his time spent there with Rebecca.

The proprietor recognized them and led them to a table right away. It was the same one in front of the window that they'd had the other times.

"Hot cocoa? Would you like a biscuit or buttered toast with it tonight?" the man asked.

Ben looked at Rebecca and she gave him a quick nod, "Yes, I think we would. How does the toast sound, Rebecca?"

"Just right."

"We'll have two buttered toasts, then," Ben said to the owner.

"Very good, sir."

The man turned to go and Ben smiled at Rebecca. "Might as well. The next trolley won't be here for about a half hour. I think this has become one of my favorite restaurants"

"The owner is very nice."

"He is. But that isn't the reason."

"No?"

"No. I love the place because I've gotten to know you better here. I've confided in you here and I enjoy having you to myself for a bit."

"I—that's very nice of you to say, Ben."

"And I need to confide in you again, if I may."

"Of course."

"My mother's abandonment of me wasn't the only time I suffered rejection…the woman I thought I'd marry turned me down before I came to live at Heaton House."

"Oh? What happened?"

"Well, I'd accepted my teaching position at the college and was so excited to tell the young woman I'd been courting. I remember the look on her face when I told her and then proposed. It was one of total disgust."

"But why? Teaching is a very honorable profession."

"It is. But it's not the greatest paying one—at least not at first. She evidently thought I'd go to work for her father and told me that she wasn't about to live on a teacher's salary and if I expected her to, I'd better think again. She walked out of my life that night and since then, between the abandonment by my mother and her rejection, I decided right then and there that I wasn't going to risk that kind of pain ever again."

"Oh, Ben, I'm so sorry. But I think you might be better off without her. She didn't appreciate your worth at all."

"Nor did Jenny's father appreciate yours. But perhaps it's time we…you and I…put all that in the past and begin to live the life the Lord has given us. I know I've been blessed in so many ways and I realize now that Mary wasn't the woman for me and I never was truly in love with her. She was the first woman I was really attracted to, but that's not the same as being in love."

The proprietor came back with their order and,

after taking a sip of hot chocolate, Rebecca said, "I believe I know what you mean. I was so young and thought I knew what love was. But I had no idea. I was attracted to Jack and believed him when he said he loved me. And I thought I loved him, too."

She shook her head. "But it didn't take long to realize how naive I really was. By then I'd made a decision to keep my shame to myself, which made my life and my daughter's much more difficult than it should have been. I am blessed that the Lord saw to it to reunite me with my family. I know I'll never have exactly the kind of life I dreamed about when I was younger, but it can be a good one."

"What makes you believe you can't have your dream?" Ben's gaze caught Rebecca's and held.

"Ben, no man—I mean—I…" She shook her head and took another sip from her cup.

Ben lowered his voice so only she could hear. "You think no man would want you because another man took something he had no right to take?"

"I wasn't totally innocent in that, Ben."

"But you expected something else, Rebecca. You thought he was a different kind of man than he turned out to be."

He could see the sheen of tears in her eyes as she nodded. "I did."

"Not all men are like him."

"I do know that. But I have Jenny to think of and I can't afford to make that kind of mistake ever again."

Ben wanted to tell her right then how much he cared. But it wasn't the right time. Rebecca needed to be courted, needed to know that when he told her how he felt, he meant it with every fiber of his being. This was not the time to move too fast.

"But you need to enjoy yourself. I need to enjoy myself. We've become friends, haven't we?"

"I think we have. I know I've opened up to you in a way I haven't anyone else."

"And you know I've done the same. So as friends, how about we go to an Italian restaurant I know of this weekend? You didn't go to the baseball game with us last summer. We all went there afterward and it became a favorite of mine. Do you like Italian food?"

"I don't know. I've never had it."

"Then perhaps you should. Maybe I'll see if Millicent and Matt want to go one of these days." He wanted to be more than "friends," of course, but no need to make her nervous about a dinner date.

"That might be fun."

"Good, I'll plan it."

"I look forward to it."

Not nearly as much as Ben did. He watched as she took another sip of hot cocoa and then a bite of the toast. She looked more relaxed now and he was glad. She smiled over at him as he took a bite of his own.

"Mmm, this is good," she said. "It goes great with the chocolate. I think they were made to go together."

Just as the two of them were. Oh, he was going to win this woman's heart or exhaust his own in trying.

Chapter Twenty-Two

The next few weeks were some of the most enjoyable Rebecca could ever remember. Ben was insistent that they put their pasts behind them and live the lives the Lord had given them, full of blessings, family and friends. If she didn't know better, she could almost convince herself that Ben was trying to woo her.

He'd corresponded with his aunt and had made plans to go meet his grandparents over spring break.

"I can't believe that I have a real family," he said on their way to class one evening. "I must admit to being envious of those boarders who have close families."

"I'm sure it'd be hard not to feel that way. I'm delighted for you, Ben." And she was. He seemed to be happier than she'd ever seen him and it was totally understandable. She knew how she'd felt being reunited with her family, but to think you didn't have a family—and then find that you did and that they wanted to be part of your life! She couldn't see how he could be anything but joyful.

Over the next few weeks, she and Ben spent more

time than ever together—not that she was complaining. She loved spending time with him, but it did have its drawbacks. Her feelings were growing for him with each passing day, and she feared as days went on it would get more difficult to hide from anyone—especially Ben—how she felt.

As a group that included the new boarders, they all went on what they were sure would be the last sleigh ride of the season when a late round of snow came, letting them know that spring wasn't quite there yet. Ben was very nice to Emily, but he treated her no differently than he did Julia or Millicent, and Rebecca was more than relieved about that.

However, she sensed that their friendship seemed to be growing. She felt more comfortable with him each day—but was that a good thing or not? Was she setting herself up for more heartbreak? Still, she couldn't seem to put any distance between them as she'd thought she must. Didn't even want to try right now. She could only pray for the Lord to help her through whatever heartache was in store as a result of continuing to spend so much time with Ben.

Michael and Violet asked her to come to dinner one night to talk about her mother's upcoming birthday the next month. "Why don't you ask Ben to come, too? That way you'll have an escort here and back, and Mother Heaton won't have to worry about you."

So she asked and was quite pleased that Ben accepted right off. Over a dinner of rib roast served with creamed potatoes and gravy, along with peas with baby onions and rolls, they started the birthday planning.

"I think Mama might like a night out to hear the Philharmonic Orchestra," Rebecca said.

"Oh that's a good idea. We all went once before Michael and I got married and she loved it, didn't she, Michael?" Violet asked.

"She did." Michael reached over and took his wife's hand. "That was a special night, wasn't it?"

"She's mentioned that she'd love to go again," Rebecca said, feeling a bit envious of the obvious love her brother and his wife shared.

"All right, let's plan it," Michael said. "See if any of the boarders want to be included. You know she'd want them to come if they want to and it will be my treat."

"I'm sure they'll all want to," Ben said. "And be glad to pay their own way. I know I'll be more than happy to."

"I know. But it'd be easier just to say it's my treat," Michael said.

"Well, I won't turn it down, then." Ben grinned. "But perhaps the boarders can all go in together for a gift for your mother."

"That would be nice," Rebecca said.

"I'll bring it up."

It was getting late by the time they left, and the night air had a bite to it, but no wind. Rebecca was glad to have Ben's arm to hold on to. It was a clear night, with a big moon and a sky filled with what looked like a billion stars.

"You know," he said, "we still haven't gone to that Italian restaurant I told you about. Want to try for this Saturday?"

Her heart fluttered. She'd wondered if he'd changed his mind. "Yes, I would. But I'll need to see if Mama minds keeping Jenny."

"You know she won't."

"Probably not." She chuckled. "Jenny loves her so much. She's quite fond of you, too, you know."

"The feeling is quite mutual. She's a great child. And the credit goes to you."

"Thank you, Ben." Rebecca felt her face flush and was glad it was dark out. Ben seemed to be complimenting her right and left lately. Not that she minded; she had a feeling he was trying to bolster her confidence after she'd confided in him.

He was the best friend she'd ever had, and she was falling more in love with him each day. She shouldn't be agreeing to every outing he suggested.

Come to think of it, there'd been several times her mother or someone at Heaton House had suggested that she and Ben do this or that together lately. Of course Ben was one of her mother's favorites, but if Rebecca didn't know better she might think they were all trying to get them together. No, that was only wishful thinking on her part.

O dear Lord, please help me. I want to be with this man every chance I get, and yet I know I'm setting myself up for heartbreak. What if he finds someone he's interested in and falls in love? She certainly wouldn't take kindly to us being best friends. Please guard my heart in preparation for when the time comes when Ben and I can't be best friends any longer.

A sharp pain shot through her heart at the very

idea. She was so into her thoughts that they were back at Heaton House before she knew it, and her mother was just coming down from putting Jenny to bed.

"Hello, dear. Did you have a good time? Has baby Marcus grown since I saw him this morning?"

Rebecca chuckled. "We did have a good time. And that baby may well have grown since this morning. He is so sweet."

"Well, of course I think both my grandchildren are the sweetest in the world," her mother said.

"Mrs. Heaton, I was wondering—I'd like to take Rebecca out to dinner this Saturday," Ben said. "But Rebecca wanted to make sure you wouldn't mind watching Jenny before I plan anything."

"Why, of course I don't mind. You know that, Rebecca."

"I told her you wouldn't."

"Well, I never want to take you for granted, Mama. I'm so blessed to—"

Her mother sliced the air with that hand, causing even Ben to laugh.

"Surely, you know what that means, Rebecca," Ben said.

"Oh, yes, I do. It means *enough*, or say no more."

"Correct," her mother said. "Just see that you have a nice time. I'm going to check in with the new boarders now and see how they are doing. Much laughter has been drifting up the stairs so I believe they're beginning to feel at home." She took off toward the parlor.

Rebecca turned to Ben. "I'm going to check on Jenny. Thank you for escorting me tonight."

"Nothing I'd rather do. I'll make reservations for our dinner."

"I'm looking forward to it. Good night, Ben."

"Good night, Rebecca."

She turned back at the landing and saw him still standing there looking up at her. The expression in his eyes had her heart doing a breathtaking double flip. "Sleep well."

"You, too. Sweet dreams."

Oh, she'd be dreaming all right—she couldn't remember a night in the past few weeks that she hadn't dreamed of Ben. They'd been such sweet dreams, she'd had to remind herself each morning that they were *only* dreams.

She made it to Jenny's room and gazed down on her sleeping child. The Lord had blessed her so much. With this precious child, in leading her back to her family and in providing such a wonderful friend in Ben. She felt bad about even thinking of asking for anything more. But if she did, it would be for those dreams to come true.

Ben watched as Rebecca descended the stairs, her mother and Jenny following behind.

She wore a dinner dress of blue-green velvet and cream lace and had pinned her hair in a little more elaborate way than she usually wore it.

"You look…beautiful, Rebecca." He watched as a delicate blush spread up her neck and onto her cheeks.

"See, I told you, Mama." Jenny whispered loud enough for him to hear.

"You did," Rebecca whispered back.

Ben had to smile at their conversation—had Rebecca wondered how she looked or what he'd think? He certainly hoped that was the case. He held her wrap for her and helped her on with it. She kissed both her daughter and her mother and he whisked her out the door to the hack he had waiting.

Once they were on their way, she turned to Ben. "I didn't see Matt and Millicent in the parlor. Are we meeting them there? I meant to ask Millicent about it, but with all that's been going on lately, I completely forgot."

"I suppose it's time to confess. I decided against asking them. With so much happening and all the new boarders—I wanted you all to myself tonight."

"Is there something you need to talk about privately?"

"There might be. But mostly, I just wanted to spend some time with you."

"Oh…that's nice of you, Ben. I like spending time with you, too."

But her tone sounded a bit distant and it was too dark to read the expression on her face. Ben couldn't let her pull away from him. Not tonight.

They arrived at the restaurant and he took her arm and helped her out of the cab, then proudly escorted her inside. The atmosphere was as warm and welcoming as he remembered, with candles lighting the tables. Ben was pleased when they were shown to a table in an alcove looking out onto the street. It felt private and open all at the same time.

They were given a·menu, but it was in Italian and

when the waiter left the table, Rebecca smiled over at him. "I don't know what any of this is, do you?"

"I've learned." He went on to explain the dishes to her. "I like the spaghetti and meatballs, but I know the lasagna is good, as is the fettuccini. At least that's what the others have told me."

"I'll just have what you are having," Rebecca said.

The waiter came and Ben gave him their order. The quiet sounds of other diners' conversations, along with the flickering candlelight and soft violin music coming from somewhere in the background, made the atmosphere seem intimate and special. At least it felt that way to him and he hoped Rebecca liked it as much as he did.

"It's very different from trying to keep up with so many conversations at home, isn't it?" she asked.

Ben laughed. "It certainly is, although I usually love that about having dinner at Heaton House, too. But it does seem a bit much at times with the new boarders. Not that they aren't very nice, it's just that I got used to the smaller group and I find myself missing it now. But I'll get used to it."

"I know. I feel the same way at times. I was worried about Jenny adapting to having more people around the table, but I believe I'm having a more difficult time than she is."

"I believe Jenny could adapt to most anything."

Their first course arrived and they had no problem keeping the conversation going between each course up through a dessert of cannoli. They talked about the weather, the new boarders and how they were both looking forward to spring.

Rebecca looked around. "I've never been to many restaurants here—a few cafés for lunch and the one where we have hot chocolate. This has been wonderful, Ben. Thank you for bringing me."

"I'm glad you've enjoyed it. So have I, and I hope there will be more times like this in the future."

"That would be nice."

"Are you ready to go?"

"Yes, whenever you are."

Ben settled their bill and asked the waiter to call them a hack. There was one waiting when they made their way outside and Ben helped her inside.

He quietly gave the driver instructions on where to take them and then settled in the seat beside Rebecca. They took off through the city streets and then entered Central Park. It had such a different look at night. There was lamplight along the way, creating shadows and pools of light. He wanted to pull Rebecca close, but didn't dare. Not yet.

After driving through the park, they headed back toward Heaton House and it wasn't long until the driver pulled up at the gate at Gramercy Park.

"I thought we'd walk through the park before going home, if that's all right with you, Rebecca," he said, after paying the driver and helping her out of the hack.

"It is. I can't remember ever visiting this park at night. But don't we need the key?"

"I brought one with me."

Ben put the key in the lock and opened the gate. The lamplight around the park, along with lights shining from windows in the homes around it, illuminated the park well enough and yet there were benches here and there that were somewhat shadowed and secluded. They walked round the small park, enjoying the quiet except for the clip-clop of horses drawing carriages and hacks over the nearby streets.

"I love the night sounds of this city," he said. "And I like that somewhere in New York City there are people awake at all hours of the night. When I was a child at the orphanage, those sounds and that knowledge somehow comforted me."

"Oh, Ben, I wish you'd had your family then." Rebecca's hand tightened on his forearm as they strolled along.

"Yes, so do I, but I've found peace with it, and without you I don't think I ever would have."

"What do you mean?"

They came to a bench partially hidden by the foliage around it, and Ben turned to Rebecca. "May we sit awhile?"

"Yes, of course." She sat down and he took a seat beside her.

Ben turned toward her and took her hands in his. *Dear Lord, please give me the right words.*

"Rebecca…that first night at the little café, where we stop after class—remember, you told me you were certain that my mother leaving me at the orphanage must have been the hardest thing she'd ever done?"

"Yes, I remember. And I'm still sure of it. But you know that now from the letter—"

"I do. But even before that, my heart was softening toward my mother because of what *you* said. And after you told me your story…I realized you really did understand how very difficult that decision might be. But you chose to accept the responsibility of raising Jenny by yourself and I know you would do it all over again."

"I can't imagine my life without her."

He couldn't imagine life without Rebecca and her daughter. "I know. And I can't begin to tell you how very much I admire you for keeping Jenny, for being the best mother you could be to her."

"Thank you, Ben." Rebecca made a funny little sound in her throat before continuing. "That means more to me than I can say."

"*You* mean more to me each and every day." It was time to tell her how he felt about her as a woman. "I… Rebecca, I know you deserve to be courted in a grand way, and my timing might be completely wrong. But I can't wait any longer to tell you that I've fallen deeply, completely, in love with you."

He heard Rebecca catch her breath as she reached out and placed her hand over his heart. Could she feel it hammering as he could?

"Oh, Ben. I don't know what to say." She suddenly jumped up from the bench. "I—never expected to hear you say those words and—"

Ben rose from the bench, his heart falling in anticipation of her turning him down. He put his hands on her upper arms and looked down into her eyes. Did he see the sheen of tears there?

Well, he'd started this and he meant to finish it. He wasn't giving up without giving it his all. "Rebecca, if you don't think you'll ever return my feelings, I'll have to accept that fact. But if there is even the slightest chance you might, please hear me out."

"Ben, I—"

"Rebecca, my feelings for you didn't happen overnight. I've seen the kind of daughter and mother you are, I know the kind of woman you've become."

He lifted one hand and ran his fingers through his hair. "I'm doing this all wrong, I know. But—I love you deeply, Rebecca. I realize this may all be too soon, but I'm asking if I may court you properly, with the intention of marrying you one day. Do you think—?"

"Oh, Ben! I was so afraid that you couldn't bring yourself to love a woman like me, who—"

"Is the kind of woman any man would be proud of and fall deeper in love with each year? I've watched you reach out to others, including me. I've held you in my arms and kissed your sweet lips. And I think I know what kind of wife you will be—" He pulled her into the circle of his arms. "I love you with all my heart, Rebecca. I want nothing more than to marry you and spend the rest of my life showing you just how much I treasure you, by being the best husband I can be to you and the best father I can be to your daughter—if you'll have me."

"If I'll have you? Oh, Ben, yes, I'll have you. I love you with all that I am and I want to spend the rest of my life being your wife."

Her words spurred him to do what he'd been longing to do for weeks. He pulled her deeper into his arms and kissed her in a way he hoped would convince her of his love for her. She kissed him back and before it ended, neither of them was in any doubt at all about what their future would be.

Epilogue

May 22, 1897

Rebecca Roth stood in her mother's garden while Millicent took photograph after photograph of her and her brand-new husband.

"Time for Jenny to join us," Ben said, and Rebecca's daughter ran straight into his arms. He lifted her up and kissed her on the cheek.

"Now I can call you Papa, right, Mr. Ben?"

"Yes, Jenny. I'm your papa now."

Her daughter wrapped her arms around Ben's neck, bringing tears to Rebecca's eyes. She still couldn't believe how truly blessed she was. To be reunited with her family, fall in love with her best friend and confidant, and find he loved her, too, and wanted to adopt Jenny so he'd legally be her father, all in less than a year, was almost more than she could absorb at times. *Thank You, Lord, for answering all of my prayers in such an awesome way.*

Millicent took several more photos of the three of

them before saying, "I think that's enough. I should probably let you enjoy your reception now."

Rebecca chuckled. "That would be nice."

Ben still held Jenny in one arm and put the other around Rebecca, pulling her close. "Yes, let's go taste that beautiful cake Gretchen and Jenny made for us."

The three hurried inside to join their guests—Rebecca's family; the boarders, old and new, who'd become family to her; Mrs. Butler from the orphanage—all were there, along with several of those Ben had helped along the way. His aunt and uncle and his grandparents who'd become so precious to her and Jenny had come from Boston, and Molly, Sarah and her husband—so many who'd come to help them celebrate this day.

Rebecca actually pinched her arm to assure herself this *was* truly a dream come true. She and Ben had decided against a wedding trip, opting instead to spend a few nights alone in their new home while Jenny stayed at Heaton House.

Then she'd move in with them and they'd start their new life as a family. At first Jenny had wanted them to all live at Heaton House, but with Ben's background in helping orphans when it was time for them to go out on their own, and Rebecca's gift for mentoring young women, and their desire to help in ways similar to how her mother had with Heaton House, they'd decided to use their inheritances to buy a house one street over from Heaton House.

When Rebecca told her mother she felt she was letting her down by moving out, her mother had sliced her hand through the air. "Nonsense! You're going to be right around the corner and I can see you anytime

I want. I will miss seeing you all each day, but I am so very thrilled that you've found true love, Becca. I'm more than happy that you and Jenny have Ben. He's a fine man and I love him already, of course. I'm overjoyed that Ben will be the husband you deserve and the papa our Jenny needs and I'm delighted to have him join the family."

"I will still keep the books for you and I can do the shopping for both of us—"

"You can do that when I can't. But we can still go shopping together and I'd enjoy that most."

Rebecca had hugged her. "Oh, Mama, so would I."

Now, as she and Ben stood with knife in both hands to cut the cake, she looked up at her husband to find his loving gaze on her. Together they sliced the cake and cut one small piece before handing over the knife to Gretchen to slice the rest.

He leaned over and kissed her in front of all their guests, then whispered in her ear. "I love you, Rebecca."

"I love you, too."

Jenny pushed her way in between them. "And I love you both! May we have cake now?"

They pulled her up into the circle of their arms and kissed her on each cheek. "Yes, we can have cake now."

Bubbling over with happiness, Rebecca laughed with all the others as she thanked the Lord above for allowing her the longing of her heart by bringing her and Ben together. She'd been blessed more than she'd ever imagined.

* * * * *

Dear Reader,

Rebecca Heaton Dickerson has been an integral part of the Boardinghouse Betrothals series since the very first book, *Somewhere to Call Home*. Even though we don't meet her in that story, we know of Rebecca and find the reason Mrs. Heaton started Heaton House was because of her having gone missing.

Then, in *A Place of Refuge*, she's found in the tenements by Kathleen and reunited with her family. In *A Home for Her Heart*, with Heaton House full, Rebecca and her daughter have moved in with her brother Michael and his wife, Violet, to make the adjustment of starting a new life easier on her daughter, Jenny.

In *A Daughter's Return*, after several boarders marry and move out, Rebecca and Jenny move into Heaton House, where the relationship with her mother continues to heal and grow, as Rebecca tries to make amends for the pain she caused her mother. She's been forgiven by God and by her family but is still having trouble forgiving herself, and while she longs for true love, she's sure no man will ever have her once they learn about her past.

Little has been known about Benjamin Roth, other than that he's a good man and fits in with the other boarders at Heaton House quite well. But Ben has a past that pains him, also, and makes him want to help single mothers with children to raise. Rebecca's daughter, Jenny, sees Ben as her hero, and Rebecca must fight to keep from seeing him as her own. But with the Lord's and each other's help, Rebecca and Ben are able to get beyond the pain of their pasts and have hope for their future.

I hope you enjoyed getting to know Rebecca and Ben better and seeing their love story unfold as much as I enjoyed writing it.

Blessings,
Janet Lee Barton

COMING NEXT MONTH FROM
Love Inspired® Historical

Available March 3, 2015

WOULD-BE WILDERNESS WIFE

Frontier Bachelors

by Regina Scott

Nurse Catherine Stanway is kidnapped by Drew Wallin's brother to help their ailing mother...but she soon realizes that she's also been chosen by Drew's family to be his bride!

HILL COUNTRY COURTSHIP

Brides of Simpson Creek

by Laurie Kingery

Maude Harkey is tired of waiting for love. But then an orphan baby is suddenly put in her care, and the generosity of her handsome rancher employer offers a chance at the new beginning she's always wanted...

THE TEXAN'S INHERITED FAMILY

Bachelor List Matches

by Noelle Marchand

When four orphaned nieces and nephews arrive on his doorstep, Quinn Tucker knows they'll need a mother. Could marrying schoolteacher Helen McKenna be the most convenient solution?

THE DADDY LIST

by DeWanna Pace

Despite their rocky history, Daisy Trumbo agrees to nurse injured Bass Parker back to health. Bass hopes standing in as father figure to Daisy's daughter might put them all on a new path together...as a family.
